"MY LADY SIR

because you came to m

He stared at her. "I never saw eyes like yours. They are the color of the turquoise waters of the Caribbean." He smiled slightly and it took her breath away.

Dominique was more afraid of him and his gentleness than when he had been insulting and cruel.

"Perhaps you are a mermaid," Judah continued, "or perhaps you truly are a siren who lures men to their doom." He shrugged. "If that be so, a man would die happy indeed in your embrace."

She did not see it coming—she should have. His lips descended, and he ground his mouth against her's punishingly.

In a panic, Dominique twisted and pushed against him, trying to get from him, but he held her fast. She had never been kissed with such passion.

Books by Constance O'Banyon

Forever My Love
Song of the Nightingale
Highland Love Song
Desert Song
La Flamme
Once Upon a Time
Siren's Song

Published by HarperPaperbacks

Siren's Song

 CONSTANCE O'BANYON

HarperPaperbacks
A Division of HarperCollins*Publishers*

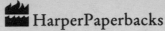 **HarperPaperbacks**
A Division of HarperCollins*Publishers*
10 East 53rd Street, New York, N.Y. 10022-5299

This is a work of fiction. The characters, incidents, and
dialogues are products of the author's imagination and are not to
be construed as real. Any resemblance to actual events or
persons, living or dead, is entirely coincidental.

ISBN 0-06-108228-7

HarperCollins®, ®, HarperPaperbacks™, and
HarperMonogram® are trademarks of HarperCollins*Publishers,* Inc.

Stepback illustration by Pino Daeni
Cover photo © Aurness-Westlight

First HarperPaperbacks printing: December 1996

Printed in the United States of America

Visit HarperPaperbacks on the World Wide Web at
http://www.harpercollins.com/paperbacks

❖ 10 9 8 7 6 5 4 3 2 1

To Elaine Barbieri, who came to the rescue when I cried: "Help, I have written myself into a corner and can't get out." I not only count you as a friend, I am also one of your most devoted fans.

Siren's Song

1

Boston, May 1801

The early morning sun reflected pale golden light across the tall roofs of the elegant houses that graced Bowdoin Square. The hour being early, a lone carriage moved unimpeded down the street and stopped in front of the three-story mansion belonging to Captain Judah Gallant.

A gray-haired gentleman dressed in sober black emerged from the carriage and, leaning heavily on a cane, made his way hesitantly up the steps that took him to the massive front door. Grasping the lion's head knocker, he rapped three times. Almost immediately, the door was swung open by a plump woman wearing a chain of keys that established her to be the housekeeper.

Mrs. Whitworth greeted the stranger cautiously. "Good morning to you, sir," she said. "If it be Captain Gallant you're wishing to see, he allows no visitors these days."

The man removed his hat and looked at her apologetically. "Forgive the early hour, Madame, but I must insist on seeing the captain."

The housekeeper did not budge from the door. "If you have a card, I will present it to him. You may return tomorrow and I will inform you at that time if he will receive you."

"Madame," the man said insistently, "my name is William York, and I have come on important business from President Jefferson. It is imperative that I have a private word with Captain Gallant, so please take me to him at once."

The housekeeper still looked doubtful, but she reluctantly stepped aside. "Come in and wait, Mr. York," she said. "I'll inquire if the captain will see you."

Once inside the huge foyer, William York stared in appreciation at the priceless treasures that surrounded him. The walls were lined with fine European artwork that included two Rembrandts, and he knew enough about art to recognize an original when he saw one. Priceless oriental vases were displayed in mahogany cases with glass fronts, and valuable Persian rugs adorned the highly polished parquet floor.

William tried to remember all he had been told about the Gallant family. They had been prosperous shipbuilders and exporters for three generations, and the treasures he saw displayed in the captain's home were undoubtedly gathered from all over the world.

Just then, the housekeeper returned, her demeanor more cordial. "Captain Gallant has agreed to see you. Please follow me."

William York fell into step behind the woman, following her through a long corridor that took them toward the back of the house.

Mrs. Whitworth paused before a door and rapped softly, entering only when she heard a voice bid her to do so.

"Captain Gallant, Mr. William York to see you."

Judah Gallant had been sitting at his desk and he came to his feet as his guest entered. He nodded at the housekeeper, who quietly withdrew, then he remained standing to impart his impatience to Mr. York. He would allow the man to express his reason for the unannounced visit and then he could be rid of him.

William meticulously examined his host. Judah Gallant had the look of a man of the sea. With his dark hair and ice-blue eyes, the young captain was a handsome rogue. He stood tall and straight, with an air of assurance about him that was usually found in men who commanded destiny—their own and others'. Then the older man observed the open bottle of wine atop the desk, and his eyes dropped to the half-filled glass that told its own story. The captain's early morning drinking was an important factor, and he should have been told about it. Somehow one did not expect such a man—a legend—to have any weaknesses.

William frowned. The information he had received about Judah Gallant chronicled the life of a man who had been shattered by the death of his wife. Since Captain Gallant had resigned his commission in the navy, he had become almost reclusive in his habits, and apparently had taken to drink. He wondered what kind of woman Judah's wife had been, whose passing had so devastated the vital young man. William's sources claimed that there had been numerous women in the captain's life since his wife, Mary, had died, but not the kind of women who would be a threat to her memory.

"Captain Gallant," he said after a long, uncomfortable silence, "I have just been reading about your exploits, including your capture of five Moorish privateers. Also, there was the time when you uncovered the dey of Algiers's sinister plot to cripple our economy by attacking American shipping. I don't know if you're aware of it, but it was primarily on your recommendation that Congress became convinced that we needed to enlarge our navy and build more warships."

There was a cynical twist to Judah's lips. "I hardly think Congress needed the advice of a fledgling naval captain to perceive the necessity of a larger navy."

"That's where you are wrong. The Gallant name is most respected. Your father was a hero in the War of Independence and you proved yourself in sinking three of Napoleon's frigates. Indeed, your family has served its country well."

There was skepticism in the blue eyes that Judah turned on his guest. "I am always suspicious of those who come to me with flowery speeches, sir. Perhaps we could dispense with the flattery and cut right to the reason for your visit."

William York smiled. "I was warned that you would not tolerate nonsense; I see I was not misinformed."

For the first time Judah focused his attention on the elderly statesman. His coat and vest were of good material, but some twenty years out of mode. He also wore his long hair tied back in a queue, rather than in the newer, short style.

"You have the advantage over me, Mr. York. You know about me, and yet, I believe we have never met."

William sat down slowly in a well-padded chair and crossed his legs, leaning toward the warm fire that blazed in the hearth. "True, we have never met, but I have followed your career with great interest. Perhaps because I have always secretly wanted to go to sea and have command of a ship."

"You are a long way from home, Mr. York. From your accent, I would place you in the South, Virginia perhaps."

"You have a good ear for dialect, sir," Mr. York declared, his gnarled hands resting on the curved arm of the chair. "I'm a Virginian born and bred. Most probably like yourself, I thought I'd done my service to my country. I would have been content to live out my days as a farmer, but President Jefferson would not have it so." He laughed jovially. "Thomas can be very persuasive—so, here I am."

Judah lowered himself into his own chair, regarding his guest with puzzlement. "You have me mystified. What have I to do with you or the president?"

William was quiet for a moment before he spoke. "When one needs a man to command, one looks for the best. It was a dark day for America when you resigned. We need men like you for the trouble that is to come."

"I know other captains who are more accomplished and more worthy," Judah said in an irritated voice.

"But none that come so highly recommended," William York told him. "It is known to us that you are a man with an uncanny ability to master the winds and currents. Besides, you are the president's preference. He is very vocal in complimenting your genius."

"Do not give me too much credit, Mr. York. I stood at the helm of my father's ship before I could walk. It is only right that I should know the sea."

"It's admirable that you take no praise upon yourself—it is fortunate, however, that others have been lavish in their tributes to your heroism."

Judah laced his hands together and studied his guest. "You are not here to talk of past victories. You have something else on your mind."

William York's expression became grim, his eyes troubled. "Therein lies the truth. President Jefferson wants you to reenlist." The foxy old man raised his eyes to Judah, his expression circumspect. "You know that we are fighting an undeclared war with the French.

They have preyed on our shipping and the president is getting damned angry."

"So I would imagine."

"Your country needs you—the president needs you! He wants someone who is young and hardy so he looked no further than you."

Judah was quiet for a long moment as he considered the older man's words. "I have retired, sir. Tell the president he would be better served to find someone else." His words took on a bitter tone. "I have already given too much for my country. It cost me all I held dear."

William lowered his voice, his eyes filled with compassion. "I sympathize with the loss of your wife and baby. Perhaps you need a distraction from your grief."

"You know quite a lot about me," Judah said in an embittered voice. "But what you do not know is that had I been with my wife, rather than chasing Moorish ships, she might not have lost the baby, and I may have been able to save her life."

William heard the pain in the young man's voice. It was tragic that he blamed himself for something he probably could not have prevented even if he had been with his wife.

"I was aware that Mary was not strong," Judah continued, leaning back in his chair and staring at the ceiling. "I should have stayed with her—she begged me to."

"You had your duty."

"I damn sure did that while she and my stillborn baby were being laid to rest. So, do not talk to me about duty!"

"I am sorry," William said, his voice soft with feeling. "It was a great tragedy."

"I can perceive no reason that my country would need me, unless it concerns the war with Tripoli," Judah said, unwilling to speak further of his personal life. "Our navy can easily outsmart the pasha."

"Tripoli is nothing more than an irritant. We have far greater troubles closer to home." William leaned forward and lowered his voice. "I must trust you—I can trust you, can I not?"

"Yes, of course, but—"

"What I am about to tell you must go no further than this room."

"I am not sure I want to be privy to any national secrets," Judah said, becoming aware of how a defenseless fish must feel when caught in a net. This man was very clever—too clever.

"Inasmuch as I have been instructed to enlighten you on certain matters, we—the president and myself—trust you implicitly."

"I'm listening," Judah said at last, although he had little interest in anything that would take him away from his self-imposed exile.

"We have just learned of a secret treaty between Spain and France to place Louisiana under French sovereignty. You can imagine the danger this poses to the United States—to have Napoleon Bonaparte for a neighbor."

Judah was clearly shocked and outraged. "My God! There must be a mistake."

"Our source is irrefutable."

Their eyes met, and held, as they both contemplated what it would mean to their country to have a hostile France in Louisiana.

"Captain, will you help America in its hour of need?" William York asked with meaning. "Are you willing to go to sea again?"

Judah was more than moderately annoyed. "Just what do you want of me?"

"We want someone to cause as much mischief as possible in the French-held Caribbean, thus distracting them from our shipping lanes."

"I have difficulty remembering from day to day who controls what island in the Caribbean. One month it is the French, the next they have been ousted by the English. It is the same with remembering who is our confederate; one year it is France, the next it is England."

"There is much truth in what you say." William's expression became cunning. "Your country needs someone to keep watch on the situation as it develops—someone we can trust to report back to the president."

Judah realized that William York's motives were suspect. "I do not believe that either France or England would welcome the American navy in the Caribbean."

"America has advanced past the time when she asks either country for pardon or permission."

Judah's eyes held a steely coldness. "The French are otherwise occupied with their extended war. On the other hand, the British may not be so distracted since their war with Napoleon is outside the Caribbean."

"Necessity often makes strange bedfellows, Captain Gallant. The British have agreed to look the other way should an American ship commandeer cargo from a French vessel. As a matter of fact, your contact will wait for you on the island of Martinique, which is at this moment under English rule. But I will tell you about that later, should you agree to help us."

Judah's brow lifted. "Help my country indeed, sir. What you are really asking me to do is spy for my country, is it not?"

William York caught a glimpse of the legend, the man who feared no foe and asked no man's pardon. In that moment he decided that he would not want to be the one to rouse Judah Gallant's ire—and he was becoming convinced that they had chosen the right man.

"You are clever and already ahead of me. If you were to agree to help us, to the world you would be a privateer. I must hasten to warn you, however, that should any foreign government make inquiries about you, the president would deny knowing anything about you or your activities."

"Let me see if I have this right—I am to assume the role of a pirate, and if caught, I will be abandoned by my country?"

"I would say that is partly . . . accurate. Although, as you are aware, a privateer is not considered a pirate, but more like . . . an opportunist." In that moment the older man smiled in realization. Judah Gallant was not a man to placate. "Call yourself what you will, pirate or privateer, the real truth is that you would be serving your country."

Judah considered what such a venture would mean to him. He had shut himself away from life, and he was aware that everyone avoided mentioning Mary in his presence. Lately, he had allowed himself to sink deeper into his own guilt. It was time to put grief aside and live again.

At last he took a deep breath and met the old man's eyes. "I will captain only a ship built in my own shipyard."

William smiled—his mission had been a success. "I suppose you will use your old ship, the *Tempest*."

"Yes, the *Tempest*," Judah said, the name rolling reverently off his tongue. "Although she sustained damage in the last battle, it would take little to have her made seaworthy."

"Excellent! I have been empowered to give you permission to outfit her to your liking." William York stood, offering his hand to Judah. "Enlist what men you deem necessary, keeping in mind that this is a delicate situation—you have two months before you have to put to sea."

Judah's shoulders seemed to straighten. He corked

the bottle of wine, then he went across the room to the bellpull and gave it a tug. The housekeeper appeared with such suddenness that William deduced that she had been awaiting the summons.

"Mrs. Whitworth, have Dickens bring the carriage around. At once."

She was astonished—the captain had not left the house in weeks—but she was too well trained to react. It was enough that Captain Gallant was smiling because he had not smiled in a very long time. "Shall I expect you for dinner, sir?"

"I think not. I will be at the shipyard. I will sleep and take my meals there as well. Do not expect me home for some time."

He spoke with feeling to William York. "Shall we go?"

And so the great ship *Tempest* came out of dry dock, refitted with fifty guns, new masts and riggings, her decks swabbed and polished. She was long, sleek, and fast, carrying a crew of one-hundred-twenty men, her mission unknown but to a few.

She was a powerful ship of grace and beauty, running boldly before the wind. With all sails gleaming and billowing in the sun, she met the tide and made for open water with Captain Judah Gallant at her helm.

It was the first time in months that he had felt any emotion but grief.

The time had come to bury old sorrows and embrace a new cause and a new reason for living.

2

Isle of Guadeloupe

Dusk had fallen as Dominique Charbonneau stood on the veranda peering into the gathering shadows with anxiety tugging at her heart. Valcour, her brother, had gone to Basse-Terre with twelve cartloads of processed sugarcane, and had not yet returned.

Dominique had not really been concerned until today. It was his twenty-fifth birthday and he had known that she had sent out invitations for a party. All their friends had gathered at Windward Plantation for the celebration, and it was difficult to mask her concern as she explained to each arriving guest that her brother had not yet returned from the village.

Night descended quickly and Dominique became even more distressed. Something was most definitely wrong—she could feel it—Valcour would never have missed his own birthday celebration. He did so love parties, especially when he was the guest of honor. If he were able, he would have come home; if not, he would have sent word to her.

Dominique's attention was drawn to the music that

drifted from the large drawing room where twenty of the island's most elite families, arrayed in their finest, were enjoying the festivities.

"Dominique, come back inside. Everyone is asking about you."

She turned slowly to Philippe Laurent, whose family had fled France seven years ago to avoid the mass executions of anyone who supported the royalist cause.

Philippe was of medium height with coffee-brown hair. His brown eyes reflected a restrained nature, although Dominique was aware that he loved her—or at least he thought he did.

Being pretty had never been of any particular importance to Dominique, but she knew that men admired her, although her outspokenness often kept them at arm's length.

Her brother had always affectionately accused her of being a wild spirit with no care for her manner of dress or deportment.

Thus far, she had met no man who tempted her to abandon her life for wedded bliss. She loved being at Windward Plantation with her brother and grandfather, and was perfectly contented to remain there forever.

"Forgive me," she replied, placing her hand in Philippe's outstretched hand. "I was watching for Valcour. I am convinced that something dreadful has happened to him."

His fingers tightened on her hand. "Put your anxieties aside, Dominique—he will be here, with his usual disregard for time and place. Your brother is a dreamer of dreams and does not always consider others' feelings."

Dominique resented Philippe's implication, and she jerked her hand free. "You do not really know my brother if you believe that," she said defensively. "And you say this when you claim to be his friend."

"I am his friend," he said softly, glad that he had finally spoken the truth about her brother's frivolous nature. "And to prove it to you, if Valcour is not home from Basse-Terre by Monday, I shall go there myself and find out what has happened to delay him." He looked at her for approval. "Will that make you feel better, Dominique?"

She shook her head. "I would only feel better if I found out for myself just what is keeping him."

Philippe looked at her with misgiving, knowing that her impetuous disposition was not unlike her brother's. In fact, it was a flaw that Monsieur Charbonneau seemed to encourage in his grandchildren.

That very personality was what had first attracted him to Dominique, and it was now the very characteristic he intended to change when they were married. He needed a wife who was settled, who would be at his side and have his children. Dominique thought nothing about rushing headlong into danger without weighing the consequences. Yet, still, he loved her and wanted no other as his wife.

He looked deeply into her eyes, wishing he could read her thoughts. "Promise me you will not do anything impulsive, Dominique."

She blinked innocently. "I never make a promise I may be unable to keep, so do not ask it of me, Philippe."

His hand slipping about her arm. "Give me your word that you will not go to Basse-Terre, looking for Valcour. It would be too dangerous for a woman such as yourself to go alone with those soldiers garrisoned at the fort."

She looked at him carefully and he lowered his eyes. "You are keeping something from me," she accused. "Do you know something about my brother that you are not telling me?"

He did not look at her. "Why should you think that?"

"You have not answered me. Have you any notion what has happened to him?"

"*Non*, I have not. But you can trust me to find out where he is and what is keeping him."

She wriggled her hand out of his grasp and clasped his arm. Something was not right, she could feel it. "Tell me what you know. Tell me now!" she demanded.

"I speak the truth, Dominique. Do you think I would keep it from you if I knew where Valcour is?"

There was earnestness in his expression and her anger cooled. "Let us go now and see if we can find him," she pleaded. "He may be in trouble, or hurt and needing me."

"Dominique, you must calm yourself." He shook his head. "You know that Valcour is always late for any engagement."

"He does lose track of time," she admitted. "But this is different. I must go to Basse-Terre, and you shall accompany me."

"How can you even consider such an unconventional action. Think of your reputation."

"Little I care for my reputation if my brother is in danger."

"If you do not care about yourself, then consider what others will think," Philippe said, his eyes boring into hers. "You know that if your grandfather were himself, he would not approve."

She considered his words before answering. "*Non*, Grandpapa would not approve. But he is very ill and cannot go himself. Much of the time his memory is faulty. There are moments when he does not even remember who I am," she said sadly. With a heavy intake of breath, she raised her chin and looked at Philippe with sadness. "Therefore it is left to me to look for my brother."

"Come," Philippe said in a jovial voice, hoping to distract her. "Valcour brother arrives home he will laugh at you because you worried so about him."

She wanted to believe him, but her fear would not go away.

Philippe studied Dominique's lovely face framed by a bountiful array of black hair. Her eyes were like the turquoise waters that surround the island and her cheeks were the color of coral. He reached out and daringly touched a stray curl that rested against her shoulder, and was encouraged when she did not pull away.

"Give me the right to protect you, Dominique," he said hurriedly, before he lost his nerve. "If you were my wife, it would be my honor to take care of your family as well."

She frowned as she looked into his earnest eyes. Philippe, like everyone else, must be aware that Windward Plantation had fallen on hard times, and his offer to help was heartrending.

Dominique wished she could love Philippe. He was a fine man and he would make a good husband. Why did she hesitate to accept him? She told herself it was because her brother and grandfather needed her, but there were other reasons. She often dreamed that a man would one day sweep into her life and bring her love and excitement.

"I am honored that you asked me to be your wife. But I cannot marry anyone just now, Philippe. My family needs me."

Philippe had long ago realized that Dominique was different from any woman he had ever known, and he had known many. She had a wild spirit and a beguiling manner that drew and held everyone's attention. When she entered a room every man's eyes would follow her around as if no other woman existed. He was not certain that she was even conscious of how she affected those around her.

"Perhaps the time will come when you will reconsider my proposal," he said with hope lingering in his heart. "I know how hard you and your brother have fought to save the plantation. Let me help you."

"Never! You must understand why I can make no commitment to anyone until Windward Plantation is free of debt. We are a proud family, Philippe. Neither my brother nor myself will accept charity. One day we shall prevail, but only because we worked hard, and did it ourselves."

"Sweet Dominique, I am very aware of the reason you and your brother are having difficulties. I would be willing to lend you money, asking nothing in return."

Her eyes hardened and her manner chilled as she glanced at him. "Do not offer me your pity. I can assure you that it is not welcome."

He chuckled and took her hand. "Pity? I think not. You see, I know that your grandfather used his fortune and even mortgaged Windward Plantation, so he could aid royalist families in their flight from France. Even those unknown to him have benefited by his generosity. And while I do not approve of your grandfather squandering his funds and leaving little for his family, I admire his reasons for doing so."

Dominique glared at him. "All that matters is that my brother and I approve of what he did."

Philippe's eyes dropped to the hem of her gown,

which was frayed and had been mended many times. To him she was more beautiful than any of the young ladies who wore the latest Paris fashions, and to him her ragged gown was only testimony of her courageous heart.

"I wonder if you would accept me as your husband if nothing stood in your way—neither pride, nor money, nor family obligations."

Dominique's grandfather had once explained to her that love, the lasting kind, came slowly, and was built and grew on a firm foundation. Perhaps he was right, and she should accept Philippe. Surely if she was going to love anyone, it would be him. But no, she thought, there must be more to love than the fondness she felt for Philippe—there just had to be!

"I cannot give you the answer you want, Philippe. For now, let us remain friends."

He resisted the urge to enfold her in his arms, to crush those tempting lips beneath his own, to speak of the love that raged inside him, but reason prevailed. "We will talk of this another day, Dominique. I have known for some time that we belong together. Some day you will realize it as well."

She had no answer for him. Philippe's was not the first marriage proposal she had received. The others had been easy to turn away, but with Philippe it was different. She cared about him, even though she did not love him.

"Let us join my guests, Philippe. I fear I have been remiss in my duties as hostess."

He reluctantly ushered her into the house, where he would have to share her with others. "I am certain, Dominique, that Valcour has met with some minor incident, a lame horse, a broken axle, nothing to fret about."

Dominique entered the room with a forced smile. She danced with several gentlemen, thinking the party would never end. She was thankful when she was approached by her grandfather's oldest friend, Bartrand Dubeau.

"I see worry in your eyes, little one," Bartrand said. "Will you tell me what is troubling you?"

She had always been able to speak her mind with this treasured family friend. "Oui. Valcour is in danger, I can feel it."

"It does no good to worry until you know there is something to worry about," he said with a shrug.

"Can you find out where he is for me?"

"I will try, if it will ease your mind." He raised her hand to his lips and smiled. "Tell my old friend that his granddaughter is ready for marriage, and he should send you away from Guadeloupe to find a gentleman who is robust and hardy, and one who will appreciate a woman such as yourself. There is not a man on this island worthy of you."

She gave him a grateful smile, knowing he was merely talking to her to distract her from worrying about her brother. "There is always Philippe, and I would not even have to leave the island if I married him."

Bartrand turned his gaze on Philippe Laurent, who was watching him and Dominique with resentment in his eyes. "Philippe is an ignominious fool who thinks only of his wants and needs. He would not know the worth of a woman with your spirit. If only I had had a son, and not three daughters, I would marry you to him. Alas, that was not to be."

She smiled and kissed his cheek. "A young version of you, I might consider."

He led her to the edge of the dance floor and handed her to Philippe, winking and whispering in her ear. "A foppish fool, a blandisher, and a boor."

"I do not like Monsieur Dubeau or his influence on you," Philippe remarked in ill humor, as the older man walked away.

"I will hear nothing bad about him," Dominique said, wanting to put some distance between herself and Philippe. "Bartrand Dubeau is like an uncle to me. Outside my family, I trust him more than anyone."

Philippe frowned at her as she moved away from him. Why did Dominique always seem so elusive? he wondered in frustration.

For the rest of the evening, Dominique avoided Philippe. She could see him watching her, and she knew he was pouting, a trait she did not admire in a man, but one she saw in him more and more. If only she could ask her grandfather what he thought of Philippe, but she would not trouble him with her problems.

At last, when Dominique was sure she could not endure another dance, the guests began taking their leave. Philippe said a frosty good-bye to her, and she answered him in kind.

She stared at the long line of torch-lit carriages that soon disappeared around the bend, to be swallowed up by the denseness of the woods.

3

Wearily, Dominique instructed the servants in their cleaning duties, then they were sent off to bed.

She was too restless to sleep, so she stood on the veranda, watching and listening for her brother. After a while she went upstairs to look in on her grandfather. A lone candle burned on his bedside table and his eyes were closed. Pierre, the man who looked after him, moved out of the room to give them privacy.

Thinking her grandfather was asleep, she bent to kiss his cheek.

"You could not sleep either, Dominique," her grandfather said, his mind clear, his eyes seeking. There were times when he recognized her, but most often he mistook her for his wife, who had been dead for many years. Even now, his eyes went to the portrait of her grandmother as a bride.

Dominique wondered how many hours he lay there staring at that likeness and remembering happier times.

"I am just on my way to bed now, Grandpapa. Can I do anything for you?"

Jean Louis Charbonneau took his granddaughter's hand and clasped it in his trembling grasp. "You must remember, ma petite, that I am quite capable of taking care of myself. Where is your brother? Does he think he is too old to tell his grandpapa good night?"

"Do you not remember, Grandpapa? Valcour has gone into town."

"Oh, *oui*." He wiped his hand across his face as if trying to remember something. "I have been lying here having very disturbing thoughts. Since Bonaparte appointed General Richepance as governor of our island, many people have disappeared, never to be heard from again."

Dominique was surprised to find that her grandfather's mind was so clear tonight, and that he, too, seemed to sense that Valcour was in some kind of danger.

"What is troubling you?" she asked, pulling up a stool and sitting down beside him.

His gnarled hand shook as he placed it on her dark head. "Many things. I have been remembering the past and I miss your grandmama."

Dominique studied him in the dim light. There was an aristocratic air about him, but where he had once stood straight and tall, he was now weak and frail. His face was framed by a shock of white hair, and his blue eyes that once sparkled with humor were now dull and lusterless.

Dominique adored him. He had given her and Valcour a wonderful childhood, allowing them freedom to express their opinions and encouraging them to think for themselves.

Jean Louis Charbonneau had come to Guadeloupe from France with his new bride, who bore him a son, Dominique's father. Dominique's grandmother had died long before her birth, but she had grown up on tales of the strong-willed woman who had worked alongside her husband, carving Windward Plantation out of the wilderness.

Jean Louis had often observed with great pride that Dominique resembled her beautiful grandmama, in looks as well as obstinacy and tenacity.

Sadness had gripped the family of Windward Plantation and a pall hung over them in the form of death. The great yellow fever epidemic that ravaged the island in 1790 had taken Dominique's mother. Then, three years later, her father had died in a hunting accident, leaving her grandfather to raise Dominique and Valcour, and to impart to them his values, chief among them that people were more important than possessions.

She placed a soft kiss on his rough hand, loving him with all her heart. It would be such a pity if he lost his home because of his generous nature in helping others escape the guillotine in France.

Dominique and her brother hid from their grandfather the fact that the plantation no longer prospered. Every day was a fight just to keep the moneylenders from taking their home.

Unlike many of the other planters on the island, her grandfather did not approve of slavery, and therefore had never owned a slave. The men who worked for them were treated fairly and paid wages, even if the Charbonneau family had to go without.

With a heavy sigh, Dominique stood up and moved to the window, pushing the curtain aside and looking once more toward the road. The trade winds that tousled her hair brought with them cooling, moist air, a welcome reprieve from the heat that had plagued the islanders for the last three months.

"You have had a long day, Grandpapa. I will go to bed now, so that you may rest." She bent to kiss his forehead. "Sleep well. I do not want you to be over-tired."

Jean Louis patted her hand. "You guard my health with the ferocity of a wildcat. But I must tell you of a strange acceptance that came over me tonight as I was waiting for you. I realized that more of my life was behind me, rather than ahead of me. My only concern in life is keeping Windward Plantation for you and your brother."

She pressed her cheek against his and his arms went around her. "All we want is for you to get well, Grandpapa."

He chuckled and put her from him. "When the body grows weaker, the mind sometimes grows muddled. Why do you suppose that is, Marie?" he asked, and Dominique realized that he thought she was her grandmother again.

She wished she could tell him about Valcour, and ask him what to do, but already he had closed his eyes and his even breathing told her he was asleep.

"You will always be the source from which I draw my strength, Grandpapa," she whispered, and tiptoed out of his bedchamber.

The house was quiet and all the servants had gone to their quarters. Dominique's footsteps were noiseless as she moved across the polished floor. Lifting a candle to light her way to her bedroom, she paused—someone was rapping on the door that led to the garden. There it was again. She decided that it was most probably one of Valcour's hunting hounds that had escaped from the kennel.

She walked to the door and opened it wide, but no one was there. She was about to close it when her eyes settled on a piece of paper that had fallen to the floor.

Puzzled, she picked it up and found that it was a note. Rushing inside, she held it to the light and read the scribbled markings.

Mademoiselle Charbonneau,

I must take this form to warn you that your brother, Monsieur Valcour Charbonneau, has been arrested and is being held at the fort. I believe it would be wise if you were to hasten there with all possible speed. He is in great peril. It is said that he is a friend to the British, and this will go against him.

It was unsigned.

Dominique was shaking so badly she had to sit down and lean her head back. Her worst fears had been realized, Valcour was in trouble—terrible trouble!

Her first instinct was to rush to her grandfather and ask him what to do, but no, she must protect him from the knowledge that his grandson had been arrested.

Quickly, she raced to her bedroom and dressed in a gray riding habit. Then she hurried to the stable to find that no one was about at this late hour. With trepidation in her heart, she saddled her own horse.

The sunlight was just topping the tall trees when she rode away from Windward Plantation and headed for Basse-Terre. Her powerful gelding's long strides kicked up dust as they raced against time.

She knew why Valcour had been arrested. He had spoken too often and too loudly about his hatred for Napoleon Bonaparte. Most probably he would be charged with treason or even spying—both offenses were punishable by death!

On she rode past sugarcane fields dotted with the new sugar mills Valcour had built so they could process and market their own sugar. He had even constructed a distillery, where rum was bottled with the Charbonneau label. Their hope had been to export the rum, but thus far they had been unsuccessful.

Dominique urged her horse on to a faster pace in her anxiety to reach Basse-Terre. Her mind was whirling ahead to what she would do when they reached the fort. General Richepance would certainly have to answer for what he had done. She would remind him that on Guadeloupe the Charbonneaus were not without influence. They had many friends who would help her gain Valcour's release.

She slowed her horse to cross a small stream and caught a glimpse of the mango trees that grew along the roadway. In the distance she could see patches of scarlet from the flame trees. She loved this island and had never been away from it, except for short boat trips to neighboring islands. It was no longer the paradise it had been before Bonaparte's troops had gained control.

When Dominique finally entered the outlying village of Basse-Terre, the town was just coming to life. She slowed her mount to a walk on the narrow streets that were soon choked with a press of humanity. There were oxcarts loaded with bananas and tobacco. She passed women who were setting up stalls to sell fruit and vegetables while their children wove baskets from dried banana leafs.

She raised her eyes to the garrison, which loomed in the distance like some dark forbidding place of evil, and tasted the bitterness of fear. Dominique swallowed her apprehension when the guard waved her inside without question. But when the heavy gate clanked shut behind her, she had a feeling of impending doom.

Dominique halted and slid to the ground, tying her mount to a post. She must not show fear, she told herself. For Valcour's sake, she must be strong.

"You there," she said to the guard on duty, trying to sound authoritative, "I insist on being taken to Governor Richepance at once."

The soldier shifted his weight, looking undecided. He

was momentarily stunned by the beautiful woman, and she was definitely a person of some importance, but her scornful manner evoked his indignation. He, like many of the soldiers who had come to this island from France, cared little for the locals whose haughty manners were reminiscent of the royalists they'd left behind.

"I cannot do that, Mademoiselle," the soldier said stiffly. "First, I must speak to Colonel Marceau's aide, Corporal Parinaud, who will in turn speak to the colonel. Then, only the colonel decides if you will be allowed to speak to his excellency, the governor."

Dominique cast a disparaging glance at the Frenchman. "Then inform the colonel that Mademoiselle Charbonneau insists on seeing General Richepance at once."

Within the walls of Fort Saint-Charles it was sweltering. A young boy waved a long-handled straw fan back and forth to cool Colonel Marceau. It was obvious by the scowl on the officer's face that he was not in a congenial mood.

With an angry growl, he shoved the young boy aside and wiped the sweat from his forehead with a lace handkerchief.

The boy scurried from the room, glad to make his escape. If asked, he could have advised the Frenchman that to dress in full uniform in this climate was the epitome of stupidity—but no one asked him.

Colonel Henri Marceau snarled at Corporal Parinaud, who had just entered the room. "Damned pesthole. How can any civilized man live in a place like this? If the heat does not kill you, the fever will. The locals scorn you and then protest when you scorn them in return."

"Colonel," the aide smiled, knowing he was about to

deliver news that his commanding officer had been waiting to hear. "Mademoiselle Charbonneau has arrived,
just as you predicted she would."

Colonel Marceau's eyes gleamed with satisfaction and
he nodded. "Is she accompanied by her grandfather?"

"*Non*, Colonel, she is alone."

The colonel poked his handkerchief back in his
pocket, his eyes gleaming with triumph. "It is unfortu-
nate that he is not with her. Send someone for him and
bring him to me by the quickest means possible."

"But sir, I had heard that the old man is ill and keeps
to his bed."

"I care not about details, just do as you are ordered—
and do it now!" His face suddenly became calm. "You
know what to do with the woman. Tend to her before
you send for the grandfather."

"Colonel," the aide said carefully, "I wonder if it is
wise to put such a highborn lady in a cell. The first
consul has insisted we deal gently with the aristocrats,
and General Richepance might not like the woman
being—"

Colonel Marceau's eyes became cold, and his neck
arched upward, reminding his aide of a fighting rooster.

"Fool! Imbecile! How dare you question my orders. I
have been trained to think and you have been trained to
obey. Besides, Napoleon Bonaparte is a long way from
Guadeloupe and has no concept of how to deal with
these people, and neither does the general—he only likes
results, and I get them for him."

The colonel's face reddened, and his dark eyes flashed
with rage as he continued his tirade.

"The reason Mademoiselle Charbonneau is to be locked
in a cell is to make her more amiable to my . . . shall we
say . . . request." He laughed at his own daring. "After a
few hours in a cell, I believe she will be only too eager to do

anything that I ask of her." His eyes narrowed. "Now go, and do as I say."

The young corporal backed out of the room, bowing every few steps. "Yes, Colonel. Right away, Colonel."

When he was outside, he drew in a sigh of relief. Colonel Marceau had lofty ambitions, and he pitied Mademoiselle Charbonneau if she refused him. The colonel could be merciless.

4

Dominique was frantic after being kept waiting in the cramped office. She watched the door in agitation for the guard to return and escort her to the governor.

As time passed Dominique became more angry than agitated. When she first arrived, she had considered using politeness to win the general over, but now she would demand that he release Valcour at once.

The door opened and a soldier wearing the blue and red uniform of a corporal entered with a flourish. "Good morning, Mademoiselle. How may I help you?"

"Was it you who kept me waiting for over an hour?" she asked pointedly.

He looked unconcerned, and she had the impression that he cared little for her comfort.

"Alas, I plead guilty. There are so many trifles to take up my time."

"What is your name," she demanded, "so I can report you to your commanding officer? I cannot believe he would approve of your actions."

He only smiled as if he was unimpressed with her threat. "I am Corporal Francis Parinaud, Mademoiselle."

"Well, Corporal Francis Parinaud, has General Richepance agreed to see me?" Dominique asked, trying to retain her patience.

He swept the door open. "Mademoiselle Charbonneau, if you will but accompany me."

"Will the general see me?" she asked again, stubbornly standing her ground.

The corporal bowed slightly to her, feeling no guilt for what he must do. "If you will follow me, all will be understood shortly."

He indicated that she should precede him through the door, which she did reluctantly. As they walked through several rooms, she practiced what she would say when she was face to face with General Richepance. But when they descended the steps that took them into a dank, ill-lit room, she became concerned.

"Are you taking me first to see my brother?" she asked in confusion.

Silently, the corporal smiled, urging her forward.

"I want to take Valcour home with me today. You see, our grandfather is ill, and my brother is needed at home to run Windward Plantation. Our sugarcane rots in the fields and—"

She broke off as a sickening odor wafted through the air and assaulted her senses. Looking bewildered, she paused while a guard with a ring of keys at his waist unlocked a heavy wooden door and she peered into a hole of darkness.

Corporal Parinaud held out his hand and the guard gave him a lantern.

As they descended the steep steps, Dominique could see only vague shadows, but they seemed to be passing cells with heavy iron doors. She was horrified to think that Valcour was being held prisoner in this appalling dungeon.

"Is my brother here?" She asked the stone-faced corporal. "Is he?"

He merely inserted a key in a rusty lock and the door squeaked open. There was no light in the cell, but Dominique rushed forward, calling her brother's name.

When she realized the cell was empty, understanding dawned on Dominique. She turned toward Corporal Parinaud just as she heard the iron door slam shut and the key grate in the lock.

"Monsieur, what have you done?" she asked, moving forward, her hands gripping the bars. She tugged to open them. "Surely you are not going to leave me here. I have done no wrong. My grandfather will see you stripped of your rank and cast in a prison cell yourself."

Her threat only brought laughter from her jailer. "As you said, Mademoiselle, your grandfather is old and ill, and I heard he is crazed." Without a backward glance, he walked away, leaving Dominique with the feeling of unreality—this could not be happening to her!

She and Valcour were French citizens and they could not be held without a reason. This had to be some terrible mistake. Perhaps this was only meant to frighten her. If that was so, it had succeeded—she was terrified!

Dominique had no notion of the passing of time as she lingered near the iron door, refusing to venture too far into the cell. The shadowy world was so terrifying that she could neither move nor catch her breath. The aide lit a torch and rammed it into a wall holder, then she heard the echoing of his footsteps disappear. Her body shook and her hands trembled with terror of the unknown.

When she felt something scurry across her foot, she did not need to see to know that it was a rat. She shivered, suddenly glad she could not see the condition of the cell. Most probably it was lice-infested. She fumbled in her reticule until she found a scented handkerchief, which she held to her nose to block out the stench left by previous occupants.

Her stomach churned sickeningly and she leaned her head against the bars as a feeling of hopelessness invaded her mind. The fact that Valcour was probably sharing the same fate gave her the strength she needed to gather her courage. She had no doubt that she would be released, but when?

Dominique became aware that there were prisoners in the other cells—she could hear them moaning as if they were in pain. What a hideous place, she thought, what human misery.

"Valcour, Valcour!" she cried.

There was no answer, but she did hear the sound of heavy boot steps, and the grating of an opening door. Her face was suddenly thrown into blinding light by the lantern carried by the same man who had locked her in the cell.

He inserted the key in the lock and the door creaked open. "Come with me, Mademoiselle."

Wordlessly, Dominique adjusted her straw bonnet atop her head and retied the green ribbons beneath her chin.

"Take me to Governor Richepance," she told the man in a voice that trembled with emotion.

He merely nodded, and she followed him up the steps, glad to be quit of the loathsome dungeon.

Although the day was hot, she shivered with dread at the thought of facing General Richepance. What kind of man would place a woman in a cell merely to frighten her? Yet she feared him for a far greater reason: he had the power of life or death over her brother.

Dominique was shown into a brightly lit office, with gilded and ornate furnishings, somehow out of place with the drab walls of the garrison. The man who sat at a desk studying the papers before him was overdressed, with wide epaulets on each shoulder and gold braid on the sleeves of his uniform. He had a thick neck and thick shoulders, the physique of a fighting man. His head seemed small in comparison to the rest of his body. For all his fastidiousness, his dark hair had an unwashed look about it.

He neither looked up nor acknowledged Dominique's presence as his quill pen darted across the paper.

Dominique could see that his actions were meant to intimidate her, but she refused to play his game. Although it was difficult to keep her anger under control, she moved casually about the room, while bitterness surged through her mind. To keep her trembling hands busy she examined a portrait that was the focal point of the room. Her lip curled in disgust at this man's audacity: he had been painted dressed like Caesar, from the laurel wreath atop his head to the golden sandals on his feet. She turned away in revulsion to stand before his desk, her hands folded demurely in front of her, silently watching him work.

Colonel Marceau had expected Dominique Charbonneau to come to him, her face tear-streaked, beseeching him to allow her to go home. He watched her from the corner of his eyes and she appeared a cold, calm beauty who demonstrated little fear of him. After a while, her urbane actions began to agitate him; he resented anyone who represented the nobility, a class of people who had always made him feel inferior about his humble ancestry.

At last he raised his eyes to hers and was momentarily struck by the calmness with which she returned his stare, and by the tilt of her chin, which demonstrated a frosty manner. She was a beauty all right, he thought, even more so than he had heard. Her dark curls peeked out of her straw bonnet, and her face was perfect, from her full, ripe lips to the sooty lashes that swept across her turquoise eyes. Her faded riding habit did little to hide her soft curves—she was precisely what he needed.

Dominique was anything but calm. Her heart was tinged with foreboding, and she was more frightened than she had ever been in her life, but she would not drop her eyes, and she would not speak to the man until he spoke first.

His baleful eyes bore into her. "So, Mademoiselle Charbonneau, we meet at last. I hope you have enjoyed our hospitality."

"I would not call your kind of welcome hospitable, Monsieur. I have been watching for some time and I have concluded that you are not General Richepance, and I expressly told Corporal Parinaud to take me to the general."

"What makes you think I am not he?"

"It is simple. General Richepance would be a gentleman, therefore he would not have had a lady placed in that vile cell."

She had his attention.

"Corporal Parinaud is a wretched fool." His eyes did not flicker as he spun his lie. "He was not acting on my orders when he placed you in the dungeon."

Dominique looked at him skepticallly. "General Richepance would have offered me a chair. Who are you?"

Anger caused red blotches to stain the colonel's face and neck, and he tapped his quill against the desk—in truth he was having difficulty controlling his fury.

"As you guessed, I am neither a gentleman nor a general, but those of you who have not heard of me will soon come to fear and respect the name of Colonel Henri Marceau!"

Dominique's words were sharp, but she kept her tone polite, fearing he might harm her brother if she truly angered this man. "I hope one day to show you the same hospitality you have shown me, Colonel Henri Marceau."

He glared at her; she was cleverly maneuvering him to her advantage. He extended his arm to her, and she reluctantly touched her fingers to his cold, clammy hand as he led her to a chair.

"The incompetence of the fools that surround me is not to be believed," he declared in an indignant voice. "How was I to know that my imbecile of an aide would place you in the dungeons? I can assure you that he will be severely reprimanded."

Dominique sat forward on the chair, wanting to demand that he tell her about her brother. It took all her will to smile at him. "Do not be too hard on yourself, Monsieur. You either have the ability to command men or you do not."

He blinked in astonishment. "What do you mean?"

She slowly and deliberately studied the man, from his balding head, to his wide girth. He was foppish, and she observed his elaborate manner of dress with contempt.

"Some men," she said at last, "are born to be leaders, like your Napoleon, and perhaps even General Richepance. I cannot imagine Napoleon being surrounded by such incompetence, can you?"

The colonel lowered his bulk into a chair and chose his words carefully, knowing just how to crack her air of dignity.

"Suppose we begin with my telling you what I know about your family."

She wanted to scream at him that the only thing she wanted from him was her brother's release. "How kind of you to take the trouble to learn about my family. I regret, I know nothing of your background."

He ground his teeth, wanting to strike that superior smile off her face. But he would bring her down from her lofty perch. He thumbed through several papers on his deck. "Your family is tied by blood to the princely house of Grimaldi of Monaco."

"I hope you are impressed."

"Who would not be overwhelmed by your family name, Mademoiselle," he said, his tone of voice sounding less than sincere. "Your grandfather held the title of count until he left France almost fifty years ago. I believe he had quarreled with his father and relinquished his birthright to his younger brother. Your father and mother are dead. Your mother was English, and you had an English governess, therefore, you speak both French and English without an accent."

"Your sources are to be congratulated," Dominique replied, feigning a yawn. "But there is much you have left out. What you may not know is that my grandfather's family did not approve of his marriage to my grandmother. She was a commoner, you see. You might also like to know that my grandfather never regretted marrying her, nor did he regret for one day giving up his title and lands in France."

"Just because he relinquished his title would not have saved him from death, had our revolution reached this island. I believe that your family in France did fall prey to Madame Guillotine, so I suppose the title has reverted to your grandfather again."

Dominique felt the pain of his words, knowing that the members of her family who had stayed in France had indeed been beheaded in the revolution. "Again your source is to be commended," she replied, trying not to show her distress.

But he was a man trained to forage out pain and weaknesses in others. He could almost see what she was thinking. He twirled the quill pen in his fingers and smiled. "Now that we have dealt with the amenities, let us speak of why you are here."

Dominique squared her shoulders. "I have come to take my brother home," she said simply.

He began scribbling furiously on a piece of paper and then shoved it at her. "What is your opinion of this, Mademoiselle?"

She shrugged her shoulders and handed the paper back to him. "It looks like an oblong box."

"That is partly accurate. It is one of my inventions. I am quite proficient in the knowledge of ancient methods of torture."

She felt fear grip her, more because of his malevolent smile than anything he said. In that moment she felt her blood chill and she forced the words through her lips. "A questionable pastime, Monsieur. One certainly not to my liking."

He glanced back at the drawing. "It is quite fascinating, really, if you understand the mechanics. May I explain the way it works?"

Dominique was growing alarmed by his half-veiled innuendoes. What was he trying to do? "I have no wish to learn about such a vile manifestation."

His thick lips settled in a line of utter satisfaction. Her poise was slipping, no matter how she tried to conceal it. He could read the fear in her eyes, fear he had caused.

Dominique Charbonneau would soon be willing to do anything he asked of her.

5

"*Indulge me in this if you will,* Mademoiselle Charbonneau," the colonel said. "I believe you will find it enlightening."

Again he pushed the drawing at her. She did not touch it, but stared at it as he spoke.

"The way this works is quite simple. Imagine, if you will, that this is a room—a very small room. If a man were to be locked in it, he would be so constricted he could neither turn, sit, nor even move his arms. Can you imagine that?"

Dread filled her heart. "*Oui.* I can imagine what you are saying."

"That is good. Now think, if you will, of the torment some poor wretch would experience if imprisoned within those limited walls."

Dominique felt as if she could not breathe. She stood slowly on shaky legs, her eyes wide with horror. "Is that where you have imprisoned my brother?"

Colonel Marceau was enjoying himself; he licked his lips, his eyes bulging with pleasure.

"How clever you are to guess the truth. But I am cruel to keep you in suspense. Your brother was placed in the box only this morning after you arrived. I forgot to mention to you that if a man remains within my little invention for a span of three days, he will lose his sanity and become a hopeless madman."

Anger ran through Dominique like a fire out of control. "I demand that you release my brother at once, and I demand to see the general."

"I cannot bother the general with little frivolities, and I cannot release your brother just yet," he said in a condescending tone. "One does not show pity to a man who has collaborated with the enemy."

"Do you think my family has no friends who will demand justice?"

Colonel Marceau's eyes gleamed slyly and he ignored her outburst. "If your brother cannot endure the box, I wonder how your grandfather would survive my little room. I have not tested my box on anyone who is already mad."

Dominique was shaking so badly that her voice trembled. "You would not dare."

"Oh, but I would dare. You see, I have already sent for Monsieur Jean Louis Charbonneau. He should be arriving here before sundown."

She shook her head, clamping her lips together, allowing herself time to think. Dropping her gaze, she concentrated on her hands clasped in her lap, willing them not to shake. As last she was able to look at him.

"Why would you do this to my grandfather? He has done nothing wrong."

"He will not suffer if you cooperate, Mademoiselle."

Her face paled and her lashes swept over her eyes as she tried not to cry. She was facing a madman, who would not hesitate to harm her brother or torture her grandfather. She would do anything this man asked of her if it would save her family.

Once more she tried to reason with him. "What proof have you that my brother has aided the British? Valcour is of French descent."

"He is only half French," the colonel reminded her. "The other half is English. I have found many on this cursed island to be of French descent, and yet they still favor our enemies. It suffices to say that your brother will be executed . . . unless you decide to help us. I already told you what your grandfather's fate will be."

He was enjoying his power over this proud beauty. "It is in my hands to say if they live or die."

"You, Monsieur, are a monster!"

His eyes bore into hers and he stood, towering over her. "I have been told this before and it does not offend me. Uninformed people simply do not understand the workings of superior minds."

Her tongue darted out to moisten her dry lips. She wanted to slam her fists against him and scream at him, to accuse him of being a hideous fiend, but she dared not. It was true that Valcour favored the British, and apparently Colonel Marceau was aware of it. She dared not provoke the man further, lest he turn his anger on her family.

"What must I do?" she asked, rising to her feet.

"Obey me."

She took a hasty step away from him, and guessing her fear, he only laughed.

"Have no concern that I will ravish you, Mademoiselle Charbonneau." His eyes ran over her slowly and deliberately, lingering on the swell of her breasts. "Although you are a tempting morsel, I have something much more important in mind for you.

"But there," he said. "You are weary and I believe I should allow you to rest until your grandfather arrives."

Dominique reached out to him beseechingly. "Oh,

please do not harm my grandfather! He is so ill—have pity. Do not hurt him!"

Colonel Marceau called out, and the same man who had escorted Dominique to the dungeon appeared at the door. "Make our guest comfortable," the colonel said, dropping his eyes to his papers as if he had dismissed her from his mind.

Dominique said not a word as she was escorted out of his office, but she was greatly relieved when she was led to a small room with a settee and chairs. She dropped down on the settee and waited for the man to leave before she buried her head in her hands and sobbed. She then leaned her head back, closing her eyes, soon to fall into a troubled sleep.

Dominique awoke with someone shaking her shoulder.

"Mademoiselle, will you come with me please?"

She stood up, wide awake, running her hand down her riding habit in a futile attempt to remove the wrinkles. She then followed the man to a wide window that overlooked the inner compound of the fort.

The guard nodded at the coach where someone was being helped to the ground. Dominique cried out, beating her hands against the thickness of the window.

"Grandpapa! No—Grandpapa!"

She watched helplessly as he stumbled, then two soldiers supported his weight, leading him out of her sight.

Her body trembled with rage and she fought to bring it under control. "Take me to the colonel," she said at last.

The man nodded, and for a moment she thought she saw sympathy in his eyes, but she did not want pity from any of these men, these minions of Napoleon Bonaparte!

This time when she entered Colonel Marceau's office, he smiled tightly and pointed to a chair.

"Let Valcour and my grandfather go free," she implored.

"I do not think I will do that—not just yet."

"How can you mistreat my grandfather, who is ill and has never done anything to harm anyone?"

"We shall keep him with us until you have done as we asked. And you should remember that war knows few friends, Mademoiselle. Now, are you ready to talk to me about serious matters?"

Dominique's shoulders slumped in defeat. "What do you want of me?"

"I want you to serve France. And remember, as soon as you have done that to my satisfaction, I shall release your brother and grandfather."

She met the colonel's eyes with all the defiance she felt. "How do I know that I can trust you?"

"You do not know this about me," he said coldly, "but I am considered a man of my word and I say to you that if you do what I ask, your family will come to no harm."

She watched as the odious man hooked his thumbs through the waist of his trousers and strutted about like a peacock, nodding his head.

"Will Valcour be released from the box at once, if I agree to help you?" she asked.

"But of course, Mademoiselle. He will be treated according to his privileged rank."

"Will my grandfather be allowed his own doctor?"

"*Oui*, I am not really the monster you suppose me to be."

Their eyes met and locked. "Just so we understand each other completely, Mademoiselle," the colonel said softly, "I will keep faith with you as long as you are keeping faith with me. If you do not, the last thing your brother and grandfather will see in life will be the inside of my little contraption."

Dominique had no choice but to do as he asked. "Explain what you want of me."

He nodded in satisfaction, a grin spreading over his face. "Very well." He returned to his desk and sat down. "Have you perhaps heard of a man by the name of Judah Gallant?"

"*Non.* I do not know that person. Why should I?"

"There is no reason you should. He is a black-hearted pirate, who preys on innocent vessels. He is causing me great distress and embarrassment, and severe reprimands from General Richepance. I will not have this American upstart interfering with the plans I have made for my future."

Dominique was trying to understand his ravings. She had come to believe he was half mad.

His face creased in a frown, then he smiled. "Should I be the one to capture Gallant, I would earn the first consul's favor."

"I do not see what this has to do with me. I care nothing about you or your first consul."

The colonel's eyes moved once more over her face, and he continued as if she had not spoken. "Everyone speaks highly of your beauty, even in France. You could well be the most beautiful woman I have ever seen."

"I want no compliments from you. Your opinion does not interest me."

Unruffled by her words, he lit a thin cigar, took a long draw, and watched the smoke disappear before he continued. "There are many rumors about this Judah Gallant. Some consider him a hero, while others tremble in fear at the mere mention of his name. I am told that he was once married and that his wife died, so he took to a life of piracy, perhaps to forget her. This I do not know. What does interest me is Judah Gallant's liking for beautiful women."

Dominique had a sinking feeling in the pit of her stomach. "Why should that concern me?"

"I have been informed that when he is ashore he is surrounded by women, and he spreads his favors lavishly. That was when I decided that I would use a woman to bring him down. I would venture that he has never met anyone with your . . . charms. He will not be able to resist you."

This could not be happening. Her legs felt so weak that she had to sit down and grip the wooden arms of the chair. "Surely you do not want me to—"

"Ah, but I do. You are to ingratiate yourself into the American's life and make yourself indispensable to him. You will be the beautiful instrument of his downfall."

"What do you mean?"

"I mean, Mademoiselle, that this pirate, this Captain Judah Gallant, will take your brother's place in my little room."

"Tell me more about Captain Gallant," she said, acknowledging defeat. "And where will I find him?"

"The man is a mystery. As I said, he is an American, and he is a pirate. Judah Gallant has the ability to strike without warning and sail away with little or no damage to his own ship. Thus far, he has avoided capture, even though there is a high price on his head." The colonel's eyes radiated hatred. "He is clever, but you must be even more clever."

"How do you know he will like me?"

"To ask a delicate question, I am assuming that you have not yet known a man?"

Dominique's face reddened with humiliation. "You go too far, Monsieur. Much too far!"

Laughter filled the room. "By your response, you have told me what I needed to know. Our captain will like you well enough, and even better when he learns how pure you are."

"I do not like you at all," she said angrily.

"And I do not care," the colonel answered casually. "When one is in my position, he gains enemies because he is forced to do many things that others find distasteful."

"I believe you like what you do all too well." She slammed her clenched fist on his desk, venting her anger. "Otherwise, you would not think up such devilish plots."

He glared at her and opened his mouth to speak, when she interrupted him.

"I will meet with this man," she said. "And I shall attempt to help you, but I will not play the strumpet for you or anyone."

"How you perform is up to you." He picked up a letter and scanned it quickly. "I have information that Judah Gallant will soon be meeting with someone on Tobago, most likely to sell his ill-gotten plunder. You will simply go there and wait until he arrives. But know that you were chosen for a reason other than your beauty."

"And that is?"

"That you can speak English without an accent. When you meet Judah Gallant, you will pretend to be English. How you do this is up to you."

"I will not take an English name," she said rebelliously.

"That too is up to you. All I care about is capturing the man everyone wants to hang."

"Why do you not just take him yourself when he arrives on Tobago?"

"Since the island owes its allegiance to England, we can hardly do that, can we?"

"I suppose not."

"You must see that Gallant's interest in you does not wane until you lure him into my trap. What we are unable to do with fire power, you must do with soft words."

Dominique was trembling with fright; the lives of the two people she loved most depended on her success with Judah Gallant.

"What if I do my best and still I fail?"

Colonel Marceau laughed in amusement. "You shall play Delilah to his Samson. Find his weakness and I will do the rest."

6

A heavy mist hung over the rough sea as the frigate *Tempest* lowered its anchor in a secluded cove off the island of Tobago.

Judah Gallant stepped out of the longboat, treading water to reach shore. He kept watch while his two companions hid the longboat beneath dense undergrowth. His senses became alert to each noise and he motioned for the others to join him behind the thick tropical vegetation until he could make certain they were unobserved.

The members of his crew who had accompanied him ashore were the two men he trusted above all others. Cornelius T. O'Brian had served as his first mate, remaining in the navy when Judah resigned. He had since been made captain of his own ship, but when Judah requested that Cornelius serve with him on the *Tempest* because he was the best navigator he knew, Cornelius had readily agreed.

The first mate was a great hulk of a man in his forties. His unruly red hair and a pockmarked face gave him a sinister look, but the tranquillity reflected in his blue eyes belied that impression. He walked with the long gait of a man accustomed to the rolling deck of a ship.

Judah's other companion, Dr. Ethan Graham, had a lofty air about him that intimidated those who did not know him. He was tall and lean, with dark hair and eyes. He and Judah had been friends since childhood, and when Judah had asked him to join the crew of the *Tempest*, he had not hesitated.

There had been a strain between the two men after Mary's death, since Ethan had been the doctor in attendance. It had not been so much that Judah blamed his friend, but that Ethan had been reluctant to face Judah.

Since boarding the *Tempest*, they had resumed their old relationship, and the thought of Ethan masquerading as a pirate still made Judah smile—a more unlikely blackguard had yet to be born.

The remaining crew members were a lawless lot, willing freebooters of questionable morality that lent credibility to the mission. Thus far, they had performed well when they had encountered the enemy, although they would just as likely give their allegiance to another if the price suited them.

"Captain," Cornelius said, fingering the dagger at his waist, "I've got a bad feeling about this place. I fought the British too long to trust them now, and they're swarming all over this island."

Judah looked at him grimly. "I cannot say I trust them either, but I do trust William York, and the correspondence I received from him assured me that my liaison would meet me here. We were forced to choose a new rendezvous since Martinique has once more reverted to the French."

Cornelius glanced up at the sky that was darkening with clouds. "Looks like it might rain, sir. What do we do now?"

Judah stood to his full height, his gaze moving out to

sea. "If you have navigated correctly, Cornelius, the village of Scarborough should be just ahead. I shall walk in that direction."

"You are going to walk?" Ethan asked indignantly, as if the notion had never occurred to him.

"Walk, Doctor," Judah affirmed. "Surely you know how to walk. Just put one foot in front of the other, one foot in front of the other."

Ethan was not amused. "Let us hope your contact has been watching for us." He slapped at his arm where an insect had just bitten him. "I do not relish staying overlong on this damned mosquito-infested island. Likely as not, we will all die of yellow fever."

Judah had to laugh at his friend, who had always had the habit of looking on the shadowy side of every situation. "It is fortunate for us, Ethan, that you are a doctor, should any of us be stricken by that malady."

"Do you not think we will look a bit conspicuous, Captain?" Cornelius asked, glancing down at his short-legged trousers and striped shirt. He removed his tasseled cap and tucked it beneath his arm and smoothed his hair.

"The two of you will not be accompanying me. One man will not draw as much attention as three," Judah said, pushing a wide branch aside and stepping onto an overgrown path that looked as if it was seldom used.

"I don't like your going alone," Cornelius said. "You might be walking into a trap. Keep your eye out for a Frenchman who might recognize you, Captain. Don't forget there is a price on your head."

Amusement danced in Judah's eyes. "And on yours as well. Be vigilant, Cornelius. I would not like to see your red hair hung on a traitor's pole."

Judah checked his pistols to make certain they were primed, then jammed them both back into the scarlet sash that was tied about his waist. "If I am not back by sundown, you can assume that your fears were not unfounded. In that event, you will rejoin the ship and set sail for America."

"We shan't leave without you, Judah," Ethan insisted. "If you are not here, we shall come looking for you."

Judah's expression hardened as he looked at his friend. "I will expect the two of you to sail for home and that's an order."

Both men watched their captain move away, knowing they would do as they were told. Even though Judah was their friend, he was not a man who would allow disobedience from his crew.

At first Judah walked along cautiously, but when he reached the main road that led to Scarborough, he joined a crowd of locals who were headed for market.

Dark-skinned women, dressed in large prints and bright colors, carried earthen jugs on their heads, while barefoot children chased each other in a game of tag. In the beginning, Judah seemed to be the object of curiosity, but by the time they reached the bustling seaport, no one took notice of him.

Judah glanced at the docks, where three British ships rode at anchor. One was a merchantman and the others flew the flag of the British navy.

Scarborough was a haven for opportunists. Pirates, freebooters, and even honest tradesmen prospered there. A more corrupt seaport Judah had never seen, and he was alert to every movement around him.

Judah turned on a man who deliberately bumped into him. "It will take more nimble fingers than yours to pick my pocket," he said, brandishing a pistol and holding it to the man's head. The pickpocket scampered away, soon to be lost in the mass of humanity that spilled into the streets.

After that, Judah kept his hand near his weapon and his eye on the crowd. He turned onto a street lined with taverns and brothels, and the filth and stench was overpowering.

A woman in a bright yellow dress and equally bright bandanna tied about her hair approached Judah, and from the way she swayed her hips, it was not difficult to guess her profession.

She drew even with him and stopped. "Ah, my handsome one," she said, moving her body in a way that made her breasts brush against Judah's chest. "Would you like to be entertained by Phylipi?"

He shook his head. "Some other time, perhaps. I have business matters to attend to at the moment."

She leaned closer and her lips brushed his ear. "You will find the man you seek within the Blue Dog Tavern," she whispered.

Judah's lips thinned and he looked at her carefully. "How will I know him?"

"He will know you." She looked at him regretfully. "What did you mean, Captain Gallant, when you said 'some other time'?"

He was not even surprised that she knew his name. His eyes swept her face and he smiled chivalrously. "I meant, some other time."

For over a month, Dominique had been residing in Scarborough, in a shabby room above the Blue Dog Tavern. She had been told that Captain Gallant would rendezvous with his contact there, but as the days passed without a sign of him, she began to despair that he would not appear.

She had nothing to do all day but wait in her room, so she had time to worry about the fate of her brother and grandfather. She spent many restless nights when sleep eluded her. When she finally did sleep, she was terrorized by nightmares in which she was stalked by the ruthless pirate, Judah Gallant.

Colonel Marceau's contacts always kept watch over her movements. Only once had she asked to leave her room to walk about the village. However, on that occasion, she had been accosted several times by unsavory characters. After that, she had not asked to go out again.

When the heavy knock landed on her door, Dominique was startled. Opening it a crack, she found one of the men who had been guarding her.

She did not like the man, and she did not pretend to. "What do you want?"

His words struck terror in her heart. "Captain Gallant has arrived, Mademoiselle. I shall escort you below, and then I will leave you to your task. Should you have need of me, I will be nearby. And later, if you wish to contact me, I can be found in the tavern every day."

Dominique had known this moment would come, and now that it had, her courage almost failed her. What would she do—what would she say to a pirate, a cutthroat? She thought of the suffering of her brother and grandfather and pushed her fear aside.

"Give me a moment to prepare," she said, closing the door and leaning against it to gather her strength. She took several big gulps of air and went to the valise under her bed. Gathering what she needed, she made herself ready to meet the infamous Captain Gallant.

When she stepped out of the room, the man nodded his approval at her appearance. She wore her hair loosely about her shoulders and she had abandoned her fashionable gown for a peasant blouse and a red skirt with layers of stiff white petticoats. Her feet were bare, and she hoped she looked like the women who walked the streets, flaunting their charms for any man who had the price to pay.

"I am ready," Dominique said.

Judah moved through the smoked-filled tavern, his eyes traveling carefully over each man's face, watching for a sign from anyone indicating that they were his contact.

Dominique clung to the shadows near the back door allowing herself a first full look at Captain Gallant. He stood as if at the helm of a ship, and even from across the room, she would know him as a man of the sea. She hugged the corner, hoping he would not notice her. But he gave the appearance that he was aware of everything and everyone around him.

This pirate was not at all what she had expected—no patch over his eye, no peg leg, no ugly scar on his face. He wore tight-fitting trousers and high-cuffed boots. A brace of pistols were tucked into his crimson sash.

At that moment, he turned his ice-blue eyes on Dominique, and she felt that he could discern her intentions by just looking at her. She dropped her head, trembling. How would she ever find the courage to approach this man?

When she glanced back to him, he was moving slowly past each table as if he were looking for someone. When a woman with a low-cut gown and blood-red lips sauntered up to him, he effortlessly sidestepped her, giving Dominique the impression that he was not looking for feminine company.

When Judah reached a table at the back of the room, a man raised a mug to him. "Set ye down and have a wee taste of ale with me, sir," he said, slurring his words.

Judah propped a booted foot on a chair, assessing the stranger. He wore rough linen clothing and a black patch over one eye. His white hair was long and tangled, and he looked as if he hadn't bathed in weeks. "I will be proud to take that drink, stranger, if you have the right words."

"Then set you down, so I may whisper to ye."

It seemed to Judah that the man no longer slurred his words. He dropped into a chair, thinking there was something familiar about him. "One need not whisper, old man, since no one could hear you in this din."

The stranger leaned forward, so only Judah could hear his words. "The tempest blows strong this storm season."

Judah relaxed and took the mug from the man's hand. This was his liaison. "So it would seem," he replied. "Pray tell me that you brought me the money I was promised to mollify my crew."

"Aye, that I have. If you ever decide to continue with your present occupation, you will be a wealthy man."

"Did the three captured ships arrive safely at Charleston?"

"Aye, that they did. Have ye anything to report?" the man asked.

"Not yet." Judah leaned back with a slight smile curving his lips. "But I haven't given up yet, Mr. York."

The older man chuckled. "How did you know it was me? I thought my disguise was so correct that even my dear wife would not recognize me."

"If you will recall, you once complimented me on my ear for accents. I still place you in Virginia." Judah took a sip of the ale and shoved it away in disgust. "Why put yourself in danger. There are others who could have come in your place."

A wide grin spread over William York's face. "I do

not know when I have enjoyed a situation so much. I will
have to tell our friend in Washington that I have a liking
for the clandestine life."

Judah slammed his fist against the table. He had great
respect for William York, and this was no place for a
man like him. "Leave this wretched occupation to others. We are better served by your diplomatic skills. This
is a dangerous business, fit only for men who do not
have your gift."

William looked pleased. "Perhaps you are right. But it
has been an invigorating experience." He glanced about
him, then leaned closer to Judah. "Let us put that aside and
talk of the reason I am here. I have foul news for you. There
is a spy about who will be watching your every move."

The pupils of Judah's eyes widened and his jaw tightened.

"Tell me his name."

"Regretfully, I do not yet know. A dispatch was intercepted some time ago from a French colonel on
Guadeloupe. The document states that he has a spy
aboard the *Tempest*. You must be alert at all times. Do
not forget for a moment that there is someone aboard
your ship who is willing to betray you."

Anger coiled inside Judah. "The hell you say!" he
exclaimed. "Then pity the poor wretch when I find
him."

"Be careful, Judah. It could be anyone. It is amazing
what a man will do for money, and there is an even
larger reward on your head than when that message was
intercepted."

"Have no concern. I will find the traitor and deal with
him. Now," he asked, "have you new orders for me?"

"Yes, but all in due time, Captain Gallant. Let's get
away from here. Since you have joined me, I feel that we
are being watched."

Judah stood, looking about for anyone who might appear suspicious. He saw movement out of the side of his eye, and turned to catch a fleeting glimpse of a woman—a beautiful woman—dressed in a red skirt. But she quickly melted into the shadows and disappeared.

William nodded toward the stairs. "Let us find seclusion in my room so I can give you the monies that represent your crew's share of the plunder."

As Judah followed William, he paused halfway up the stairs, and caught a glimpse of the woman in the red skirt again. This time, she stared boldly back at him.

She was very unlike the other women who frequented the Blue Dog Tavern. She had a refinement about her, but her eyes were inviting all the same.

He caught up with William, who was already opening the door to his room. He had no time for dalliance—he had to find a French spy. And one thing was certain, when he discovered the man's identity, he would deal severely with him.

7

Puddles of water from a sudden rainstorm glistened on the cobbled streets. Although it was still two hours until sunset, dusk had fallen over the town, and the narrow passages Judah walked through were cast in shadows. His mind was on his conversation with William York, so he did not see the woman who ran toward him until her body slammed into his.

Judah could hardly make out her features in the gathering darkness, but he had the impression she was very young. He placed his hand on her shoulder to steady her and felt the tremor that shook her body.

"Please," she cried in English, "help me. Help me, kind sir!" She clutched his arm. "I am in grave danger. Some men are chasing me—evil men who mean to do me harm. Will you not help me?"

A burst of crimson seemed to linger on the horizon and Judah was impatient to rejoin Cornelius and Ethan before sunset. With resigned patience, he gave his attention to the girl, staring at her with a hawklike glare while she looked back at him with a stricken gaze.

His tone of voice reflected his irritation. "What did you expect, when you frequent these streets without escort?"

She ducked her head and answered him evasively. "You are an American. I have heard that men from your country are chivalrous to a woman in danger. Is that not so?"

Judah looked up and down the street but saw no one who appeared to be a threat to the woman's safety. "Go home to your mother and father where you belong, little English miss. Whoever was pursuing you has gone now."

"I have no mother or father," she said softly. "I have no one."

For the first time, he looked at her closely, and recognized her as the woman who had been watching him in the tavern.

Even though he suspected that she had sought him out, she appeared vulnerable, and he took pity on her. "Show me where you live and I will escort you there. But we must hurry."

"I live at the Blue Dog Tavern, but I can never go back there." The lies did not come easy to Dominique's lips, and she faltered over the next words. "The . . . landlord forces me to . . . work for him." Her face reddened and she looked piteous. "I am not a bad girl, and I do not . . . like what me makes me do. Please, sir, take me away with you."

Judah's lip curled in contempt. "I have never met one of your kind who didn't claim that she was forced to ply her trade." He reached into his pocket and withdrew a gold coin and tossed it at her. "Go and trouble some other poor fool with your sad story. I do not believe you."

Dominique grasped his shirtfront and he could sense a desperation about her. "Take me with you. I promise I will be no trouble."

He pried her fingers loose and gently shoved her away. "Where I am going, no woman can go. Trust my word when I tell you that you will be far safer where you are than with me."

"I will cook and scrub for you," she said desperately. "I will be anything you want me to be, only please do not leave me here. If you do, something terrible will happen."

There was such terror in her voice that Judah was momentarily inclined to believe her. Then he looked at the artificial blush on her cheeks and the painted mouth and frowned. "An ingenious approach, Madame," he said with contempt. "I am sure you will find a man to accommodate you before the night passes."

Without a backward glance, he stepped around her and moved away, while she watched helplessly. She had failed! What would she do? Then Dominique gathered her courage and walked silently after him, taking care to stay far enough back so he would not see her.

Once Judah glanced behind him, and she held her breath, fearing he had discovered her presence, but he turned away and with long strides left the village behind.

When Judah reached the shore, Dominique stayed at a distance while he conversed with two men and then all three boarded a longboat and rowed toward the huge ship swaying at anchor.

Then with a determined gleam in her eyes, she walked into the water until she caught the tide. Being island-born, she was a strong swimmer, but her heavy skirt and petticoats hindered her, draining her strength.

The sun had set and it was a dark night without moon or stars. Dominique kept her eyes on the small pinnacle of light emitted by the ship. Breathless, with her arms and legs feeling like iron weights, she was sure she could go no further—but she had to.

She felt overwhelming relief when she bumped into the hull of the ship. But the real danger lay ahead of her.

She had to get on board without being discovered—how she did not know.

Dominique counted herself fortunate that the sea was calm, so she could cling to the side of the ship until all was quiet. If only it weren't so dark, then she could find a way to climb on board. As if in answer to a prayer, she felt a rope dangling from the side of the railing and grasped it in her hand. She did not know what danger awaited her on that ship, but nothing could be worse than what her family would suffer if she did not succeed with Judah Gallant.

Slowly, Dominique began to pull herself upward, hand over hand until she reached the railing. She waited a moment to get her bearings, then climbed aboard. A lone lantern swayed with the rocking motion of the ship and she kept well out of its light as she surveyed the deck. She saw no one, but suddenly she heard voices, so she slipped behind several barrels to hide until two men passed.

Her hands were raw and bleeding from the rope, her clothing was ruined, and she was dripping wet, but she had overcome her first obstacle and was on board the *Tempest*. She must not be discovered until the ship was far from land and the captain could not put her ashore.

Of course, since meeting Judah Gallant she was quite certain that he was capable of anything. He was the kind of man who would not hesitate to toss her overboard just because she was a woman.

After a while, Dominique inched along the railing until she came upon several longboats. Taking great care, she climbed inside one of them and pulled the canvas cover back in place.

Dominique shivered from cold and from fear. Everything rested upon her success with Captain Gallant, but already he had rejected her, even though she had presented herself as the kind of woman she thought he would like. How could Colonel Marceau have thought that the pirate would find her appealing?

Huddled in a dark world where danger lurked everywhere, Dominique closed her eyes and fell into an exhausted sleep.

Tom Beeton was as able a seaman as had ever walked the deck of a ship. But the jagged scar that ran from his forehead to his jaw gave him a sinister look. Women and children shrank away in fear whenever they encountered him. This was the face that greeted Dominique as the canvas was thrown aside.

Rough hands grabbed her and pulled her from the longboat. "Here now, girly," Tom said, placing her on her feet. "So, we got us a stowaway."

Dominique raked her tumbled hair from her face with a trembling hand, refusing to meet the man's eyes.

"I caught me one of them mermaids," he said, leering at her, his fingers digging into her arm.

"Let me go," she demanded, jerking her arm free. "I demand to be taken to your captain."

By now, several men had gathered about, and one of them laughed at her suggestion. "You'd be safer with us than the captain. He don't take kindly to anyone coming on board his ship without an invitation."

"What goes on here?" Cornelius's voice boomed out, and the men cleared a path for him. When he stood before Dominique, astonishment creased his rugged features and his eyes widened in disbelief. "How came you here, Ma'am?" he asked in a hard voice. "And who are you?"

She tried not to show the fear that quaked through her body. Without blinking, she looked into the man's eyes. "My name is not important. Take me to your captain so I might talk to him."

Other members of the crew had joined them by now—frightening-looking men who she could tell at a glance were pirates. They leered at Dominique while jabbing each other in the ribs and making lewd remarks, until a harsh command from Cornelius sent them scurrying away to attend their duties. Only after the last man had retreated did Cornelius turn his attention back to Dominique.

"Captain Gallant is otherwise occupied, Ma'am," he said, his face red with anger at the disruption she had caused. "You'll talk to me and no one else."

Before Dominique could protest, he gripped her arm and steered her belowdecks. He flung open a door and led her none too gently inside. The cabin was cramped, with room for little besides the narrow bunk bed along the wall, and a small table that appeared to serve as a desk. There were very few conveniences. She watched as he went about gathering possessions and cramming them into a trunk.

Then he lifted the trunk and shoved it out the door. "This is my cabin but you will be occupying it until we decide what to do with you." He spoke to Dominique sternly. "Now, you have some explaining to do."

"I'll talk only to your captain," she repeated stubbornly.

In exasperation, Cornelius moved to the door. Before he exited, he removed a key from a chain that he wore about his ample waist. "I told you that's not possible. You'll be remaining here until we can put you ashore."

"How dare you treat me like a criminal. I have done nothing wrong, and I have the right to see your captain. Look at my clothing," she said piteously, hoping to gain his sympathy. "My skirt is ruined and it is all I have with me. What shall I do?"

The manner in which Cornelius twisted his body and placed his hands on his hips warned Dominique that he was trying hard to control his temper. "Ma'am, do you think it matters what you wear on this ship? As it is, you will have to be locked in for your protection against the crew." He dropped the key in her hand. "Have you any notion what might have happened to you if I had not come along when I did?"

"Who is to protect me from you?"

Cornelius studied her face, realizing for the first time how young she was—couldn't be more than twenty, he thought. "I am flattered if you see me as a threat, Ma'am. But you have nothing to fear from me. I like my women willing, plump, and sweet-tempered—you are none of these."

He gripped the door as if to close it and Dominique realized that when he was gone she would be alone and no nearer her goal. It was not in her nature to be dishonest, but she would say anything, do anything to get her family released from prison. And to accomplish that aim, she must stay on board this ship and win the captain's confidence.

"Wait! I will tell you what you want to know."

Cornelius nodded and closed the door, moving to stand beside her. He motioned that she should be seated on the only chair in the room, while he dumped clothing off a stool and lowered his bulk.

"Let's start with your name," he prodded.

She saw no reason to hide her true identity; no one on board this cursed ship would have heard of her or her family. "I am Dominique Charbonneau."

"You are English, and yet you have a French name."

"That is because my father was French. That could be said of half the women of Tobago."

He stared at her as if he could tell by looking into her eyes if she were telling the truth. "Why did you stow away aboard this ship?"

"I was frightened because I was being pursued by someone and I had to leave the island. I hoped your Captain Gallant would help me."

"Why would you think that?" Cornelius asked doubtfully.

She met his gaze. "I encountered your captain in Scarborough and he seemed a . . . proper gentleman. I felt I could trust him."

Cornelius inspected her with suspicion. "Do you know who he is?"

She blinked her eyes innocently. "He is captain of this ship. Any ship would have done as well. I had to leave the island—to escape."

"Where is your ma and pa?"

At least on this she could be truthful. "They are both dead."

"Then what were you doing on Tobago?"

She had practiced her story over and over for just this moment. Could she be a good enough actress to fool this suspicious man? "I . . . served tables at the Blue Dog Tavern."

His eyebrows rose in disapproval and he spoke curtly. "I know about the serving wenches at that tavern. They are required to do more than just serve rum and ale to the men."

Her face flushed with color, and she bent down as though to examine her feet so he would not see her embarrassment. It was hard to keep from defending herself against his accusations. "A woman has to do many things she does not like to survive—but you would not know about that."

There was disgust in the first mate's expression. "A

whore. You will surely rue the day you came aboard this ship. If the captain don't throw you to the sharks, the crew may well have their way with you."

She threw back her shoulders and tilted her chin. "I can take care of myself."

"So it would seem." He pointed to the key he had given her earlier. "Still, I would lock the door if I were you."

When he left, she did just that, then she leaned against it, trying to still her beating heart. She had met the first obstacle, but there would be others. The worst, she was certain, would be when she had to face the notorious captain of the *Tempest*.

Cornelius rapped on the door of the captain's quarters and entered only when he was invited inside. The cabin was not what one would expect if one believed Judah Gallant to be a pirate. It reflected a man of meticulous habits, with a love of the written word. Maps were neatly stacked on the corner of the massive desk and leatherbound books lined a three-tiered bookshelf. The bed was wide and had been built to fit the cabin. Through the door to the right was a formal dining room where the captain and Ethan had just finished their meal.

Judah nodded to a chair, "Sit, Cornelius, and help yourself to the food. There is plenty left."

"Begging your pardon, Captain, but I'm here to report a stowaway."

Judah rose slowly, wondering if this could be the spy that William had warned him about during their meeting. "A stowaway on my ship," he said grimly. "Bring him to me at once!"

"It isn't exactly a him, Captain—it's a woman."

Judah threw his napkin on the table, his eyes blazing and his jaw tightening. "Who was on watch when this happened?"

"She came aboard last night, that would be Tom Beeton's watch."

"Did she give a reason for stowing away aboard my ship?"

Cornelius remembered he still wore his cap, so he snatched it off and tucked it beneath his arm. "Well, Captain, she said she met you on Tobago and felt she could trust you. Said she worked at the Blue Dog Tavern."

Ethan grinned. "And I thought you said you went into the village to meet a man. You must have been at your most charming to cause her to sneak on board just to be with you." The grin did not leave his face as he looked at the first mate. "You said she felt she could trust him? Are you sure she did not confuse the captain with someone else?"

Judah glared at Ethan, but made no comment. He wondered if it was the same woman who had asked for his protection. How the hell had she boarded his ship?

"The men are a superstitious lot; they are not going to like having a woman on board," Judah said. "Keep her away from them until we can put her ashore."

"She said she'd like to talk to you," Cornelius said.

"All I want to see of her is the back of her head as she leaves my ship. Is that understood!"

"Aye, Captain," Cornelius said, then he turned to leave. The captain had taken it better than he'd expected, still he would not want to be Tom Beeton, who had been lax on his watch. On a ship with such an undisciplined crew, punishment must be swift and certain.

Judah stood on the quarterdeck, his arms folded, his eyes riveted on Tom Beeton, who was tied to the mast with his shirt ripped to the waist to expose his naked back. Cornelius unfurled a cat-o'-nine-tails, while the rest of the crew stood by, having been ordered by the captain to observe the punishment.

The whip snaked out, cutting into the man's flesh, but he made no outcry. Once more the whip struck, then again. This time, Tom Beeton did scream. Twice more the whip slashed across Tom's back before the punishment was fully executed.

"Let this be a lesson to all who are gathered here not to be lax in your duty," Judah said, his voice like a whiplash cutting across the grumbling of the men and shocking them into silence. "A crime against one is a crime against all—remember this. Now you are dismissed. Go about your duties."

As ship's doctor, Ethan had Tom cut loose and ordered two crew members to carry him to the infirmary.

Cornelius stood beside his captain, his eyes watchful for signs of trouble.

"The men don't like the flogging, Captain. You heard the dissent. You should have let me set him adrift with food and water."

"That would have proven nothing," Judah said impatiently, ready to put the distasteful incident behind him. "Discipline is the only thing they do understand. Had I allowed Tom to get off without punishment, I would have looked weak in the eyes of the others. They may not like what I did, but they respect it—and they expected it."

Cornelius nodded. Still, he would watch the crew closely for signs of trouble. They were a scurvy lot, and he did not trust any man jack of them.

Even in her cabin belowdecks, Dominique could hear the man's screams and the sound of the whip striking flesh. She covered her ears and huddled on the bed, trembling with fear.

She should have expected brutality from these black-hearted pirates, but still, she wondered what the man's crime had been.

She remained in her cabin, trying to gather enough courage to face Captain Gallant. She passed long, lonely hours lying on the hard bunk before she could make herself unlock the door. Even then, she did not dare take one step outside the cabin.

What would be her fate when the captain turned his eyes on her? Would she live long enough to complete her mission? She was not so certain.

And if not, what would become of Valcour and her grandfather?

8

Although Dominique had been warned to remain in her cabin, she quietly unlocked her door and crept up the narrow steps. She was willing to chance encountering some horrible cutthroat just to escape the stuffy cabin.

When she reached the deck, she was captivated by the dawn dancing upon the waves with the brilliance of shimmering diamonds. As she breathed in the cleansing sea air, her head seemed to clear.

Suddenly, she heard voices above her and pressed herself against the railing, fearful that someone would discover her presence. Only after a moment of apprehension did she glance up at the quarterdeck to see Captain Gallant himself, speaking to one of his men.

"How fares Tom Beeton, doctor?"

"His wounds are deep, but they will heal. I would watch him if I were you, Judah. He has made some threats."

"Tom Beeton does not concern me. Let us hope he learned a lesson and never again allows a stowaway on board my ship," Judah said grimly.

The man who had been referred to as doctor moved

away and the captain turned his head in Dominique's direction. She quickly jumped behind a roll of canvas in a panic, but when a few minutes passed, she realized he had not seen her.

Dear God, what she had heard the night before was a man being punished because of her. What kind of a monster was this pirate captain? And how could she bear to get close enough to such a man to glean secrets from him?

Dominique leaned forward so she could have a better view of the godlike captain who seemed impervious to his surroundings, his gaze centered on the rising sun.

His hair was black and short-cropped, curling at the nape of his neck. The white shirt he wore was full-sleeved; the lacings across his chest opened just enough to show his bronzed skin.

In that moment, Judah turned his head so his face was in profile and she could study him more closely. His mouth was full and his nose straight, in harmony with the rest of his features. If he were not a man, she would have called him beautiful.

He looked dashing and noble, quite unlike a pirate. His bearing was straight and tall, his stance arrogant, his presence overpowering. How could a man so handsome have such a black heart? she wondered.

Judah Gallant seemed to dominate the very air she breathed, and she was completely at his mercy. Dominique was even more frightened of him than ever.

Unconsciously taking a step, she did not see the rope lying on the deck until it was too late. Her foot tangled in the jute coils and she fell forward, hitting the deck with a hard thud.

When Dominique lifted her head, trying to shake off the pain, all she could see was a pair of black, shiny boots. Slowly, she raised her eyes and they clashed with the stormy blue eyes of Captain Gallant himself.

When he made no attempt to help her rise, Dominique scampered to her feet and faced him bravely, even though her heart was thundering with fear.

"What are you doing on my deck?" Judah asked, his nostrils flaring in anger.

"I . . . came out for a breath of air. I did not think there would be anyone about."

"Then you are a fool. Do you believe that the ship sails itself?"

Dominique felt her own anger ignite, but she struggled to control it. She was there to woo the pirate captain not battle with him, no matter how tempting it would be to put him in his place. She was not exactly certain what Captain Gallant found attractive in a woman, but she supposed sweetness and charm would be more persuasive than stinging words, no matter how well deserved.

From their brief encounters, Dominique had discerned that the captain was a man of intelligence, even though he was a lawless scoundrel, a murderer, and a thief, if not worse. Most likely he liked depraved women. Could she make him believe she was a woman of low morals and still keep her virtue?

With the sea breeze ruffling her hair, Dominique moved toward him, allowing her hips to swing enticingly as she had seen the women do in the tavern. "Captain," she said softly, "surely you remember me."

"How could I forget?" he said dryly. "I believe you were trying to convince me that you were in your . . . profession against your will."

Dominique's stomach tightened with anxiety, and she quivered when his eyes raked her boldly, lingering on her low-cut blouse, then moving to her softly rounded hips, which were covered by the wrinkled red skirt, now shrunken and showing her ankles.

She met his steady gaze. "I . . . cannot help the way I look; my clothing was ruined when I swam to your ship."

"You swam?" he asked in disbelief. "That was a dangerous thing to do—the undertows, the sharks—are you crazed?"

Dominique shrugged. "I told you I was desperate, that I had to leave Tobago."

His jaw tightened. "Ah yes, I believe you said someone was chasing you. Did it occur to you that—"

Dominique interrupted him. "Believe what you will, Captain, but I was in grave danger." Dominique's face burned with humiliation and she laced her hands together and stared down at them, afraid to look at him lest he read the deception in her eyes, "I am in great fear for my safety," she assured him. That at least was true, but the person who frightened her most at the moment was the captain himself.

"Madame," Judah said, "it was I who was speaking. What made you think you could seek sanctuary aboard my ship? You would be far safer with men who are willing to pay for your . . . charms. My crew would not be so inclined."

"You speak of your crew, but what about you? Need I fear you, Captain?"

His lip curled in contempt. "You have nothing to fear from me, unless you leave your cabin again without my permission. If you do, I can assure you that your door will be locked from the outside. I have enough problems without worrying about your effect on my crew." His eyes pierced hers. "Is that understood?"

Lowering her eyes, Dominique paused for a moment in silent despair. Then she gathered her courage and raised her eyes to his. "I had heard that you were more appreciative of a woman's charms."

He watched her closely. She was a woman of contradictions. She would have him believe that she had loose morals, but there was an air of innocence about her that did not quite fit the part. He was immediately suspicious, thinking she might have been planted aboard his ship.

"What else did you hear about me?"

"I have heard that even though you are a pirate, you are both feared and admired. And I was told that you like the company of women."

"If you were told that I would be drawn to someone of your special . . . qualities, you were badly misinformed."

Dominique realized that she had approached him wrongly. "So what kind of woman do you prefer?"

Judah's eyes swept past her and out to sea. "A lady of my own choosing."

For some reason she was hurt by his harsh words. He had won this time, but she would regroup and approach him again. She had to—she had no choice.

"If you find my company so offensive, then I will take my leave of you, Captain," she said stiffly.

"Wait!" Judah stopped her. "I don't know what folly induced you to come aboard my ship, but you were told to keep to your cabin, and you will do so. Do not make me warn you again."

"And if I disobey, what are you going to do with me?" she challenged. "Have me whipped like the poor creature I heard screaming in pain last night?"

"It would be no more than you deserve," Judah said coldly. "If you were a man, there would be no question of it. I would have Cornelius lay the lash to you with no compunction. Unfortunately, there is nothing I can do about you at the moment."

He took her arm firmly and escorted her to the steps leading down to her cabin. "Go below and lock yourself in. But be warned that we will be engaged in a battle by dawn tomorrow, and you may regret ever having stepped aboard my ship."

"A . . . a battle?"

"That's what we do, you know. If you are alarmed by that prospect, you should have considered the consequences before you sought sanctuary aboard the *Tempest*."

"I never thought—"

Judah held his hand up to silence her. "You have met my first mate, Cornelius. He will see to your needs. You can trust him, as well as Dr. Graham. But do not open your door to anyone else."

Dominique nodded mutely, then fled to her cabin, glad to have escaped with no more than a scolding. Once inside, she sat on the bed, her mind going over her untimely encounter with Judah Gallant.

A sea battle, he had said—they could be sunk or killed! Would this nightmarish ordeal never end? One thing was obvious: Captain Gallant did not like her. Perhaps if she had come to him as herself and begged for his help— No, that would not have mattered to him. And it was too late to feign innocence. She had already convinced him that she was a woman of questionable character.

She shivered, wondering what her fate would be if he ever discovered her plan to betray him. She must be very careful.

There was a knock on the door, and when Dominique unlocked it to admit Cornelius, he was carrying a tray of food.

"Ma'am, I thought you might be hungry. Cook made you a special dish," he said cordially.

She moved away from him, angry because the captain had implied that it was Cornelius who had beaten the poor crew member.

"I do not want anything."

"The captain won't take kindly if you refuse to eat and make yourself ill. You'd better reconsider. I have some nice fruit for you here. At least eat that."

"Why didn't your captain have me whipped instead of the poor man who did no wrong? I was the guilty one. I made sure he did not see me come aboard."

"So you heard about that."

"Your captain treats his men no better than animals. He is a beast."

The first mate set the tray down on a chair and stood to his full height. "If you are looking for someone to blame for what happened, you might want to look to yourself. 'Twas you that stowed away and raised the captain's ire. We are in enemy waters here," he said a little more kindly when he saw her face pale. "If a man does not do his duty, it could mean death to us all."

"I do not understand why he should be punished so severely," Dominique said, only slightly mollified.

"Then you know nothing of the laws of the sea, Ma'am. Here on board the *Tempest*, the captain is master. His word is law, and if any break those laws, they pay the consequences."

"Why did he not have me whipped?"

"Suppose you ask the captain." Cornelius picked up the chair with the tray and moved it toward her. "Now, why don't you be a good lass and eat. It may be a long time before we get close enough to land to put you ashore. You could get a mite hungry before then."

Dominique nodded, more to placate him than from any need of sustenance at the moment.

He nodded his head in approval, then left. Dominique went to the door and turned the key, wondering if she would be safe even with the locked door between her and the nest of pirates.

Restlessly, she moved to the porthole and stared out at the serene white clouds that floated in a bright blue sky. Who would have guessed that she would ever be aboard a pirate ship, and at the mercy of a madman like Judah Gallant?

9

Judah stared at the distant ship that was no larger than a dot on the horizon. He tossed his eyeglass to Cornelius, who stood beside him on the quarterdeck. "Tell me what you make of her."

Cornelius squinted into the eyeglass, surveying the ship carefully. "It's hard to tell from here, Captain. But I'm betting she's French."

"Lower the sails and turn into the wind. We will allow her to gain on us."

"Aye, Captain," Cornelius replied, calling out an order below. Men sprang into action and excitement ran high as they sensed a battle in the offing.

Time passed, and by late afternoon, the frigate was within sight and it was easy to see the French flag waving atop her mast.

"Run up a French flag," Judah ordered his first mate, "and have half the men dress in French uniforms and the other half remain out of sight for the time being. Also, have fifteen casks of wine brought up from the hold so they can be transferred to the French ship. Make certain the wine is some that we commandeered from a French vessel."

Cornelius grinned, reading Judah's mind. "Aye, Captain."

Dominique stood on tiptoe and looked out the porthole, staring in stark surprise at what she saw: a French ship bearing down on them. This must be the battle Captain Gallant had predicted. She squeezed her eyes tightly, waiting for the sound of cannon shot, but it never came. Soon the ship had sailed out of her view, but she knew it had not gone away. Why had Captain Gallant let it pass unchallenged?

Mystified, she crept out of the cabin and climbed carefully up the steps to the deck. Dominique was shocked when she saw a number of the *Tempest* crew wearing French uniforms.

She raised her eyes to the quarterdeck and saw that Captain Gallant was also wearing a French naval uniform. To her surprise, he was shouting across to the other ship, speaking flawless French.

She listened in stunned silence.

"Captain du Plissis, of the good ship *Bonheur,* I have long heard of your daring exploits," Judah called out amiably. "It is a pleasure to meet you at last."

The captain of the *Bonheur* was obviously flattered. "I am sorry I have never heard of you, Captain. But I have been battling Nelson, the English dog. Alas, I have not seen home waters for these last two years."

"Then allow me to offer you some wine from my private stock," Judah told him. "Perhaps it will help make you less lonely since it comes from our own Auvergne Valley. I will include enough for all your crew."

"Why, thank you. I am most grateful to you for your kindness, and I accept your gift gladly."

Dominique hugged the shadows, listening to the conversation between the two captains. She had only to call out and warn the French that this was a pirate ship and that they were in danger. But she would say nothing that would jeopardize her own mission.

She rushed back to her cabin, feeling physically sick. With a groan, she lay her head back on the bunk. What had she come to?

Hours later, sleep still eluded Dominique. She could hear the drunken laughter coming from the French ship. Even though she did not like Napoleon, she felt pity for the French sailors all the same. They were unsuspecting—that a viper waited to strike.

It was just after midnight that the captain and crew of the *Tempest* went over the sides of their own ship and easily boarded the *Bonheur* and overcame her drunken crew.

No shot was fired, and soon the drunken captain and his officers were locked in the brig, while a crew from the *Tempest* was placed at the helm to take their prize to a safe port and deliver it into American hands.

Judah removed the offensive French coat and tossed it aside. It did not sit well with him to trick a fellow officer, even if he was the enemy. He would much rather meet his foe in open combat.

There was a rap on his door and, thinking it was Cornelius, Judah invited him to enter, while he unbuckled his belt and stripped his shirt over his head.

"I know what you are going to say, Cornelius, and I agree with you. I do not like pretending to be a friend and then taking prisoners. But lives were saved tonight, those of my men as well as the French—"

He broke off when he saw Dominique standing just inside the door, her face flushed, her eyes cast downward. He pulled his shirt back in place, his face a mask.

It had taken all Dominique's courage to come to him,

and even now she wanted to flee, but she stood her ground, unwilling to allow him to intimidate her.

"I thought I told you to remain in your cabin," Judah said sternly.

She raised the most dazzling turquoise eyes to him, and he was immediately struck by her beauty. He had not really seen her as a woman until now.

"Captain," she said softly, "please do not chastise me. I had to come because I am troubled."

He noticed that she looked pale. "What is bothering you?"

"I need to know what has happened to the French ship and crew. Did you sink the ship and slay all the men?" Her eyes were round with horror as she waited for his answer.

"If you must know," Judah replied in irritation, "the *Bonheur* is headed for friendlier waters, her unharmed crew with her. They will suffer no more than the effects from drinking too much wine when they awake in the morning—and perhaps hurt pride at being so easily taken."

"Then they were not harmed?"

"Ah, I see. Cornelius told me that your father was French, so I suppose you feel a kinship with those men. Are you an admirer of Bonaparte, as well?"

Dominique gave him a haughty look. "Do not imagine that just because I am half French, I believe in Napoleon Bonaparte. I can assure you that I do not. My family has suffered greatly at his hands."

Judah smiled sardonically. "So, what does a woman like you believe in?"

Dominique had forgotten for a moment that she was playing a role, and almost blurted out that she believed in honorable men like her grandfather and her brother.

Catching herself, she forced a smile and pushed her

tumbled hair out of her face, while allowing her blouse to slip off her shoulder in a deliberate move to be provocative.

"I believe in making men happy, Captain."

He stared at her reflectively. "Unfortunately, you can't do anything for me. I don't know what happiness is."

She felt drawn to him. There was something about Judah Gallant that reached inside of her and pulled at her heart. This was not supposed to happen, not with a pirate—a man with no honor.

"I could try to bring you happiness," she suggested, not knowing how she could accomplish such a feat.

Judah was trying to separate the seductress from the innocence he had seen in her earlier. "Cornelius told me your name, but I have forgotten it."

"I am Dominique Charbonneau," she answered, walking toward him purposely, even though each step was forced. "If you have not found happiness, then you have not been looking in the right places." Her voice was breathy, more from embarrassment than by design. "I could please you, for a day, a week . . . or perhaps even longer."

Judah startled her when he eased his hand about the back of her neck and brought her face into the lantern light as he searched each feature.

Dominique trembled, wanting to pull away, to run, but she merely smiled.

"I believe, lovely one, that you could please most men, but I am destined for a life of hell. You cannot help me. No one can."

She stared into clear blue eyes that were filled with— what? sadness? What had happened to him to make him so melancholy? Suddenly she felt like taking his dark head and laying it against her shoulder to comfort him.

"Perhaps you do not want to be helped, Captain. Has some woman wounded you so deeply that you close your heart to all others?"

In that instant, the blue of his eyes deepened and his hand slid from her neck to cup her face.

"My Lady Siren I shall call you, because you came to me from out of the sea to tempt me." He stared at her. "I never saw eyes like yours. They are the color of the turquoise waters of the Caribbean." He smiled slightly and it took her breath away.

Dominique was more afraid of him in his gentleness than when he had been insulting and cruel.

"Perhaps you are a mermaid," Judah continued, "come to enchant man, or perhaps you truly are a siren who lures men to their doom." He shrugged. "If that be so, a man would die happy indeed in your embrace."

She did not see it coming—she should have. His lips descended, and he ground his mouth against hers punishingly.

In a panic, Dominique twisted and pushed against him, trying to get free from him, but he held her fast. She felt her head swimming and her heart beating rapidly. She had never been kissed with such passion. With a suddenness that caused her almost to lose her balance, he released her and stepped back.

He pulled her blouse back on her shoulder and smiled regretfully. "Run along, Dominique Charbonneau, before I oblige you and take what you offer."

She did indeed want to run away. The glimpse of his unleashed passion frightened her. Taking a big gulp of air, she faced him bravely. Her voice trembled with emotion. "Suppose I want to stay on the *Tempest*? Suppose I want to be with you?"

"Then you are a fool," he said scathingly. "There is nothing for you here. I am a man with no heart and no conscience. Run away while you still can, little girl, lest you live to rue this day."

Now Dominique did run. She fled as fast as her legs could carry her. She raced across the deck, and down the steps, then yanked open the door to her cabin and locked herself inside. It took a moment before she could stop the quaking of her body.

The disquiet in her mind was another matter altogether.

How would she ever entrap the captain? He did not seem to want her. He had only been toying with her.

Even her fear for her brother and grandfather was not strong enough to prevail over the fear she felt for Captain Judah Gallant at the moment.

Judah's thoughts were of Dominique. She would most probably be a pleasant diversion, but he had neither the time nor the inclination to learn more about her. All he wanted was to have her off his ship, but that would not be possible just yet. He had a mission to accomplish and that must come before anything else.

Still, he could not help thinking that she was a rare beauty.

10

Dominique tossed upon her narrow bed as restless sleep caught her in its grip. There was a strange fever in her blood and a longing in her breasts that she did not understand as the face of Judah Gallant haunted her dreams.

"No," she groaned. "Go away, I do not want you. Leave me alone."

The ship's bell woke her and she noticed it was still dark. Why was she so hot? She kicked off the covers and tried to rise, but fell back trembling. Groaning, she wished her head would stop hurting. And why was the ship pitching and rolling?

Dominique did not know how much time had passed, or how long she had been confined to her bunk. She heard voices, but what they said was a jumble to her.

"I found her this way, Captain," Cornelius said. "When she didn't answer the door, I knew something was wrong, so I used my key."

She felt cool hands on her forehead, and someone was forcing her mouth open.

"She is not infected with any contagious illness," the doctor told Judah. "I suspect hers is nothing but a mild ailment, no doubt brought on by her swim to the ship. I will start her on a treatment that should have her up and about in no time."

"Stay with her until she is improved, Ethan," Judah said, concerned by how pale she looked. "As it is, I will have difficulty convincing the men that she hasn't brought some dread disease on board."

Judah left abruptly, and when he reached the upper deck, as he suspected, most of the crew had already gathered there and were mumbling among themselves.

"I have just left the woman," Judah told them. "She is only mildly ill and Dr. Graham has assured me she is not contagious."

"We don't want no woman on this ship," one of the men complained, drawing nods of agreement from the others.

"Cast her adrift," another chimed in. "Women bring nothing but bad luck on a ship—they're marked for trouble. We'll most likely all die from whatever it is she's brought aboard."

"Hear me," Judah said, raising his voice and speaking with authority. "Have I not always been honest with you? Would I not be the first to tell you if the woman posed a danger to either this ship or crew? Is there anyone here who doubts my word?"

The men looked at each other and talked among themselves, now satisfied that what the captain had told them was true.

Tom Beeton, however, still held a grudge against the woman and wanted to see her punished. He spoke up, his voice filled with hostility. "I done took me a beating 'cause of that woman. She's nothing but trouble, and I say she goes before she causes any further harm."

Judah's eyes moved over Tom with such intensity

that, although he was not a coward, he cringed. "Who are you," Judah said at last, "that you think you can give commands aboard my ship?"

"None of us like the woman being here, Cap'n," someone spoke up in Tom's defense.

"Who among you blame this woman instead of Tom? Was it not his carelessness that allowed her on board in the first place? If any one of you had been so remiss on your watch, don't you think Tom would want to see you punished?"

There was a nod of heads. "Ye be right enough, Cap'n," one of the men agreed. "Still, that don't change the truth that women are poison on a ship."

"On that I will agree," Judah said. "But I will not put a helpless woman to sea on her own. If there is any among you who is willing to send her to certain death, step forward."

There was a long silence, and no one moved.

Judah nodded in satisfaction. "Now that we understand each other, you have my word that I'll put her ashore as soon as we are within sight of land."

Tom felt grudging respect for the captain, who held the men together by sheer will. "Seeing as it's my fault, like you said, Cap'n, that she's on this ship, I wouldn't feel right putting her adrift. It's all right with me if she stays aboard 'til we reach a port."

Judah nodded, knowing that a revolt had been averted. However, he had a feeling that if he did not get Dominique off his ship, other complications would ensue.

"Go about your tasks, men," he ordered. "Tonight each of you will have an extra ration of rum."

In her fevered condition, Dominique became aware of a man with a soft-spoken manner and gentle hands. As the days passed and she grew stronger, she came to know Dr. Ethan Graham. Sometimes when she awoke at night, she would find him sitting at her bedside, his eyes on her face.

One morning Dominique awoke to find herself alone. Feeling well and rested, she sat up in bed and stretched her arms over her head.

The door to her cabin swung open, and a man entered, his face easing into a smile when he saw her sitting up.

"I am glad you are feeling better. In another day or so, you will be your old self again."

The man was slender, and his dark hair was swept across his wide forehead. His dark eyes were filled with compassion.

"You are Dr. Graham, are you not?"

"I am, indeed. And you, Miss Charbonneau, have been a very ill young woman."

Dominique had to know how much valuable time she had lost. She was no closer to her goal than she had been when she first came aboard the *Tempest*. "How long have I been ill, Dr. Graham?"

"Three days. But you were never in danger." He smiled kindly. "However, I must caution you against swimming such long distances. I am amazed that someone as delicate as you would even attempt it."

Three days, Dominique thought with growing distress. That could be a lifetime for her grandfather, who was so ill. She had to convince the doctor that she was well enough to leave this cabin. Otherwise, how could she hope to win her way into the captain's favor?

"Dr. Graham, if only I could walk about—I mean outside, I am certain that the sea air would go a long way in speeding my recovery."

Ethan pulled up a stool and sat beside her. "You may

be right. I'll talk to the captain about it. Any decision on that matter must be his."

She looked into the doctor's clear honest eyes and wondered what he was doing aboard a pirate ship. "Your captain is mean-spirited, and I fear he might not allow me any privileges."

Ethan chuckled and then laughed with abandon. "You may be the first female who ever saw Judah in such an unfavorable light. How amusing."

"From my own experience with him, I have not found that he cares overmuch for a woman's feelings."

The doctor became serious, and he was speaking more to himself than to her, although she could not have known that. "You should not judge him too harshly. Judah was once a good and faithful husband. When his wife died, he became a changed man, the one you see today."

Dominique remembered Colonel Marceau mentioning that Captain Gallant's wife had died, but she could not think of him as a man who would grieve over a woman. She was not certain that the doctor knew him as well as he thought.

"You defend him, but I wonder if he would thank you. He is, after all, no more than a vicious pirate."

Suddenly it seemed as if a secretive veil crept into the doctor's eyes and he stood, his demeanor less friendly. "All of us on board the *Tempest* are no more than vicious pirates. But then you were aware of that fact when you came aboard." He looked weary as he moved to the door. "I will speak to the captain on your behalf. I am certain he will allow you to walk about if you are escorted."

Dominique felt that she had somehow offended the doctor, and that had not been her intention. "You seem so different from the other men. I cannot believe that you would even condone their actions against humanity."

Ethan paused at the door and looked back at her. "Are any of us what we seem?" he asked solemnly. "Take you, for instance. You have admitted freely that you worked at the Blue Dog Tavern." His eyes searched her face. "Yet, to look at you, one would hardly associate you with such an occupation."

Dominique lowered her head so her hair would curtain her face. Once more she was forced to endure the degradation brought on by her lie. She did not want the doctor to think ill of her, but she dared not tell him the truth. No matter how kind he had been to her, he was, after all, the captain's man.

When she raised her head and looked at Ethan, her eyes were incredibly sad. "We all do what we must, Doctor."

"You do what you must, and the captain does what he believes is right." His words were spoken kindly and without any intent to chastising her. "You might want to remember that when you judge him, Miss Charbonneau."

When the doctor departed, Dominique slipped out of bed to find that she was wearing a man's shirt and it came all the way to her knees. She could only suppose the doctor had dressed her while she was ill. Taking the blanket off the bed, she draped it about her shoulders and moved about the cabin, searching for her own garments.

Someone knocked on the door, and when Dominique opened it, Cornelius entered, carrying what appeared to be a bundle of clothing.

"The captain has given permission for you to walk about the deck with either myself or Dr. Graham. I foraged through everyone's trunks until I found something suitable. Mayhap the men will be less inclined to take notice of you if you are garbed as a sailor."

She held up a pair of faded blue pants with white stripes and inspected them carefully. "Surely you cannot expect me to dress in trousers. It would be . . . disgraceful, unseemly— No, I cannot do such a thing!"

Cornelius looked at her carefully, taking in the embarrassed flush to her cheeks. How could a woman with her jaded past, who made her way by pleasing men, care how she was garbed? He never would understand the workings of a woman's mind.

"I'm sorry, Ma'am, but the captain's orders are that if you want to walk on deck, you must be inconspicuous."

"Where is my own clothing?" she asked pointedly.

"Cook thought he was doing you a good turn when he washed your skirt and blouse. He feels real bad that they just fell into rags." He held up a pair of scuffed brown boots. "Look," he said proudly, "I even managed to find you footwear. These boots once belonged to a cabin boy and they look just about your size."

Dominique made a quick decision: the only way to reach the captain was to get out of this cabin. And the only way to do that was to dress as he commanded. She sighed. "I do not wish to seem ungracious after all your trouble on my behalf. I shall wear them."

"Then make yourself ready. I'll return in a bit to escort you on your walk."

Dominique felt exhilarated as she moved across the deck beside the first mate. Her slender form was artfully concealed beneath the baggy trousers and her hair was stuffed beneath a bright red cap. She did, however, receive some heated glances and snarls of discontent from several of the men, which she chose to ignore.

"It is such a lovely day," Dominique said, basking in

the warm sunlight. "Being island-born and -bred, I love being outside. Unlike most of my friends, I never cared overmuch for sewing and other genteel tasks. I prefer to ride across the plantation—"

She paused, fearing she might have just given herself away. But when she glanced up at Cornelius to see if had heard her, she was relieved to find his attention was otherwise occupied.

"You there, mister," the first mate called to one of the crew, "retie that rope and see if you can do it tight this time. You know the captain doesn't allow slovenliness on this ship."

Cornelius moved away from Dominique to inspect the man's work, so she allowed her attention to stray to the quarterdeck. Yes, the captain was there, still godlike, still observing everything around him. His eyes rested on her only briefly and then he looked away as if she was beneath his notice.

At that moment, a sudden gust of wind struck with a force that ripped Dominique's cap from her head and deposited it on the edge of the railing. To her dismay, the cap was just out of reach.

Hoping no one would take notice, she leaned forward and reached out for her cap. But just when it was within her grasp, her hand slipped on the wet railing. Unable to regain her balance, she plunged forward and then downward into the water below.

She hit with such a force that it knocked the breath from her and she felt the water close over her head as she plunged deeper and deeper into the salty brine.

In a panic, she fought and kicked her feet, trying to get to the surface, but she feared that she would never reach it in time. Her trousers and heavy boots were dragging her even further downward.

Just when she thought her lungs would burst from lack of air, she felt a strong arm go around her and she was swiftly guided upward toward the surface.

Her first breath of air was painful and she coughed and sputtered, grasping the neck of the man who had rescued her. Her strength ebbed, and she weakly laid her head against her rescuer's shoulder, believing it was Cornelius.

She tensed when she heard Judah's harsh voice.

"Miss Charbonneau, are you all right?"

"I . . . Yes, I believe so."

When she looked up at him, she saw the disapproval in his expression.

"Whatever possessed you to do such a fool thing?" he demanded.

"My cap," she said, collapsing against him in fatigue. "I lost my cap."

"A siren right out of Homer's *Ulysses*," he muttered, reaching for the rope ladder that Cornelius had dropped. He handed her to his first mate when they reached the deck.

"Cornelius," Judah said harshly, "keep this woman out of trouble and attempt to keep her out of the water. Next time, I'll let her drown."

"Aye, Captain," the first mate answered, looking Dominique over carefully. "Are you hurt, Ma'am?" he asked, setting her on her feet.

She only had the strength to shake her head as he led her forward, supporting most of her weight. After a few steps, she collapsed and would have fallen had not Judah reached for her. Since his cabin was the nearest, Judah lifted Dominique into his arms and carried her to the quarterdeck.

Cornelius raced ahead of him and grabbed a blanket from a chest, which he wrapped about her while Judah gently deposited her on the bed.

"Go get Ethan. I want him to make certain she has not harmed herself in the fall."

Dominique opened her eyes to find the captain standing over her, his expression almost soft. "You have not had an easy time of it, have you?"

For some reason, his kindness brought tears to her eyes, and she was glad her face was wet so he would not know she was crying. "You could do with dry clothing, Captain," was all she could think of to say.

"So I could," he agreed. He quickly rummaged through a trunk for clothing and boots, then moved to the door, grasping the knob in his hand. "You will remain in my cabin until the doctor says you are steady enough to return to yours."

She raised up on her elbows, looking at him with concern. "This is your cabin?"

Guessing that she was suspicious of his motives in bringing her to his quarters, he frowned and turned back to the door. "You need have no fear of me, Miss Charbonneau, I have my duties to perform."

Dominique could not keep from noticing the way his wet shirt clung to his broad chest, and when she watched him rake a hand through his dark hair, she diverted her eyes, somehow feeling shy. "Captain, thank you for saving me. I would surely have drowned had you not come in after me."

He looked at her grimly. "You seem to spend a great deal of your time in the sea. A habit I would suggest you rectify."

Without another word, he swept out of the cabin.

Dominique rolled her head to the side, looking about the room. This was her opportunity—she was alone in his quarters! Perhaps she would have time to search through the captain's personal papers before anyone came in.

Much to her dismay, Dr. Graham chose that moment to enter, and after examining her closely, pronounced her none the worse for her dunking.

She had no choice but to allow him to escort her back to her own cabin, where he urged her to change into dry clothing, then left to make his report to the captain.

Somehow she must get back into Judah's quarters. She was convinced that she would find the information Colonel Marceau wanted there.

11

The days of Dominique's life passed in virtual solitude, bringing her to the painful realization that she had come on a fool's mission. She spent long hours pacing the narrow confines of her cabin, planning how best to approach Captain Gallant. But she never caught more than a glimpse of him in the distance, and it almost seemed as if he was purposely avoiding her.

She was beginning to despair, fearing that the captain was never going to allow her near him.

She was permitted only a brief time each morning and evening to stroll about the deck with either Dr. Graham or Cornelius. As the first mate had predicted, she blended in with the crew, and found herself enjoying the freedom her new garb allowed her.

However, dressed as she was, how would she ever get the captain to look at her as a woman? She had to make herself desirable to him, although such a notion was abhorrent to her.

Dominique had never liked lies and deceitfulness. But she was caught in a trap and there was no escape. The only way she could gain her brother and grandfather's release was to help her own enemy bring Captain Gallant to justice for his crimes against France.

* * *

Dominique picked up the three books that Dr. Graham had brought her. Two of them were in English, and she had already read them each three times. The third book she had pushed aside since it was Homer's works in the original Greek, a language she had no knowledge of. Of course, she had once read a French translation of Homer, so she knew the stories. She reached for the book and noticed that it was beautifully leather-bound, with pages embossed in gold. She was impressed with Ethan's ability to read Greek.

Absently, she turned to the front of the book and read the personal inscription that had obviously been written by a feminine hand. It was inscribed, not to the doctor, but to Captain Gallant.

> To my dearest husband, Judah, knowing how fond you are of Greek myths, I send this along to you with my love. I pray God will hasten the days so we can soon be together.
>
> Lovingly, Mary.

Dominique felt like an eavesdropper as she read the tender sentiment from a wife to her husband. So, the captain not only spoke French, he could read Greek as well. More and more, she was confused because he refused to conform to her vision of him. Who was he—what was he really like?

She was so caught up in her thoughts that she was totally unaware of the tumult that was taking place aboard the *Tempest* at that very moment.

She was almost thrown to the floor when the ship turned sharply and excited voices reached her consciousness. She was alarmed when she heard cannon fire.

They were under attack!

She heard Judah give the order to fire a broadside at the French vessel as she sailed boldly within range of the *Tempest*'s guns.

"Cap'n," the watch called down from his lofty perch, "there'll be another ship off the starboard. She's closing in fast."

Judah swung around and viewed the second ship through his glass. "Damn," he growled, slamming the eyeglass against his hand and turning to Cornelius. "Curse me for a fool, but I led us into this one. The second enemy ship will overtake us in minutes."

"What'll we do, Captain?" his first mate wanted to know.

Judah took the helm and turned toward the nearest ship, aiming for her bow and attempting to rake her with a hard broadside. Splintering wood and the cries of agony came from the enemy ship, and the *Tempest* shuddered and groaned, but her timbers held fast.

The second ship was now within cannon range and was firing at the *Tempest*'s riggings. With a loud splintering sound, the riggings and the main mast fell, amid cries of agony from the men crushed beneath them.

"Prime cannon and look sharp," Judah called loudly. "Hold your fire men— Hold it. Hold it— *NOW!*"

Dominique clamped her hands over her ears to mute the deafening sounds. It seemed to her that there was continual bombardment and she was sure they would be sunk.

Presently Dominique became aware of the injured, and knew she must do something to help. Heedless of any danger to herself, she ripped open her cabin door and ran up the companionway, making her way on deck.

The sight that met her eyes was horrifying. The deck was littered with debris and men lay bleeding and dying.

In shock she watched Tom Beeton ram a rod down the muzzle of a cannon, and then another man load and a third man light and fire it.

She had no notion how long she stood there. She cried out when Tom fell to the deck, wounded by a sharpshooter's bullet.

Her eyes went to the other vessel and she saw the French flag waving above its mast. However, she felt no kinship with the men of Napoleon's navy. To her they represented the enemy and Colonel Marceau.

She could hear Judah's voice calling above the noise. "Continuous firing, men! Keep a steady volley!"

With an anger that took her by surprise, Dominique ran forward, grabbed up the rammer Tom Beeton had dropped, and performed the motions that she had seen him do before he was cut down.

She sponged out the muzzle of the cannon, clearing it of hot debris, then the startled seamen loaded, primed, and fired. This was repeated over and over, and Dominique mechanically performed the duty as if she had been born to it. She felt that every shot that came from the cannon was aimed at the heart of Colonel Marceau.

An acrid pall of smoke lingered in the air and it looked to all concerned that the *Tempest* would lose this battle. Judah did not notice that Dominique had joined his crew in defending the ship. His only thought was how to outmaneuver the enemy.

His jaw tightened in a grim line, and just for a moment, a smile lingered on his lips as he gauged the distance of the two French ships approaching from different directions.

"They believe they have us, Cornelius, but they have just signed their own death warrant! Look sharp," he warned as the two ships bore down on them with cannons firing.

With a quick maneuver leeward, the *Tempest*'s bow arched and it seemed as if the ship was propelled upward, between wind and water. Men tumbled across the deck and machinery slid abaft as Judah fought to compensate for the perilous movement. With super-human strength, he managed to maintain his grip on the wheel and bring the vessel under his control.

When the *Tempest* cleared the path of the enemy ships, the deafening sound of cannon fire continued. A cloud of sulfur smoke was so thick that it was impossible for Judah to see what was happening behind him.

He turned the *Tempest* against the wind and grabbed up his glass to see if his plan had worked.

Slowly, the smoke cleared and his face was grim, but he nodded in satisfaction.

"I never saw the likes, Captain!" Cornelius said, grinning widely and shaking his head in amazement. "I thought we were goners the way the French had us trapped between them. Damned if you didn't slip out of their reach and their wayward shots hit each other. This day will be spoken of long after we are all gone."

A yell of triumph went up from the crew as they saw the extensive damage to the enemy ships. One was list-ing badly from a gaping hole at her waterline. The other vessel had sustained extensive damage and was on fire. They were both sinking.

Judah watched as small crafts were launched and the French sailors clamored over the sides of their ships, fighting for a place in the longboats.

"Do we fire on them, Captain, or do we take prison-ers?" Cornelius inquired.

"Let no man fire, and leave them to their own devices. The enemy has lost, and we shall not add to their woes."

"We'll take no prize from them," the first mate observed as the burning ship went under.

Judah glanced about his own ship. Wounded men lay bleeding on the decks, some who were pinned beneath broken masts were dead. "Get us underway, Cornelius. Take us to safe harbor so we may lick our own wounds."

Dominique was bone-weary, but she saw that there were wounded who needed tending. Wordlessly, she knelt beside Dr. Graham and assisted him while he tied a tourniquet around Tom Beeton's injured arm.

"Doctor, you see what the little miss did?" Tom said, grinning despite his pain.

Ethan glanced at Dominique, whose face was black and her clothing shredded. "Did you join in the fight?"

"That she did, Doctor." Tom answered for her. "Miss Dominique was so fearless, that no man could have done better," he said with pride.

Ethan motioned for two men to take Tom below to the infirmary. There was no time to dwell on the battle— the wounded needed immediate attention. As he moved from man to man, doing what he could, Dominique stayed at his side, lending her aid. She wrapped shattered limbs, cleansed gaping wounds, and held the hands of dying men.

It was hours later before she could escape to her cabin. Then she was so weary, she fell asleep at once.

After Judah surveyed the damage to his ship and made certain she was seaworthy, he went to the infirmary and walked among the wounded, pausing at each man to give him a word of encouragement. Although they had taken no prize, each man considered today a decided victory.

Judah stopped to converse with Tom Beeton, who wore his arm in a sling. "How goes it with you, Tom?"

"I'm doing right fine, Cap'n, sir. We had ourselves a hell of a battle this day."

"I understand from the doctor that you took a hard one in your arm and had some deep splinters, but that no bones were shattered."

"That be so, sir. But it would have been worse if not for the little lady."

"I have been told that Miss Charbonneau helped during the battle." Judah smiled at the man's changed attitude toward having Dominique on board ship. "Everyone seems to be singing her praises."

"She's mighty fine, Cap'n. Miss Dominique was a ministering angel, helping Dr. Graham with the wounded. Most women would have been squeamish when it came to wounds and blood, but not her."

"Well, Tom, she seems to have found a champion in you, hasn't she?"

"That she has. It's kinda like she's brought us luck, Cap'n. If anyone ever tries to cause her harm, he'll have to deal with Tom Beeton first."

Judah saw no reason to remind Tom that he was the one who had cried the loudest that having a woman on board would bring disaster to them all. Next, he thought, Tom would be bragging that he was the one who brought Dominique onto the ship in the first place.

"If that be so, Tom, then we owe the battle to Miss Charbonneau."

Tom rose up on his elbow. "No, Cap'n, the battle belongs to you, and by all that's holy, I never saw anything like it. I do recall a legend about a captain, can't call his name to mind, but he was one of those heroes from the Revolutionary War—don't know if he was a real person or just some tale. He was said to have done the same maneuver you did today and with the same results. Never heard of anyone else pulling such a stunt, and never expect I will again."

Judah looked reflective. "The man you speak of did in fact exist. He was known only as the Raven, and he was a friend of my father's."

The hour was late as Judah went below to see about Dominique. Her door was ajar, so he entered the cabin to find her asleep. He stood over her for a long moment, studying her features. Her face was blackened, and her clothing was torn and bloodstained. He tried to imagine her as she must have looked today, manning a cannon and tending the wounded.

He though of his dead wife. Mary would have fainted at the first sounds of battle, let alone the sight of blood. Over the years, he had learned to measure every woman by Mary's character—but not this woman. She was different from anyone he had ever known.

Even beneath her blackened face, he could see the smooth even features. Her form was slender and her hands dainty. What would make a woman with her kind of courage turn to prostitution? he wondered, resenting the fact that she had been handled by countless men.

He reached down and picked up a blanket and pulled it over her.

Dominique only sighed, but she did not awaken.

There were many things he did not understand about her, but he would never believe, after her heroic deeds today, that she had fled to his ship in need of protection.

There was another reason she was there, and he intended to find out what it was.

12

Dominique was jarred awake by the rumbling sound of cannon fire. In a panic, she jumped off the bed and raced upward to the deck. It took her a moment to realize that they were not under attack.

Instead, Captain Gallant was conducting a solemn ceremony in honor of the men who had died in battle. She pressed her way forward and was surprised when the crew members stepped aside respectfully to allow her to pass.

Moving to stand beside Dr. Graham, Dominique looked up at the quarterdeck, where all eyes were trained on the captain.

"Rest in peace, noble warriors," he said with feeling, "until the sea shall give up her dead."

Dominique glanced about her, noticing the look of respect on the faces of the men. They might be hard-hearted pirates, but they did appear to honor the man who commanded them all.

The ceremony seemed to be over, but everyone still stood at attention, waiting until Captain Gallant dismissed them.

Dominique looked up at the doctor in remorse. "I

must have slept through most of the ceremony. I am sorry for that."

Ethan gazed down at her and smiled slightly when he saw that her face was still black from the cannon smoke. "You have nothing to apologize for, Miss Charbonneau. I would say you deserved your rest. Have you any notion what a heroine you have become to this crew?"

"I have?" she asked in surprise.

"I can assure you I was told a dozen different versions of how you single-handedly saved the ship."

"While I was helping you, I heard nothing but talk of the daring of your Captain Gallant. I would say the day belonged to him."

Ethan nodded. "In truth, Judah is known as a brilliant strategist with a quick mind. Even so, I am as amazed as everyone else at how he outsmarted two ships that outgunned and outmanned us. Some men are born with abilities far beyond us other mortals—he is one of those men."

"You like him," Dominique observed.

"Indeed I do. And if that's a crime, I plead guilty."

Her eyes widened with sudden wonder. "I did not realize that we had been attacked by two enemy ships."

"The way I understand it, you were a bit busy helping load the cannons."

There was misery in her eyes. "I never thought I would help take a human life."

Ethan put a comforting arm about her and steered her around a broken timber. "Do not blame yourself. It was the French ships that destroyed each other. Our captain merely maneuvered out of their path so they could take the cannon shots that were meant for us."

Dominique swallowed hard. "Were there . . . Were many lives lost on those ships?"

"Not near as many as there would have been, Miss

Charbonneau, had not the captain allowed them to take to their longboats. I wonder if they would have been so generous if the circumstances had been reversed?"

Dominique was troubled by yet another side of the complex Captain Gallant. Why couldn't he be the cold-blooded pirate she had been led to believe he was? "Doctor, why do you think he allowed them to escape?"

Ethan's voice softened with kindness as he inspected her face and hands. "You will have to ask Judah that yourself. But for now, you should return to your cabin. I'll have bathing water brought to you."

Her hand went to her face, and for the first time she thought of her own appearance. "I must look a fright." She hurried away from him, feeling the heat of her humiliation in the very depths of her soul.

She did not see the adoring way the crew looked at her as she passed, and neither did she see their captain, whose eyes followed her until she disappeared from sight.

Dominique had bathed and was now clothed in clean trousers and shirt. When she heard the hesitant tap on her cabin door, she had just finished brushing her hair and laid the brush aside. She opened the door, startled to find Tom Beeton, with an uncertain grin on his face.

"Miss Dominique, the first mate gave me permission to speak with you."

"How is your wound, Tom?"

"It's less than a scratch, Ma'am. I've had much worse."

She had not expected the man who had been punished because of her to show such kindness. "I am glad. I was concerned about you."

He cast his eyes downward and stared at his scuffed

shoes. "Ma'am, I made you this necklace and I wondered . . . if it . . . if you'd like it."

He extended his prize to her: a necklace made of polished shells and threaded on a leather string. She could only imagine how painstaking it must have been for him to complete the task with his injured arm.

She smiled, and lifted it over her head. "I have never had a finer gift, Tom. I shall treasure it always."

His eyes were shining and he took two steps backward. "Ma'am, if you ever need anything, me and the men—especially me—will . . . Well you know."

"Thank you, Tom. I shall remember that."

"Night, Ma'am."

"Good night, Tom."

Dominique smiled as she closed the door, wishing she could win Captain Gallant over as easily as she had Tom Beeton.

The sun was like a magnificent ball of fire against the backdrop of an azure-blue sky. Gentle waves lazily kissed the sandy, white beaches. The *Tempest* was anchored off a hidden inlet where she was undergoing repairs.

Several crewmen were carrying buckets of pitch they had found in a nearby lake to caulk the ship, while others were cutting timber to replace the masts that had been shattered.

Dominique sat on the deck beside Tom, who had attached himself to her as her protector. Hennings, the sailmaster, sat upon his bench, observing their work with a watchful eye. All three were wearing special thimbles to force the needles through the tough canvas sails.

After a while at the tedious task, Dominique became bored and stood up to move about the ship. She leaned against the railing as her eyes traced the path of a colorful blue bird until it dipped down to the tropical forest and was lost from view.

Then her eyes were drawn to the man who stood atop a hill, apart from the others, yet aware of everything that went on around him. He was stripped to his waist, and she could see the rippling muscles, his bronze skin glistening with sweat, and again she was reminded of his godlike pose. Could any woman reach his heart? He said not, but he had been married, and surely he had loved his wife.

Now, she could feel the intensity of his gaze upon her, and she could not breathe. Even from this distance, she was affected by his commanding poise, the strength of him. She felt something else, his displeasure, and it was aimed at her.

Suddenly the cart that had been built to transport logs broke loose and careened down the steep incline, scattering men before it, and the logs went flying in every direction.

Judah ran down the hill to help right the cart and reload the logs. Tom and the sailmaster abandoned their task and rushed down the gangplank to lend their help as well.

After watching for a while, Dominique decided it would take them hours to reload the cart. She glanced about her, and found she was alone on board the ship. Her heart was beating wildly—there could be no better time to search the captain's quarters.

But first, she hurried to her own cabin and scooped up the book of Homer. If the captain came back unexpectedly, she could pretend to be returning it.

She was shaking as she made her way cautiously to the quarterdeck. She forced herself to slow her steps and try to calm her breathing. Before entering the captain's quarters, she paused to see if anyone was watching her, but they were all too busy on shore.

Cautiously, she opened the door and stood transfixed for a moment. It had never been her habit to pry, and this was much worse. It was spying on a man who had never done her harm.

At first she stood undecided in the doorway, reluctant to enter the captain's sanctuary, but time was her enemy and she could not cower on the threshold.

She hurriedly moved to the desk in the corner of the sleeping quarters, wishing she dared light a lantern because it was dark in the cabin. Quickly, she thumbed through a neat stack of papers only to find that they contained nothing more than inventories of loot taken from captured ships. The desk had several pigeonholes that contained maps and charts, but nothing that indicated what the captain's future plans were.

Neatly, she returned everything, taking care to leave nothing out of place.

She moved about the cabin, looking for anything that would tell her about the private man, the part he kept hidden from others. All she knew about his personal life was that he had been married to a woman named Mary, who had died. Strange that there were no pictures of his wife in his quarters.

Dominique glanced down at the book in her hand. Obviously he had cared enough to keep this as a treasured memento of his wife.

Her eyes fell on a chest in the far corner. She went down on her knees, tugging at the catch, but it was locked. It probably contained the logbook with all the captain's entries. Surely if she could get her hands on that, it would placate Colonel Marceau.

She considered breaking the lock, but thought better of it. Poor Tom had been flogged, and his offense had not been nearly as serious as searching the captain's private papers.

In that moment, she heard the sound of heavy boot steps and she trembled. It was the captain—no one else would dare come to his quarters.

There was nowhere to run, nowhere to hide.

Suddenly Dominique realized what she had to do. She must convince Judah that she had come to wait for him, no matter how distasteful she found the ruse.

The footsteps were drawing closer, so she snatched up the book, hurried to his bed, and lay back as if she had been reading.

The door opened with a flourish, and Judah stood before her, his eyes blazing with suspicion. He was silently accusing as he looked probingly into her eyes.

"What, may I inquire, are you doing in my cabin?"

Clutching the book in front of her as if it were a shield, Dominique looked up at him with a forced smile. "I came to return your book and became so engrossed in reading it that I almost fell asleep."

"I see."

He walked deliberately toward her, and she flinched when he sat down on the bed beside her. He took the book from her and turned through the pages. "Here, read this part to me—it is my favorite passage."

She glanced at the printed words on the page he held before her, but they meant no more than scribbling to her. She had forgotten that the book was written in Greek, but her mind was working fast, and she had to distract the captain before he became too suspicious.

He poked his finger to the page. "Read it," he commanded.

Dominique tossed her head and wet her lips, allowing her hand to steal up his arm to his shoulder, which was tight and tense beneath her touch. "You have already guessed that I cannot read Greek. I came here to wait for you."

He grabbed her hand and held it in a tight grip. "Do not provoke me, woman." He was suddenly stone-faced, and she could not tell what he was thinking. "Do I look like a fool?"

She came up to her knees, bringing her body so close to his that she could feel his heat. "No one would ever accuse you of being a fool, Captain."

Lifting her eyes to him, she smiled ever so slightly, wearing what she thought was the face of a seductress, but in reality, her features were etched in innocence. "You have found me out, and I am forced to tell the truth."

"And what is the truth, Miss Charbonneau?"

"I have come to see if you are a hero, as your men have proclaimed, or a villain, as the French would have it."

His hot glance burned through her as if he could see what she looked like beneath the mannish attire. "And if I am a villain? You are here at my mercy, are you not?"

Dominique knew that she must not step outside the part she played. He must not see how frightened she was. This was the time she had to separate her mind from her body, so she moved up against him and parted her lips. "Then I am at your mercy, Captain. But perhaps not unwillingly. You did find me here waiting for you, remember?"

Judah was not a man to be easily duped. "So, your reason in coming here was merely to see me? It could not be that you were snooping in my belongings, could it?"

Her shimmering turquoise eyes were guileless.

"How can you misjudge my intentions? What must I do before you will take notice that I am a woman?"

He grabbed her by the wrist, and when she tried to

get free of him, his grip only tightened. "Who do you report to and who sent you?"

Now she was truly frightened. "I do not know what you are talking about." She threw back her head and gave him what she hoped would be an alluring look. "You are a handsome man. I like strong," she bent her head so her lips brushed his, "exciting men."

Judah released her wrists, and his hands moved up her back to clasp her head. "Do you now?"

His lips slid softly across hers, causing her to tremble weakly. "Let us just see how far you are willing to go to prove it to me."

She closed her eyes as his lips glided down her neck to rest at the curve of her breasts.

"If you will tell me what you like," he whispered, "I will know better how to please you."

Dominique wondered why she heard anger in his voice. Was it because he did not believe her? Somehow she had to be more convincing. Gently, she took his hand and placed a kiss on the palm. In quivering delight, and with a boldness that took her by surprise, she placed his hand on her breast.

She had been watching him to see his reaction, and it was as if a sudden fire had ignited in his blue eyes.

"Oh, lady, you do so sorely tempt me." His voice was deep and raspy. He slowly ran his thumb and forefinger over her nipple, causing it to strain against his hand.

Judah grabbed her, bringing her body against his and pressing her to him. "Your song is so sweet, little siren, so sweet."

There was a quick knock on the door, and Judah released her with a frown of impatience. "Wait here and I will send whoever it is away."

Dominique watched him move to the door and jerk it open.

"Well," he said impatiently, "what do you want?"

"Begging your pardon, Cap'n," Tom said. "I'm looking for Miss Charbonneau. She's supposed to be helping me mend the sails, and she's been lax in her duty."

A grateful Dominique welcomed the interruption. Now she could escape without the captain being suspicious. She scooted off the bed and hurried to the door. "Tom, I am sorry if you had to come looking for me. I know you need my help."

Tom took in the condition of her tumbled hair and reached out his hand to her, which she quickly took. "Come with me and go about your chores and stop annoying the cap'n."

As she hurried out the door, she was surprised to hear Judah's laughter. His response was most unsettling, and it piqued her a bit that he was not more disappointed to see her go.

When they were safely out of hearing, Tom halted. "Miss Dominique, I don't know what you're doing on this ship and I'm not even going to ask. But if your reasons concern the cap'n, you be playing a dangerous game."

"I know, Tom."

"If you have any notions . . . you and him . . . well," his face reddened and he focused his eyes on a spot just above her head. "I have heard it said that the cap'n will never love a woman because his heart was buried with his dead wife." Now he did look at Dominique, with warning in his expression. "The cap'n is a man with healthy appetites, and he's had his share of women, so I would advise you to have a care. I can't always watch over you and rescue you like I did today."

"I'll try to stay out of trouble, Tom. But there is something I must do."

"What is it?"

"I cannot tell even you."

"I know not what game you play, but the cap'n's a smart one and no one is going to best him. You remember that and stay far away from him. You've got to promise me that you won't go into his cabin alone."

She inhaled deeply, thinking how close she had come to being discovered today. "Tom, I can only promise you that I will be more careful in the future."

"And you won't see the captain alone?" he prodded.

She shook her head. "Not if I can help it. He frightens me."

"Then you learned something today," Tom said, nodding his head in satisfaction. "Go on to your cabin and rest now. I'll see that no one bothers you."

Dominique moved away, suddenly feeling very weary. She was confused by troubled thoughts that she did not understand. There was a part of her that was deeply disappointed that she had not stayed with the forbidding Captain Gallant.

13

There was a festive mood in the air because the *Tempest* had been repaired and was ready to sail with the morning tide.

Everyone had gone ashore to celebrate but for Tom, who was on watch, and two men who were still too ill to participate. Tom grudgingly observed the merrymaking from his post. A great bonfire had been built and the flames were licking high, while rum and ale were passed around in liberal amounts. Two men played fiddles, while many of the others danced and sang.

Dominique stood atop an incline so she would not interfere with the men's pleasure but could still watch the festivities. She was tapping her foot and humming along with the music when she heard someone behind her. She turned to see Dr. Graham approaching.

"Good evening, Miss Charbonneau. I see you have a good view from here. May I join you?"

She smiled affectionately at the man she had come to respect. "Yes, please do." Then she looked at him inquiringly. "I recall that the captain said he would put me ashore at the first sighting of land, yet he does not seem inclined to leave me here."

"He won't. This island is uninhabited but for a native tribe," Ethan informed her as he leaned against a spidery tree, watching her closely. The flames of the fire were reflected on her face, and he was touched by her delicate beauty. Even the oversized male garb she wore could not hide her slender form.

He did not believe for one moment that she was a woman of the streets. He had spent enough time in the Caribbean to recognize the difference between aristocratic speech and a common dialect. She was definitely from the upper class, no matter how she tried to hide it. Like the captain, Ethan was convinced that she was hiding something.

Unaware of his thoughts, Dominique turned to him. "When I first came aboard the *Tempest*, I thought the crew were all murderous pirates with little care for human life. Now, I know them all by name, the names of their wives and sweethearts, and I find nothing about them to fear."

Ethan wanted to ask her why she had crept aboard the ship if she felt this way, but he suspected that if he did, she would no doubt become secretive again.

"Your first impression of the crew was not a mistake, Miss Charbonneau," he said dryly. "They are, to a man, treacherous cutthroats, who give their allegiance only to someone who is strong enough to control them and win their respect." He saw that he had startled her. "But you need have no concern," he hastened to add. "You have won them all over, and there is not a man among them who would not defend you with his life."

The night, the stars, the sound of music, put her in a flirtatious mood. "What about you, Doctor? Would you defend me with your life?"

His eyes met hers, and he stared at her for a moment, wondering how anyone could ever think she was other than an innocent. "I, like the others, would place myself between you and harm's way. That is why I must warn you to be careful."

She looked at him inquiringly. "But you just implied that I have nothing to fear from the crew."

He nodded to a cliff in the distance, where the captain sat alone. "I was not speaking of the crew."

"I thought Captain Gallant was your friend?"

"I never had a better one. That is why I can warn you about him. He is not like other men, for he has guilt and dark misery locked in his heart. There have been many women who have thought they could reach that heart and change him, but they met with only disappointment."

Her gaze settled on Judah Gallant. She could not see him very well since he was half in darkness, but she could feel his eyes sweep across her. "I do not want his heart, Dr. Graham, and I have no interest in freeing him from the memory of his dead wife."

"Then what do you want?"

She fixed her gaze on the fiddle player, wishing she could tell Ethan her secret, but knowing he would never allow her to betray his friend. "We all have something we are running away from, Doctor." She turned back to him. "Except you, perhaps. I believe you know exactly who you are, and you are content with yourself."

Ethan moved closer to her and took her hand. It was raw and chapped from the work she had done aboard ship, not smooth and soft as it had been when she had first arrived. "I wonder, since you have acted as my nurse, and I have come to count myself your friend, if we might call each other by name. I hasten to mention that even Tom uses your familiar name."

She allowed his fingers to clasp hers. "Tom just fell into it as his natural right. By not protesting I gave him that right." She smiled. "You already know that my name is Dominique."

"And I am Ethan." He bowed to her. "At your service, Dominique."

They turned their attention back to the dancers. After a while, Ethan spoke. "Something is troubling you. Can you tell me what it is? I might be able to help."

She looked at him with sadness in her eyes. "You cannot help me. No one can."

Thinking to lighten her mood, he tugged at her hand. "How long has it been since you danced?"

She remembered the night of her brother's birthday party, the night she found out he had been arrested. "It has been far too long, Ethan."

"Then come along—tonight you make merry."

When they reached the bonfire, Ethan whirled her around in time with the music. Suddenly her troubles dropped away and she was laughing and dancing.

One of the crew members came up to her shyly and asked if she would dance with him. Before long she was being passed from partner to partner and her laughter and merriment joined with theirs.

Judah observed all this with cynicism. But he followed Dominique with his eyes, wishing it was he who had made her laugh. There was a heat in his loins and thundering in his heart. He wanted her, and he despised himself for that weakness. While he watched her go from one man to another, wondering which one she would choose to share her bed that night, he found himself becoming incensed at the thought of another man sharing intimacies with her.

A sudden awareness left him stunned. He resented every man who touched Dominique, and he even glowered at Ethan as he swung her around. Then they joined hands, bending to move through an arch formed by the others.

Judah turned his back and deliberately walked away, leaving the sound of merriment behind him.

After a while, the fire died down and the dancers began to return to their duties. Ethan had to go aboard to see about a patient, so Dominique found herself walking along a stretch of sandy beach beneath a bright full moon.

She smiled, thinking of how chivalrously the men had treated her. Somewhere along the way she had stopped thinking of them as pirates and cutthroats. The doctor was a gentleman, as was Cornelius, despite his rough ways. Then there was Tom, her self-proclaimed protector, as well as many others who had shown her kindness and respect.

Dominique paused to look out to sea, wondering which direction she would have to sail to reach her home. She was overcome with melancholy when she thought of her brother and grandfather, and what was happening to them in her absence. She lived every day with the terror that she might not be able to save them, and she was more determined than ever to lure Captain Gallant into her trap. Perhaps, if she could gather the courage, she would even go to his cabin tonight.

On a sudden impulse, and hoping to find momentary peace, Dominique looked about her to make sure she was alone. When she was satisfied that no one was about, she removed her clothing and waded into the sea. The gentle tug of the waves felt wonderful against her naked body. She dove under water, rode the waves, and then swam to a rock that jutted out of the churning tide. With wild abandon, she climbed up onto its slippery base, allowing the tropical breeze to blow through her hair.

She was a child of the sea and had always drawn her strength from her island home. Captain Gallant had called her a siren, and perhaps she was. Leaning back against the rock, with the moon as her audience, she hummed an old song her English nurse had sung to her as a child, then she

raised her voice and the sweet melody blended with the
wind and the night sounds of the sea.

> *Oh lonely my heart, I cry for a man to come*
> *hither—*
> *come hither and take my hand. But no man came,*
> *my lifeto save;*
> *so I threw myself to the wind and my heart*
> *to the thundering waves.*

Judah listened, spellbound, as Dominique sang. She
was a siren, and her song wound its way about his heart
and tore at his mind, bending his resistance to her will.
He could not look away when she stood naked and
poised, the moonlight turning her body silver.

When she dove into the waves to swim to shore, he
was actually trembling like an eager youth, waiting for
her to emerge. He ached to touch her soft skin, to tangle
his hands in her hair, to see if her lips were as sweet as
he remembered.

Dominique saw the outline of a man as she raised
out of the water, and she could tell that it was Judah.
Without an awareness of her nakedness, she walked
toward him, unresisting, as if he had cast a spell on
her.

With water streaming down her hair and body, she
stood before him, her eyes fused with his.

"So," he said, "you have chosen me this night."

She did not understand his meaning, but when he
extended his arm to her, she placed her hand in his.
Slowly, he pulled her to him. Her breath felt tight in her
throat as she waited for contact with his body.

Judah bent his dark head and lay his cheek against her
wet face. "So, little siren, your song was for me and you
caught me in your snare after all."

She made no sound as he scooped up her discarded garments and then lifted her in his arms, carrying her away from the sea. She lay her face against his chest and found that her heart was beating at the same rhythm as his.

She could not say when the feeling made itself known to her, but it seemed so right that she and this man should be lovers. She was ready to give herself to him tonight without regret.

It did not matter to her that he was a man who made his way by breaking both the law of God and man. She had found in him a man of honor, a person of high principles, and a man who made her tremble with longing every time he looked at her.

When they reached a secluded glen, Judah lay her among fragrant white ginger lilies and red orchids. Their sweet aroma blended into a delicate scent that added magic to an already enchanted night.

He looked at her, starting from her head, pausing at her pointed breasts, then slowly and lingeringly across her stomach. His gaze moved lower, to her most private core, and she had the sensation that he caressed her there, though he did not make a move. She felt the heat rising in her face, brought on by the excitement of his nearness.

"How many men have told you that you are beautiful?" Judah asked, his hand going to his shirt and pulling it loose from his trousers.

Dominique fought against a sudden shyness as she watched Judah pull his shirt off and then bend to place it beneath her head.

"Well," he prodded, "how many?"

Her lashes swept over her eyes. "They have been too numerous to count."

He came out of his boots and then unbuckled his belt.

"And how many men have tasted the fruit of your body?"

She chose to play the siren he believed her to be. "None that asked so many questions, but again, there have been many."

Again, Judah resented that Dominique had been with others before him. "Just as I thought," he said, stepping out of his trousers and standing naked before her. "Well, then, one more will make no difference to you, will it? And you should know numerous tricks to hold a man's interest."

Silvery moonlight touched his body, this man who was so commanding and powerful. The mesmerizing way he was looking at her made Dominique want to press herself against him and allow him to master her body.

He came down beside her, and she went into his arms, as if she had always belonged there. He expected her to be knowledgeable about a man's body, and she must pretend that she had done this many times before.

Instinctively, she seemed to know what to do—how to allow her fingers to glide over his corded back while she pressed her hips toward him, her body melting against his swelling hardness.

She was almost weak with longing when he clasped her face between his hands.

"You little vixen. You know just how to make a man ache."

In a daring move—and she did not know where it came from—Dominique leaned forward and softly touched her tongue to his lips. And with further boldness she outlined their fullness, excited and weak when she heard him groan with pleasure at her boldness.

"Do you know I have dreamed of this moment?" he asked, turning her to her back and hovering above her.

Somewhere in her subconscious, Dominique wanted to prolong his torment, because for the first time she had control of him. She rolled out from under him and pushed him to his back. "How do we know that this is not a dream," she said in a throaty voice. "Perhaps I shall disappear in a puff of smoke with the coming of the new day."

Reaching over his head, she plucked an orchid and stroked it ever so gently across his lips, while he watched her, wondering what she would do next, and trying to keep control over the urge to grab her and plunge deep inside her, to bury himself in her sweetness.

Oh yes, he thought, as she stroked the soft petals of the flower lower, past his stomach, past the V of dark hair and stroking, circling, tantalizing, and teasing his quivering flesh.

Judah licked his dry lips and jerked her forward. "I will again taste those lips that have mocked and taunted me for so long."

Her mouth parted invitingly, and his lips were only inches away. She could hardly breathe because their eyes joined as their lips would soon join, then there would be the uniting of their bodies.

"Miss Dominique!" Tom called loudly. "Where are you, Miss Dominique—answer me." Then his voice was louder, sharper, and filled with anxiety. "You could get lost out here. If you hear me, call out."

With regret, she pulled away from Judah and laughingly tucked the orchid behind his ear. He was speechless as she rose and reached for her clothing.

"My watchdog is calling. I had better go or he will come looking for me."

"What!? You are going to leave me when you—"

She bent to touch her lips lightly to his. "Here is your kiss. Perhaps another time we will finish what we started tonight, Captain."

She quickly dressed and then ran down the beach. He could hear her voice calling in the distance.

"Here I am, Tom. I was just out for a swim."

Tom looked her over carefully, noticing the blush to her cheeks and the shirt that was half out of her trousers. He had come looking for her as soon as he discovered the captain was away from the ship. Had he come in time? From the looks of her tumbled hair and shining eyes she was not immune to Captain Gallant's powers of seduction. He'd just have to keep a closer watch on her before she really got into trouble.

Judah raised himself up and muttered beneath his breath. "Damn that woman."

He slowly dressed, feeling unfulfilled and empty. The next time she would not get away so easily.

On his way back to the ship, he was in a temper, cursing not only Dominique, but all women. When he reached the quarterdeck, he found Cornelius waiting for him.

"'Tis a fine evening, Captain," the first mate observed cheerfully. "A mighty fine evening."

"I had not noticed," Judah replied sourly, moving into his quarters and taking the logbook Cornelius offered him.

"The men enjoyed the diversion."

"Humph."

Judah signed his name with a flourish and then thrust the log at Cornelius. "Lock this in the chest and then call a meeting of the watch. I want to sail with the morning tide."

Cornelius looked downward, trying to keep a straight face, but Judah saw his smile.

"Do you find something funny, mister?" he barked.

"No, Captain, sir," Cornelius protested, "it's just that . . . before you meet with the men . . . well you might want to—"

"What, damn it?"

Cornelius pointed to Judah's ear, so Judah reached up and found the orchid Dominique had placed there earlier.

The two men did not look at each other, and the first mate hurried away while Judah crushed the orchid beneath his boot, wishing he could vent his fury on Dominique.

14

Alone in her cabin, Dominique attempted to examine her changing feelings for Judah. She peeled back the layers of her emotions, like lifting the fragile petals off a rose. She had wanted to be with him tonight, and if Tom had not intervened, she would have given herself to Judah all too willingly.

Had she acted so wantonly because he expected it of her, and she must convince him that she was the kind of woman she pretended to be?

She closed her eyes, remembering how his hard body had glistened in the moonlight. Oh, he had been magnificent. If she had met him at some formal party on Guadeloupe, and he had been from a respectable family, would they have noticed each other? Yes, she would have noticed him in a room filled with handsome men. He was such a strong presence, a commanding force, how could any woman resist him?

Dominique undressed and ran her hands over her body. What had he seen when he looked at her?

With a sigh, she pulled on her nightdress, which was nothing but an oversized shirt, and lay back on the bed.

If only there was someone she could talk to about the

questions that haunted her. She was not entirely igno-
rant, having grown up on a plantation where she had
witnessed the coupling of animals. Perhaps if her mother
had lived, she would have been taught how to behave
with a man. What did her feelings matter, though. She
had been forced to play the wanton, and that was what
she must do.

She extinguished the lantern and lay there in the
darkness, watching the moon make a pattern through
the porthole. "Valcour, Grandpapa, you just have to be
all right. I will help free you, I promise I will."

So troubled were her thoughts that she was still
awake when the *Tempest* caught the morning tide and
took to sea.

Dominique did not see Judah for the next week. In fact,
she was about to decide that he would not want to see
her again, when Cornelius approached her on his captain's behalf.

"Miss Charbonneau, Captain Gallant wishes me to
extend to you an invitation to dine with him tonight at
eight bells," he said in his most formal manner.

Dominique had been concerned that Judah had
ignored her until now. Even so, she spoke out of pride,
before she thought. "Tell your captain that I will be dining alone tonight," she said haughtily.

Cornelius nodded, wondering if any woman had ever
refused Judah before. "I will relay your message to him,
Miss Charbonneau, but you have disappointed me, and I
am certain Dr. Graham would have enjoyed your charming company as well."

"You and Ethan will be dining with Captain
Gallant?" Dominique asked, wondering what game the
captain was playing.

"Indeed we shall, as is our custom." He moved away from her to attend his duties. "I'll give the captain your regrets."

"Wait!" she called, stopping him in his tracks. "I may have been a bit hasty. I have changed my mind, Cornelius. You may tell Captain Gallant that I will be pleased to accept his invitation."

He smiled and tipped his cap as he went on his way. Life on the *Tempest* had been tedious before Miss Charbonneau had come aboard. Her mere presence made each day more interesting, especially now that she had put the captain in a tailspin. Cornelius chuckled. Dinner tonight was sure to be an adventure.

It was later in the day when Dominique returned to her cabin after helping Ethan set a broken leg for one of the crew.

She was surprised to find a gown lying across the foot of her bed. She gently touched the pink linen creation as if it were the most beautiful gown she had ever seen. She smiled when she saw the large uneven stitches and realized that the sailmaster, Hennings, must have made it for her. It had full gathers at the waist and a high neck—decidedly not stylish, but a treasure all the same. She hugged it to her, thinking of the man's kindness, and knowing she would wear it proudly.

Hennings's had not been the only kindness. Dominique reveled in the tub bath that Tom had provided, and she wondered where he had obtained the sweet-smelling salts to scent the water.

She brushed and styled her hair and tied it away from her face with a piece of ribbon she had found folded with the pink gown. Sorrowfully, she knew she would have to make do with the scuffed leather boots to complete her ensemble.

Pressing her hand against her heart to quell its beating,

she moved to the door of her cabin. She had not expected to be so excited at the prospect of seeing Judah again.

When Dominique stepped onto the deck, she found Ethan waiting. He extended his arm to her. "I have been given the honor of escorting you to the captain's table."

She dipped into a curtsy. "How handsome you look, Doctor."

His voice took on a serious tone. "Are you certain it is wise to attend tonight?"

It was apparent that he was aware of the tension between her and Judah. "I want to, Ethan."

She could have added that when he found out about her intentions, he would despise her. But she could not turn back now. Time was precious; every day Valcour and her grandfather were in the hands of that French monster was like a sword in her heart.

Ethan led her forward, pacing his stride to match hers. "If you walk on the edge of a volcano long enough, you are bound to feel the earth tremble beneath your feet."

She made no reply; they both knew he was warning her about Judah.

Dominique saw the sailmaster watching her with pride and she stopped in front of him. "I have you to thank for this lovely gown, have I not?"

He grinned and nodded. "I made it from some tablecloths belonging to the cap'n. He won't miss 'em."

"Thank you," she said, brushing her lips against his rough cheek and drawing a toothless smile from him.

Dominique and Ethan entered the captain's dining room, which was separated from his private sleeping quarters only by the bulkhead.

Cornelius was the only one present, and he greeted her warmly. "You look pretty as a flower, Miss Charbonneau," he said courteously.

"Thank you kind sir," she replied, noticing with surprise the elegance of the captain's table, where bone china, polished silver, and crystal glasses gleamed in the candlelight. Then it occurred to her that he was probably displaying stolen booty.

Dominique could feel the moment Judah entered the room, even though her back was to him. Slowly, she turned to face him, wondering how he would react to her after what had passed between them. He wore white trousers and a green silk coat that fit snugly across his broad shoulders.

"Miss Charbonneau, it is so good of you to grace us with your presence," he said stiffly. His bold glance took in her appearance, the soft rose blush to her cheeks, the softness of the dark curls that lay wispy against her forehead, the slender outline of her body that was revealed by the old-fashioned linen gown. "Extremely lovely," he murmured. "But then you already know that."

Dominique looked into his eyes, and for the moment, she forgot that there were others in the cabin. "A compliment, Captain Gallant."

"Not at all. That gown would be but a rag on anyone but you."

Their lips were moving, they were making polite conversation, but there were deep undertones between them and their eyes spoke of other matters—of moonlight, gentle touches, and unrequited passions.

Judah moved to a chair and pulled it back for her. "Will you be seated?"

She slid into the chair, conscious that his hand brushed against the back of her neck. It was difficult to make polite conversation when her knees felt weak and her heart was thundering against her breasts.

When everyone was seated, a member of the crew appeared with wine to fill the glasses. When he stood before the captain, Judah placed his hand over the glass. "None for me. Serve the others."

He smiled at Dominique's questioning gaze. "I could at one time drink with the best of them, but lately I have had little liking for spirits, especially when I have a beautiful woman to intoxicate me."

She raised her glass to her lips and took a sip before answering. "A pretty speech, Captain," she said, playing her part. "I'll have to take care that you don't turn my head."

"Dominique, why don't you tell the captain how you came by the gown," Ethan encouraged her.

"I have your sailmaster to thank, Captain. Was it not kind of him?"

"I never knew Hennings was so creative," Judah said bitingly. "Perhaps I should set him up in a shop to style women's garments." Then he turned on Ethan, his features stormy. "At what point did the two of you decide to exchange first names?"

Ethan dared not smile, but he wanted to. "Dominique kindly gave me permission to use her name. We have become well acquainted since she began helping me in the infirmary."

"Touching," Judah said in a tone of voice that indicated his disapproval.

At that point, they were interrupted by the crewman who was placing serving dishes on the table.

"Miss Charbonneau," Judah said whimsically, "it might interest you to know that your friend, Tom Beeton, has duties tonight in the hold, rearranging stores and supplies. He should be occupied most of the night. I thought I would tell you in the event that you wondered why he was not skulking around."

A slight smile curved her lips and she stared down at her plate, better understanding the captain's moodiness.

Was he warning her that Tom would not be around to intrude tonight?

As the dinner progressed, Judah had the opportunity to observe Dominique carefully. He noticed that she knew exactly the correct eating utensils to use with each course. Her manners were impeccable, her conversation intelligent, her demeanor refined. This was no mere tavern wench, so why was she pretending to be? He was even more baffled than before—who was she, and what she was doing on his ship?

Dominique did not seem to be aware of Judah's silence as she laughed and talked easily with Ethan and Cornelius. If the men thought it strange that the captain did not join in their conversation, they did not show it.

At last Cornelius stood, making his apologies to Dominique. "I have the night watch and must leave now. It has been pleasurable dining with you, Miss Charbonneau. I hope that we can look forward to your company again."

"Good night, Cornelius," she said, nodding her head. "And please, call me Dominique."

After Cornelius left, an uncomfortable silence followed, until at last Ethan stood. "I must also leave your charming company, Dominique. Two men have developed a fever and I must see to their needs before I retire." Bowing, he took his leave.

Dominique turned to face Judah, who was looking at her enigmatically. "It would seem that we are alone at last," he said.

She pushed her plate aside. "I should be leaving also."

He stood, coming around behind her, his hand falling heavily on her shoulder. "Abide with me a while. I believe we have unfinished business, you and I."

She felt his lean fingers caress the back of her neck and move down to her shoulder, to linger there.

"You are wrong, Captain. There is nothing unfinished between us."

"Why do you speak to me so formally, and yet invite Ethan and Cornelius to call you by name?"

"They are . . . different from you."

He pulled his chair up beside her and sat down. "In what way?"

"They have been kind to me."

"They have that. What else?"

"I have no answer for you. If you want me to call you by your name, I shall do so, and I shall give you leave to speak my name as well."

He lifted her chin. "Still so formal. I would think you unfeeling and distant if I had not held you naked in my arms."

She ducked her head, but he once again raised her chin and looked into her eyes. "You want me as badly as I want you. Do not deny it."

Dominique attempted to avoid his gaze, but it was impossible. She felt compelled to warn him about her mission, although she could not have said why. "You think you know me, but you do not. If you are wise, you will turn from me and never seek me out again."

He rubbed his finger across her lips, gently and sensuously. "You are probably right, but you see, it is too late for that. I have stood beneath the moon with you and heard your siren's song."

She was immediately indignant. "You mock me."

"No, never that."

There was passion in his blue eyes as they picked up the glow from the candles, and she was caught in those eyes as they pulled at her, making her ache inside.

"You know as well as I do, Dominique, that something happened between us that night on the beach."

Oh yes, she knew it only too well. Even now, she

wanted to go into his arms and feel the passion of his hot kisses on her lips.

In that moment, a shadow fell across Dominique's face and she looked up into Tom's amused eyes.

"Sugared confection, Miss Dominique?" he asked with exaggerated politeness, injecting a silver server between her and the captain. "I believe you will find them delicious. And how about you, Cap'n—would you like one?"

Dominique was flooded with relief because the spell Judah was weaving about her had been broken by Tom's levity. She had been so close to succumbing to Judah's undeniable charms, and if she had surrendered to him, she would have felt compelled to confess her deception and the reason for it.

She raised her head, her eyes meeting Tom's inquisitively. "I thought you were on duty belowdecks tonight."

He answered her, unperturbed by the captain's silent fury. "That I was, Miss, but I traded off with Jack Dobson. You see, he likes it in the hold, practically begged me to let him finish my duties. Begging your pardon, Cap'n, but Dobson has strange habits."

Laughingly, Dominique came to her feet. "It has been a lovely evening, Captain. I hope you will invite me again."

Judah said nothing, but his lips were pressed in a tight line and his eyes blazed with anger.

"I am sure you will not mind if I ask Tom to walk me to my cabin. You did not need him anymore tonight, did you, Captain?"

Judah waved them away. At the moment, he wanted nothing more than to put his hands about Dominique's lovely throat and shake her until she begged for mercy.

15

The Tempest was running before the wind with all sails flying, cutting through a rough sea, her destination known only to her captain and his first mate.

Below in her cabin, Dominique could no longer ignore her flagging spirits. It had been over a fortnight ago that she had dined with Judah, and since that time he had neither sent for her, nor had she laid eyes on him.

Perhaps she should have stayed that night, she chided herself. She had mocked him when she should have been more agreeable. Now, he had lost interest in her, and there was no one to blame but herself.

Judah lowered his spyglass and then turned to Cornelius. "There's the *Josephine*, the pride of the French navy. She boasts seventy-two guns and is reputed to be the fastest ship under sail. Let us see if we can take her."

"Do we close the gap now, Captain?"

Judah shook his head. "That would be foolhardy since we are ill equipped to meet her full on. Lower the sails so we can drop back. The *Josephine* is running high in the water, which means she's low on supplies. I know where she will make port. We shall not be far behind."

The first mate grinned. "Aye, sir. No ship is a match for us when we've got the advantage of surprise."

It was a dark night when the *Tempest*, with Cornelius as her navigator, sailed through a narrow inlet, silently staying well out of view of the *Josephine*.

Two hours before dawn, Judah ordered the oars muffled and the longboats lowered over the side. Men armed and ready for a fight noiselessly maneuvered the shallows until they came alongside the French ship.

Silently, Tom climbed aboard the *Josephine* and came up behind a sleepy guard, clamping his hand over the man's mouth and rapping him hard across the back of the head. Then Tom attached his grappling hook to the railing and threw a rope over the side. Soon he was joined by a second man, who performed the same deed, and then another and another, until they were all on board.

It was a surprised French admiral who awoke with a pistol aimed at his head.

"Yield or die, Admiral," Judah said, smiling.

The admiral sat up slowly, trying to shake off the effects of sleep. His fleshy face was red with indignation, his nightcap askew. "Who dares enter my cabin with such a ludicrous demand? Do you not know who I am, Monsieur?"

"No," Judah said mockingly. "Suppose you tell me."

"I am the Marquis de la Taille," he said haughtily, "and this is my ship."

"Wrong on at least one count, Marquis de la Taille. This ship now belongs to me." Judah pulled back the hammer on his pistol and placed the barrel at the man's temple. "You have two choices: You can either go ashore—and I hasten to add that your men are already there—or you can accompany your ship, in which case you will be under my command. I do not believe you will like the last option."

"Who are you?"

Judah bowed to him with a flourish. "I, Marquis de la Taille, am the new captain of the *Josephine*. Now I grow impatient. Which is it to be—do you stay or shall I put you ashore?"

The Frenchman threw his covers aside and stood up to his full height. "I will see you in hell for this, Monsieur."

Judah picked up the man's trousers and waistcoat and tossed them at him.

"You will have to fall in line, I believe there are other Frenchmen ahead of you."

William York hunched his shoulders, trying to appear inconspicuous until he saw Judah Gallant threading his way through the throngs toward him. William brightened at the sight of the young captain he had come to like so well.

"Is it true that you captured the *Josephine*?" William asked in amazement, hardly giving Judah time to sit down before barraging him with questions.

"You will find that she is manned and ready to make her voyage to the United States, awaiting only my word to sail. I thought you might want to return home aboard her."

William's eyes glistened with excitement. "That I do. This is indeed a victory. An admirable addition to our fleet and the best prize you have taken thus far."

Judah watched the door, a habit he had developed whenever he was ashore. "William, when I agreed to take on this mission, I had the impression that I was to aid in discovering Napoleon's plans for Louisiana. It was never my aim to furnish captured ships for the American navy. I am a shipbuilder, remember?"

"I understand how you feel, but consider this as a great strike against Napoleon." Seeing the frown on Judah's face, William decided it was best to speak of other matters. "Have you no news for us?"

"No, but you might be interested in a plan I discovered on the *Josephine* detailing Napoleon's strategy in his naval war with Lord Nelson."

William's eyes gleamed. "Excellent! I shall pass the information on to the president and he can decide how best to use it."

"You have the money for my men?"

"I do. They are gaining wealth while playing at pirating."

Judah's eyes suddenly darkened. "Let this be understood, William. My men are not playing, as you put it. They have risked their lives many times and have not once asked why. What I want from the president, more than money, is a full pardon for every man who has sailed with me."

"I am not sure I can accomplish that. You must be aware that some of your men are dangerous fugitives."

"Be that as it may, I must insist that every man jack aboard the *Tempest* be granted a pardon, or I will sail for Boston this very day."

William could see that Judah meant exactly what he said, so he made a quick decision. "You have my word I will try."

"Try isn't good enough. *Do it!*"

William sighed in resignation. "I believe that the president will act on my recommendation. But I must warn you that his is the final word."

"I understand that, but I trust you to convince him that these men have earned their freedom." Judah leaned in closer, his expression grim. "There will, of course, be one man who will be excluded from the pardon. I trust you have discovered the identity of the spy aboard my ship."

William looked perturbed. "Not precisely. The word is that the culprit is not a man at all, but a woman, and I do not know how that could be. I questioned the validity of the information, but I was assured that it is reliable."

Judah's eyes narrowed. He had to be the greatest fool who had ever drawn breath. "So," he said under his breath, "all this time I have suspected that one of my men was a turncoat, when all along it was—" He slid his chair back and stood up abruptly. "If you have nothing further to tell me, I have matters that need my attention."

William was profoundly disappointed and could not understand why Judah had suddenly become so agitated. "But, I had hoped to hear the account of how you captured the *Josephine*."

Judah braced his hands on the table and leaned forward. "I shall send you a detailed report. Meanwhile, I want you to see if you can find out anything about a woman by the name of Dominique Charbonneau. Begin your search here on Tobago, since this is where I first encountered her."

With many questions unanswered, William nodded, then watched in astonishment as Judah stalked across the taproom in obvious anger. He would not want to be the recipient of Captain Gallant's wrath.

Dominique stood at Judah's desk, her hand hovering over his logbook as her mind ebbed and flowed like the waves that lapped against the ship. She needed the information from that book, but at the same time she was appalled at the thought of prying into his secrets.

She found herself facing a painful decision in which she must choose between saving the lives of her family or delivering Judah into Colonel Marceau's hands. She wanted to lay her head on the desk and cry, for if she chose to betray Judah, she would be going against everything her grandfather had taught her—she would be without honor.

Her hand ran across the smooth leather binding of the logbook and, reluctantly, she opened it. She immediately glanced upward, unable to look upon the words that would be written in Judah's own hand.

With tears gathering in her eyes, she made her decision. Slowly she closed the book, praying that God would save her brother and grandfather, because she could not.

"So," a deep voice spoke up behind her, "did you find all you needed to know?"

She gathered her courage and slowly turned to face Judah. "I was waiting for you."

His features were savage, and there was something dangerous about him. "I believe we have played this scene before—but not to its conclusion."

As she stood there looking into ice-blue eyes, she became aware of the reason she had been unable to betray him—she loved him! That realization came to her with a suddenness that left her stunned.

"I am glad you are here. There is something I must tell you."

When Judah did not respond, but merely looked at her with an expression she did not understand, she gave him a questioning gaze. "You were not ashore for long."

His laughter was bitter. "Did I return too soon?"

Dominique's expression was guarded. She had been prepared to confess everything to Judah and to beg him to help her free her family. But he was so cold and distant, she dared not confide in him. He was frightening her in a way he never had before.

"Come here, Dominique," he demanded harshly, holding out his hand.

Although she ached for his touch, something told her there was danger here. She shook her head, bewilderment showing momentarily in her eyes, and she backed against the desk, oblivious of the fury she aroused in Judah by denying him.

He walked to her and held out his hand, and finally, she reluctantly reached out to him. His touch burned through her quaking body and she tried to pull away.

Judah regarded her coldly, as his hand clamped painfully about hers. "You said there was something you wanted to tell me—a confession, perhaps?"

He had come too close to the truth, and she realized that he was regarding her with scorn.

"I . . . have nothing to say," she faltered.

"Ah well, I have oft times observed that a woman changes her mind as frequently as the wind changes course."

She had never seen his eyes so devoid of warmth or his manner so intense. "Is something bothering you, Judah?"

He looked at her through veiled lashes. "Should there be?"

He was strange, cold, lofty, and angry—but why? "You are acting—"

"Yes?"

"Different?"

He gave her a long, level stare before continuing.

"Why do you suppose that is?"

"Perhaps you could tell me."

"I believe now would be a good time for you to tell me why you sought sanctuary on my ship." He watched her closely. "Tell me, Dominique."

She shifted her weight and glanced down at the floor.

"There are many things I would like to tell you that I cannot."

"That is always a female's argument when she is hiding something. What secrets are you trying to conceal?"

Her head snapped up and she stared at him. "What do you mean?"

He smiled tightly. "Suppose we speak of other things for the moment. I thought you might like to know that Tom Beeton has sailed with the *Josephine*."

Now she was frightened. "Why did you send Tom away?"

"So he can no longer interrupt us at inopportune moments." He jerked her forward and her body slammed into his. "Can you guess what it is like to desire a woman as I desire you?" His hand moved to the laces at the back of her gown. "Yes, a woman of your profession knows how to heat a man's blood."

She shook her head, unable to speak—she wanted to stay and she wanted to flee. "Your daring is only exceeded by your audacity, Captain," she said, in an attempt at bravado.

His eyes raked her dark hair and he touched it, allowing it to sift like raw silk through his fingers. "You have been like a fever in my brain, consuming my mind, almost to the point of madness. I must have you or there will be no reprieve from this torment."

"I . . . do not want to do this."

He tilted her chin and stared intensely into her aqua eyes. "Yes, you do. You have wanted this from the beginning, or so you led me to believe. Have you been deceiving me, Dominique?"

He had deftly unlaced her gown and it fluttered to the floor. His lips traced a trail across her cheek and down the arch of her neck, igniting her desire with each stroke of his hand, each whispered word.

"Lovely, lovely temptress, nothing can keep us apart now."

He studied her in silence for a long breathless moment as his mouth moved slowly toward hers to meet in a flaming kiss—his hungrily, hers timorous and quivering. He lifted her in his arms and carried her to his bed, tossing her down while he removed his clothing and joined her there.

She stared at him wide-eyed. One moment he spoke to her of desire, and the next she sensed a hidden fury within him. What did it mean?

She could not think clearly as she was assailed by glorious feelings that rocked her body to the core when Judah pressed his naked form against hers.

"Sweet siren," he murmured, "I am about to partake of the fruits of your body."

His mouth swept across the crest of her breasts, and she felt desire beyond her wildest imagination. Her skin seemed to tingle all over and she was finding it difficult to catch her breath.

But more was to come as his hand swept downward, circling, tantalizing, then jabbed inside her, causing her to moan at the sensation that riveted through her body.

He suddenly drew back, not wanting her to find pleasure in their coupling. She was, after all, merely a whore who had been paid by one of his enemies to seduce him, and he would treat her as she deserved. "Are you ready to receive me?" he growled in a hard voice.

The words seemed ripped from her lips. "Yes, oh, yes."

Before she understood what was happening, he was atop her and he rammed forward, penetrating her, causing her unexpected pain.

When Judah felt the tightness of her as his drive ripped her maidenhead away, and she uttered an anguished cry, he was startled. She had never been with a man!

The fact that she had lied to him about that, too, only fueled his anger. But the silkiness of her enveloped him and he could not have stopped if it meant his life. He grasped her waist and plunged deeper into her, stilling his movements only when she cried out in pain. He gentled his movements and curbed his passion until he found blessed relief from his need of her.

Abruptly, he rolled to his side and stared at her. She looked somehow like a crushed flower, and he could guess why. The first time was never pleasant for a woman, unless the man wooed her gently. Had he known that she was a virgin, he would have made it enjoyable for her. He was suddenly ashamed of himself. Dominique should have been taken with tenderness and love, but he had none of that to give her.

Well, he thought, trying unsuccessfully to wrestle with his guilt, it was her fault for allowing him to think she had a jaded past.

By way of apology, he bent to her and placed a chaste kiss on her lips.

The casual way he kissed her seemed to mean nothing to him, and Dominique was humiliated. She could not blame him because she had encouraged him to make love to her.

"I have matters to attend to," Judah said coldly, poking his shirt into his trousers. "Do not wait up for me."

She raised unhappy eyes to him. "You expect me to stay here and wait for you?"

"I insist on it. From this day, you will remain here with me, where I can keep my eye on you."

He went to his desk, picked up his logbook and dropped it down beside her. "You appeared interested in this earlier. I give you leave to read it at your leisure."

The book dropped from her nimble fingers to the floor and she turned her face to the wall. Something had happened when Judah went ashore today, something that had made him angry, and that anger had been directed at her.

She tried to empty her mind so she could think clearly. She had always known that she would have to give herself to Judah, so she had no regret on that account. But as far as she was concerned, the act of love-making had not been as wonderful as the imagining of it.

She pressed her hand over her eyes, unable to stop the sudden flow of tears. She had failed. Now the only thing to do was to return to Guadeloupe—and she must do it soon.

16

Dominique made no attempt to leave Judah's cabin. Although it was not locked, she felt like his prisoner all the same. She had bathed, then dressed in her trousers and shirt, and was now sitting on a padded window seat, her legs curled beneath her.

The sun had gone down hours ago, and still she waited for Judah to appear. She closed her eyes, hoping to wipe away images of him that kept creeping into her mind unbidden and unwelcome. Images of him touching her, his lips kissing her, and then . . .

Restlessly, she closed her mind to the memories. It had only been the night before when she had given herself to Judah, and instead of the joy she had expected to experience, she felt emptiness.

Perhaps the actual act was more enjoyable for a man than it was for a woman. Or perhaps there was something wrong with her!

She decided to pretend that she liked it when he made love to her. Otherwise, he might guess that he was the only man she had ever been with.

At last, the cabin door opened and Judah entered. His dark hair was windblown, and she had the strong urge to run her fingers through it and sweep it back into place.

He looked at her clothing in disdain. "You should not have felt that you had to dress for me."

She feigned a bored yawn, but in fact she watched him move toward her with a lithe grace.

"How have you passed your day, Dominique?"

"Wishing I was somewhere that you were not," she said, turning away from him and pretending to be interested in the contents of his bookshelf. Yet, as she ran her hand down the titles, she did not see them; she was only aware of Judah.

Dominique's audacity nettled him, but he would allow her to play out her game—at least for a while. "Have you supped?"

"Yes," she replied, refusing to be drawn into a conversation with him.

He stared at her for a moment before he spoke. "Is there anything you would like?"

"No. I want for nothing."

At that moment, there was a knock on the door and a crewman entered, carrying a wooden tub, while several others carried pails of steaming water to fill it. Dominique noticed that they studiously avoided looking at her as they went about their tasks.

After they had gone, Judah began stripping off his clothing, so Dominique hurried to the door, intending to leave the cabin.

He caught her hand. "Don't go."

"I thought you might like privacy."

He looked at her sardonically. "There is nothing private between us, is there?"

She shook her head. "Not after last night."

He sat down and removed his boots. "Do I hear accusation in your tone?"

"No. Why should you think that? I was honest from the beginning about the kind of woman I was. You should not have been surprised that I—"

He watched her carefully. "What kind of woman do you think you are? As I recall, you indicated that you could not even remember how many men you had been with."

She gracefully raised her shoulders in a shrug. "No more than you can recall all the women who have lain beneath you."

He set his expression into a tight frown—it was either that or laugh and he dared not do that. She was even more innocent than he'd thought. She had no notion that a man could tell when a woman was a virgin. Before him she had been untouched by any man.

He stood, wearing only the tight trousers that outlined his magnificent body. "You did not enjoy our time together, did you, Dominique?"

"I do not want to make you feel inadequate, but I have been with better men." She looked at him innocently. "I did not hurt your pride, did I?"

It was all he could do to keep from laughing out loud. "Perhaps you should reserve your judgment." He raised a finely arched eyebrow. "I believe I can change your mind."

She shrugged as if it was of no consequence to her.

When he started to remove his trousers, she turned away discreetly until she heard the water splash.

"Hand me the soap there, will you, Dominique?" he asked, pointing to where it had dropped on the floor. Of course, had she watched as he lowered himself into the bath, she would have seen him drop it deliberately.

She retrieved the soap and gave it to him, and had turned to leave when she felt his hand wrap around hers.

He pulled her forward until, being thrown off balance, she fell into the tub right on top of him.

She sputtered and choked. "You did that deliberately," she accused, very aware of the warm, naked body beneath hers.

"Yes, I did," Judah admitted, tugging at her wet shirt and tossing it aside.

Her face was flushed and she trembled as she waited to see what he would do next. He deftly untied her trousers and they soon joined her shirt on the floor.

When she was naked, he turned her so she was sitting in his lap, and she thought she would faint right there in his arms.

Dominique reminded herself that it was the wooing and not the final act that stirred her body.

Even so, she clamped her lips together tightly to keep from groaning in pleasure as his lathered hands gently slid down her shoulders and cupped her breasts.

"Have other men done this to you?" Judah whispered.

"No." It was almost a sob. "No one has."

With a strength that surprised her, he turned her over, fitting her to his body. "I am glad."

She looked into his eyes and saw fire reflected there. His hand slid over her hips, her buttocks, pressing her tighter against him. Then he lifted her just enough so he could penetrate her body, and she bit her lip as he slid into her.

Something wildly passionate took hold of her and she waited for him to give her further guidance, for she did not know what to do next.

This time there was no pain when he moved deeper inside her. Instead, an explosion of excitement filled her body. With some part of her mind, she thought it must be improper to feel such delicious pleasure.

Judah's lips were moist from the steam that rose from

the tub and he ran them across her mouth. He pried her lips open with his tongue and it darted inside, and wilder sensations rocked her all the way to her toes.

She did not know the joy that was yet to come because Judah had merely rested inside her, kissing and caressing, slowly deepening his penetration, until she squirmed around and then gasped, as he sensuously stabbed deeper.

Judah threw back his head and bit his lip, attempting to keep from giving her his whole length. He never wanted to hurt her again.

Her eyes were wide with amazement as he grasped her hips and slid her forward and back rhythmically. With wild abandon, she rode the high wave of passion that struck at the very essence of her being.

He played her like a crescendo, spinning, turning, filling her, and then withdrawing. She had no substance of her own outside the man who pumped his life into her body.

A tide of sensations, one after another, wove their way through her, and she had no control of her movements.

Her hands sliced through his dark hair, then down his back, across his taut buttocks.

Arching her head back, she allowed him with his ravenous appetite to control her every move and dominate her every thought. When he dipped to catch her nipple in his mouth and play and gently tug at it with his teeth, she cried out his name.

How foolish she had been to think the act of love was only for a man. He brought her such pleasure, such intense bliss, that it left her breathless. How effortlessly he played her body as if he were the master and she the finely tuned instrument.

Lips met, hands clasped, and they breathed as one.

The union of their bodies was so powerful that they clung to each other, trembling. Lips sought lips as they found boundless delight in each other.

And finally, Dominique collapsed and lay limp and breathless against his chest.

Judah's strong hands ran up and down her back. "Did I redeem myself?" He smiled against her ear, knowing the answer. "Did I?"

In answer, she could do no more than press her lips against his chest.

But he knew what she was feeling, and he also knew that he would have her again and again and go on having her. She touched a place inside him that no woman had ever been allowed to reach. She was like an angel who could heal his tortured soul and save him despite himself.

In that moment, the love Dominique felt for Judah grew until the beauty of it was almost more than she could endure. She closed her eyes, listening to the thundering of his heart.

She buried her face in the curly black hair on his chest, wishing she could die rather than betray him—but betray him she knew she must. Otherwise, she would be trapped there forever, with a lie between them that could destroy them both.

Judah gathered her close to him, closing his eyes and pressing his lips against her cheek. God in heaven, he had not wanted this to happen. He had not wanted to care so deeply about any woman—especially not this one.

Ethan came up beside Judah and was silent for a moment, wondering how to say what was on his mind. "You have taken Dominique into your cabin. Do you think this was wise?"

Judah gave his friend his reluctant attention. "I do. I need to keep her where I can watch her movements."

"Why is that?"

"I discovered the identity of our spy."

Ethan looked confused. "What has that to do with Dominique? Surely you cannot think it is she?"

"Dominique Charbonneau is the spy. The evidence was there for me to see all the time, but I just was not looking."

Ethan was clearly disturbed. "Why don't you just send her away?"

"This does not concern you, Ethan," Judah said, glaring at his friend.

"And I say it does. I care about what happens to her. I will not allow you to—"

Judah's brows met in a frown. "You will not allow me to what, Ethan? The last time I looked, I was captain of this ship, not you. While you are aboard the *Tempest*, you, like everyone else, will do as I say. Is that understood?"

To Judah's surprise, Ethan spoke softly and without anger. "I have known you all our lives, Judah. I knew you wed Mary without loving her. And I watched you bury your heart with her because you were eaten up with guilt."

"I am warning you, Ethan. Do not say any more about Mary. We both know that if I had remained at home as she begged me to, she would still be alive."

"We do not know that, Judah. Mary was not strong to begin with. I'm a doctor, I know." He gripped Judah's shoulder and made him look at him. "You are not going to like hearing this, but I insist you listen to me anyway."

"I'm listening."

"Judah, I never told you that Mary came to me the week after you had taken ship for Tripoli."

"Why would she do that?"

"She begged me to give her something to . . . to make her lose the baby."

Judah looked disbelieving. "I do not understand." His shoulders slumped and he shook his head. "Did she hate me so much that she did not even want my baby?"

"You never understood her, did you Judah? She loved you obsessively. She did not want to share you with anyone, not even a baby."

"What are you saying, Ethan?" Judah asked in a ragged voice.

"You want to talk about guilt, Judah. When I would not help Mary get rid of your baby, she went to some woman who gave her what she asked for. I had hoped I would never have to tell you this, but I must." He took a long pause before continuing. "Mary died because the medicine the woman gave her not only killed the baby, but also poisoned her. I know this is the truth because she asked her doctor to send for me. She seemed to take great pleasure in telling me what she had done, and why."

Judah turned so the cleansing wind would hit his face and hopefully rid him of the sickness he felt inside. "My God, was she mad?"

"Perhaps. But it seems she won anyway, for she has had you more in death than she ever had you when she was alive. In your remorse, you closed your heart to everyone and everything."

Judah was silent for so long that Ethan started to walk away, but his friend's next words made him pause.

"You cannot guess the guilt I have carried with me. I blamed myself for her death because I knew she had blamed me as well. Can you imagine for one moment what that feels like? I have had thorns in my heart, ripping at me every day since Mary died. Not because I loved her—but because I did not."

"I can well imagine what you have felt, because I have had to watch you suffer and keep my secret. You will have to understand that, at the time, I thought that the truth would be worse than the lie you believed. I was wrong, and for that I am truly sorry."

Judah looked up at the sky that was studded with millions of stars. Years of guilt seemed to melt away and he felt free at last.

"Perhaps all women practice deceit, Ethan?"

"I'd like to think not. I know my mother and sisters are kind and truthful."

"Ah, well, there is always that, the relatives," Judah said without humor. "My mother was something of a paragon, herself. I doubt that she ever had a selfish thought enter her mind." Ruefully, he smiled at Ethan. "Perhaps a son views a woman differently from a husband or . . . lover."

"What are you going to do about Dominique?" Ethan asked, determined to close the book on Mary's death.

"Find out the truth of what she has been trying so hard to hide from me. And what she is really doing on my ship."

"Judah, do not hurt her. I feel she has already known great turmoil in her life."

Judah closed his eyes for a moment and then opened them, glancing at his friend. "I believe our little French spy has her lovely claws in me, more surely than Mary ever could have. Perhaps you should be concerned lest she deal me a mortal wound."

Judah turned and walked away, leaving Ethan to ponder his words.

17

Dominique was a woman desperately in love. No matter how carelessly Judah touched her, it sent her heart soaring.

At the moment, he was seated at his desk, his quill dipping into ink as he made his entries in a logbook, while she lay across the bed, pretending to read, but secretly watching him.

Judah was a man of contradictions. She had seen him in battle and had witnessed the destruction he wrought upon his enemies. He controlled his unruly crew with an iron hand and easily bent them to his will. But she had also felt the gentleness in him and he had touched her soul.

In a time when a little corporal had become the leader of France, why did a man such as Judah reach no higher than piracy?

He glanced up and smiled at her. "You were staring at me so intently, what were you thinking?"

Dominique marked her place in the book she had been reading and sat up, resting her arms on her knees. "I was merely speculating on why you took to a life of piracy."

He lay aside his quill. "Were you now? And what conclusion did you reach?"

"You are a very intelligent man, Judah. You could be anything you wanted to be."

"Is this to be one of those reprimands that women are always giving a man, urging him to mend his evil ways?"

"No, it's not that. I just think it's a waste of aspiration. You are obviously a man of education and intelligence. Why a pirate?"

"It is a profitable enterprise." He walked toward her and sat on the bed. "One might say the same about you. Why did you choose your profession?"

It was becoming increasingly difficult to pretend to be a strumpet. She ached to confess the truth to him, but Judah would probably not believe that she had never been with a man before him.

She avoided his interrogating glance. "As you said, it is a profitable enterprise."

"And yet, you have not asked me to pay for the pleasure of bedding you. Why is that?"

She felt sick inside at the thought of taking money from him. "No, I want nothing from you."

He moved to a small chest on his desk and removed a gold piece, then returned to her and dropped it in her lap. "For services rendered."

Judah had not expected her to react with such rage. She bound off the bed and threw the gold piece across the cabin. Then she turned turbulent eyes on him, and took a deep breath.

"As long as you live, never do that again! You made me feel soiled and dirty, and I hate you for it." Tears brimmed in her eyes and blurred her vision. "You do not know me at all. I was not always as you see me now. As a young girl, I had hopes of one day finding and marrying a man I would admire, and who would admire me. Now that can never be, for no decent man would want soiled goods as the mother of his children."

Judah was stunned and it took him a long time to gather his thoughts. This was the first time he had seen Dominique cry. Strange, he thought in reluctant reminiscence, Mary had cried almost daily, and after a time her tears had ceased to moved him, although he never lost the ability to feel guilty and blame himself for them.

But to see tears in Dominique's turquoise eyes was like a pain in his heart. He had really hurt her, and that had not been his intent.

He caught her hands and held them firmly, trying to stop their trembling. "I beg your forgiveness, Dominique. The gold piece was merely meant as a jest."

She turned her back on him, standing rigid, her arms folded, tapping her foot in continuing displeasure.

Judah guided her resisting body down beside him and slipped his arm about her, pulling her against him.

"Will you forgive me, Dominique?"

She shook her head, ashamed of the fresh tears that misted her vision. "You had every right to treat me that way. It is no more than I deserve."

She turned her head and looked at him, catching him unaware, and seeing a tenderness in his eyes that she had not expected.

His lips brushed her cheek and he tasted the saltiness of her tears. "Sweet Dominique, will you not smile for me?" he coaxed.

She nodded and tried to smile, but it came out as a sigh. "I am sorry for the tears, I do not know what is the matter with me. My grandfather taught me that men do not like to see a woman cry."

Judah tucked a tumbled curl behind her ear. "What else did your grandfather teach you?"

Dominique forgot to be on guard. She missed her grandfather and her brother and it was comforting to speak of them. "My grandfather is a very wise and kind man. He raised me and my brother after our parents died."

The gentle but calculating prodding continued. "Is that your only family—a grandfather and a brother?"

She was still unaware that he was gleaning information about her past. "Like most Frenchmen, grandfather was very romantic. I believe my grandmother was a fortunate woman."

"Why is that?"

"Because he gave up everything to marry her. He left France and never went back. Together they built a life on the island."

"And where would that be—Tobago?"

"It is—" She shook her head, realizing that she had already said too much. "I do not wish to talk about myself. Let us speak of you instead."

Judah nodded, thinking he would steer the conversation back to her gradually. "That's only fair. What do you want to know about me?"

"Have you a family?"

"I have a brother named Jason. He is younger than me by two years. He resides in the Orient at the moment."

She smiled, forgetting her earlier unhappiness over the gold piece. "It is difficult to think of you with a family. Does your brother know that you are a pirate?"

"I confide everything to Jason."

"Will you tell him about me?"

He took a long time to answer, as if he were compiling his thoughts. "I do not believe I shall. You see, Jason is far too appealing to women, and I would rather keep you for myself."

Dominique glared at him, rising quickly to her feet. "You mistake me if you think me so easily wooed. Just because I allowed you to bed me does not mean I offer myself to everyone else. Your brother would be safe from me."

Judah could feel her pulling away from him. "Dominique, I have been making a poor attempt at humor. Forget about what I said and come back and lie beside me," he cajoled.

She shook her head. "I do not want to."

A fraction of a smile curved his finely chiseled lips. "I believe you are the first woman I have ever known who could keep her own counsel, and I want you to tell me more about your life. I know so little about you."

He stroked a shimmering curl, his eyes lightly brushing her face. "Let me see if I can piece together what I know about you. You grew up on an island. For the moment, we will assume it is Tobago."

"No. I did not grow up there."

"Then where?"

She shrugged. "Another island, not so different from Tobago."

"Your mother was English and your father French. It was your father's father who raised you."

She answered before she thought. "Yes, that is right."

"Then his last name is Charbonneau?"

"Of course." She looked at him strangely. "I told you my real name, Judah." She had to distract him, he was becoming far too inquisitive about her, and far too knowledgeable. She turned to him, pressing her lips to his and drawing a satisfied whisper.

"I have no resistance to you, my little siren."

His hands were gentle as they lingered at the ties across her breasts. Then with one swift tug, the laces gave way and her breasts spilled out, drawing his admiring glance.

Judah dipped his head, his moist lips caressing, his tongue making the sensuous circle around her nipple, urging it into a sharp peek. She tossed her head back and forth as he repeated the same mind-shattering skill on the other breast.

"You tempt me beyond reason," he growled against her ear, his warm breath stirring a lock of hair.

She was becoming alarmed by the power he had over her. One look from those flashing eyes, one touch from those long, lean fingers and she fell beneath his spell. She opened her lips and invited his kiss; she opened her body and invited his. Her mind, her soul, her very being belonged to him and there was danger in this—she knew that, but she could not resist.

Suddenly it occurred to Dominique that she had become the kind of woman she pretended to be—a woman of loose morals. And oh, she welcomed his lips on her, his hand in hers, his body merging with hers. He had become so much a part of her that, even when she was not with him, he was always in her thoughts.

In a sudden panic, she pushed him away and rolled from the bed.

"Dominique, what are you doing?" Judah asked in frustration.

She straightened her clothing and hurried to the door, fearing that he would follow her. She needed to be alone to think. "Leave me alone! Do not touch me!"

She threw the door open and fled. She slipped past the man at the helm and found seclusion behind the bulkhead. The moon was a crescent and gave off but little light, so the night sky was as soft as black velvet with thousands of stars reflected in an equally black sea.

She felt a slight salt-tinged breeze touch her lips, and her eyes became misty as she cowered in the darkness. She sensed rather than heard Judah behind her. His hands gripped her shoulders and he turned her to face him.

"Why did you run away from me?" he asked gently.

How desperately she wanted to press her face to his rough cheek, to feel his arms about her, holding her so the world could not come between them.

"You have not answered me," he said.

Reluctantly, she raised her head and looked into blue eyes that were softened by longing, and in that instant she was aware that he desired her as much as she desired him.

Judah's arms closed around her and he held her to his heart. "Can you imagine what it is like to love a woman to the distraction of all else, Dominique?" The confession was torn from his lips, taking him by surprise.

She misunderstood him. "You . . . speak of your wife," she observed sadly.

"No, Dominique. I spoke of you."

She shook her head in denial. His confession should have made her happy, but instead she was struck with such a pain that she cried out in protest. "Do not love me, Judah."

Judah watched the different emotions play across Dominique's face, not understanding her reaction. "Perhaps I should not have spoken of love so soon."

She pressed her face to his chest. "Put all tender feelings for me aside."

"Dominique," he said with understanding, "I know you have secrets that you cannot share with me. Perhaps someday you will realize that you can trust me, and even accept the love I offer you."

With his index finger, he lifted her chin and stared into her eyes. "You know that we belong together and I will never let you go."

If only they could sail to some deserted island and never allow the world to intrude upon their lives, but Dominique knew that could never be. Their destinies lay in different directions.

As much as she wanted to be with Judah, she could never take her happiness at the expense of Valcour and her grandfather. Why had she been chosen to betray the only man she would ever love?

Her fingers trembled as she touched his face, knowing that hers could well be the hand of his destruction. The time would soon come when he would despise her as much as he thought he loved her tonight.

"No matter what may happen in the future, Judah, I implore you to always remember that I love you," she admitted softly.

"Then I have won the prize," he said, laughing and hugging her to him. "But I will not have to remember because you will always be at my side to remind me. We were meant to be together, Dominique."

She could only stare at him in wonder.

"I would like you to be my wife."

"You would want me to have your . . . children?"

"I must be honest with you, Dominique, I do not know how I feel about children. To say I court the notion of fathering a child would not be truthful. Some day I will tell you why, but not now."

She already knew why— because he had lost a baby when his wife had died. A sob caught in her throat and she turned away "Do not say any more at this time, Judah." She squeezed her eyes together tightly, hoping he would not discover that she was crying again. "Give me time to think."

He placed a kiss at the nape of her neck. "I am asking you to be my wife, and I will give you all the time you need," he said, feeling certain that she would accept his proposal. The minute she agreed to marry him, he would tell her the truth about himself and insist that she be honest about her life as well.

* * *

Judah steered the *Tempest* into the waters of the hidden cove that he had used on his other visits to Tobago. The ship would lie off the island until the crew that had delivered the *Josephine* to Charleston rejoined them.

It had been three weeks since Judah had asked Dominique to marry him, and she grieved because they could have no future together. Each night he would take her in his arms and make love to her, as he waited patiently for her answer.

Dominique walked slowly to Judah's desk and touched the small wooden chest he kept there. He had only recently started leaving the chest unlocked—it was his way of showing that he trusted her.

Oh, how ill placed that trust had been. Hesitatingly, she raised the lid and reached inside. There was a need for haste because it would soon be dark, and Judah could return at any moment. With a heavy heart, and her eyes filled with tears, she began to read a letter she found there.

> Dear Captain Gallant:
> I just wanted to take the form of this letter to thank you for your devotion to duty. Your country is proud of your accomplishments, and, as Admiral of the Navy of the United States of America, let me add my praise to that of a grateful nation and to President Jefferson's.

She could read no further, for her eyes were blinded by tears, so she replaced the letter in the chest and turned away.

So Judah was not the pirate he wanted everyone to believe—he was a man of honor serving his country.

Colonel Marceau would give much to get his hands

on this information, and Dominique had no doubt that
she could use it to gain her family's release. She tried to
think with her head and not her heart. She must leave
this ship as soon as possible. Tomorrow night would be
soon enough. Tonight, she would steal just a little more
happiness before her world was shattered.

As if he had sensed her yearning, Judah appeared in
the doorway. He smiled and held his arms out to her,
and she ran to him.

"I could not keep my mind on my duties," he whispered, running his tongue along the shell-like curve of
her ear and causing a shiver of delight to dance on her
nerve ends.

With eager hands, she unlaced his shirt and he
removed hers.

She was impatient to have him hold her and make
love to her, to chase all her demons away, if only for
tonight.

Passions ignited, their bodies were aflame. They were
soon naked on the bed, and when Judah entered her,
Dominique gripped his shoulders, meeting his thrusts with
her own upward motions. Passion swept through her like
the hurricanes that had so often plundered her island home.
Pleasure beyond any she could have imagined rocked her
body until she collapsed beneath Judah, crying his name.

The next morning, Dominique walked about the cabin,
her mind clear for the first time. After reading Judah's
letter and realizing that he was a man of honor, she was
certain he would want to help her devise a way to rescue
Valcour and her grandfather from Colonel Marceau,
their common enemy.

She would confess her real reason for coming aboard
the *Tempest*, and assure Judah that she could never have

betrayed him. She smiled happily—she would agree to marry him if he still wanted her.

Hearing a commotion outside, and the sound of scurrying feet, Dominique hurriedly left the cabin and joined the crewmen who were already on deck. She discovered that three boats filled with native men and women selling fresh fruit had come up beside the ship. Apparently the secluded glen was no longer a safe haven for the *Tempest*, if the natives had discovered them.

One man had a small monkey that was perched on his shoulder, turning flips and entertaining the crew. Dominique laughed as the man whispered something to the little animal and pointed at her. She was amazed when the monkey scampered up the side of the ship and deposited a plump, ripe papaya in her hand.

The smile left her face when she glanced back at the man to find he was not a native at all—he was Colonel Marceau's aide, Corporal Parinaud!

Fear robbed her of the ability to think clearly when he called up to her, trying to imitate the local accent. "Slice the fruit deep, lady, you will find it to your liking."

She did not stay to hear more. Clutching the objectionable object, she rushed to the cabin. With trembling hands, she reached for Judah's sword that hung on a peg on the wall and sliced the fruit.

Her endeavor was met with success, for in a place where the core should have been was a piece of paper.

With dread, she read words that chilled her to the bone.

We are watching for Gallant, just see that he comes ashore and we will do the rest.

So much for her plans to remain with Judah. She must find a way to warn him, then she must leave the ship, so she would not be a danger to him.

She lowered her head into her hands, sobbing. Everyone she loved was in peril because of Colonel Marceau.

With determination, she raised her head, her eyes hard and cold. Now, she must find a way to save not only her grandfather and Valcour, but also Judah.

18

Judah was occupied with Ethan and Cornelius on the lower deck, so Dominique found her chance to escape.

But first she picked up a quill and wrote a letter to Judah. She could not put in all that was in her heart, but she could warn him of the danger he faced.

> Judah,
> I am honored that you asked me to be your wife and I am sorry I must refuse. But I must warn you not to go into Tobago, for there is danger for you there. I am sorry that I was forced to take your gold piece, as well as four others, after all. I do not believe we shall meet again, but I beg you to leave this island as soon as possible—you have enemies here.
>
> Dominique

She propped the letter against the small chest on his desk, and then, looking about the place where she had known such brief happiness, she silently left the cabin.

As she crept along the shadows of the deck, she was grateful that it was a night without a moon, for it would make it easier to escape without detection.

Dominique made no noise as she slipped over the side of the ship and gripped the anchor, lowering herself into the water.

It was good that she was a strong swimmer because the tide was against her and kept pushing her back toward the ship. It was like an omen, or her heart warning her not to leave the man she loved.

Wet and bedraggled, Dominique made her way down the deserted beach, skirting the town of Scarborough and especially the Blue Dog Tavern, where no doubt Corporal Parinaud would be waiting for her. She would go instead to one of the smaller coastal villages. There she would hire a boat to take her directly to Guadeloupe.

Somehow, she would find a way to defeat Colonel Marceau—she had to.

As she walked along, her thoughts were of Judah. Each step carried her further from him. Judah Gallant had offered her his greatest gift, his heart. He would never know that he was her one and only love.

She had come to realize that Valcour and her grandfather would not want their freedom at the price of Judah's life, and it was a price that she was not willing to pay.

After trudging for over two hours, Dominique became so exhausted that all she wanted to do was to lie down and sleep. But she must reach her destination before anyone realized that she was missing.

It turned out to be more difficult than she had thought to find someone willing to take her to Guadeloupe; everyone was frightened of the French soldiers at the garrison there.

It was almost noon before she finally persuaded an old fisherman to help her. She gave him the five gold pieces and they set sail in his battered old boat, which smelled strongly of fish and did not appear to be sea-worthy.

Tired and hungry, she curled up in a damp corner and closed her eyes. At last she was going home.

Before she drifted off to sleep, her last thought was of Judah, and she hoped he would take her warning seriously.

Judah crushed the letter in his fist and closed his eyes. He had thought Dominique loved him, but if she had, she would not have left without saying good-bye.

"What is it?" Ethan asked, noticing Judah's stricken expression.

Judah thrust the letter at his friend and watched as he smoothed it out and read it.

"I have been the worst kind of fool, Ethan. I allowed myself to forget that Dominique was a spy."

He turned away, thinking how cleverly she had played him, then like a thief in the night, she was gone.

Bitterly, he wondered how she intended to spend the reward she would no doubt receive for his capture.

Ethan reread the letter, trying to discern its meaning. "She says that there is danger for you on Tobago. If she did not care for you, she would not have mentioned that. Perhaps we should do as she warns and set sail right away."

"Don't be deceived by her words, Ethan. She is clever, and she knows I will tear the town apart looking for her. There is nowhere she can hide that I will not find her."

Ethan placed the letter on Judah's desk and walked

out of the cabin. It would serve no purpose to try to talk him out of going ashore. The best he could do was to accompany Judah and watch out for any trouble that might come.

Under the cover of darkness, Judah and Ethan climbed out of the boat and waded ashore. They had no way of knowing that they were being watched.

"You wait by the boat, Ethan. As always, if I do not return by dawn, leave without me."

"I won't do it this time, Judah. We both know that you are in danger."

"You will do as I say—that's an order."

Judah stepped into the road, making his way toward Scarborough. He had but one aim in mind: nothing would stop him from finding Dominique.

He heard a noise, but he never saw the blunt instrument that struck him from behind. Pain exploded in his head and he fell to the ground.

Ethan heard a commotion and came running to help. He stopped when he saw the gun aimed at him. Then a bullet grazed his head, knocking him to the ground. He lay there dizzily, wishing the world would stop spinning so he could help Judah.

In a haze of pain he heard French voices.

"Fool, you hit him too hard."

"*Non*, he is merely unconscious. Pick him up and we shall take him to the ship. Colonel Marceau will be glad to see this American, no matter his condition."

"What about his companion?"

"Leave him, he is dead—did I not put the bullet in him myself?"

Ethan tried to call out in protest, but blackness enveloped him.

* * *

Judah regained consciousness to discover that his arms were in shackles and he lay upon a straw-covered floor. From the swaying he felt beneath him, he realized that he was on board a ship.

When he tried to move, he felt dizzy and groaned in agony, falling back against the wall.

He tried to remember what had happened. He had been talking to Ethan. No, he had left Ethan and had gone only a short distance when he had heard a noise. After that, he remembered nothing else.

Slowly, Judah rose to his feet, using the wall to help him. With doubled fists, he pounded against the door, but no one came. There was such silence that he had the feeling he was alone. In anger, he picked up a chair and slammed it several times against the door. The chair splintered into pieces, but the lock held fast.

Not one to give up easily, he went to the porthole, but it was useless to think he could escape by that route.

As far as his shackles would allow, he paced the small, dark cabin like a predatory cat, often bumping into objects he could not see in the all-consuming darkness.

He felt the moment the wind filled the sails and the ship got underway. He had no notion of where he was going, but he did know that he was a prisoner of the French, and they had many reasons to want to see him hanged.

There could be only one person who had known of his hidden cove, only one person who could have betrayed him to his enemies.

Dominique Charbonneau! Damn her treachery!

What hurt almost as much as her betrayal was that he had trusted her, had opened his heart to her and asked her to be his wife, even though he suspected what she was.

"Fools deserve what they get," he muttered, feeling so weak that he fell to his knees.

He pulled against the chains at his wrist and gave a strangled cry of impotent rage. All he wanted was to live long enough to get his hands around Dominique's lovely neck. That was the thought that would keep him going, the thought that would dull his pain, the thought that would keep him sane.

Somehow they would meet again, if not in this life, then surely in hell, and he would show her no mercy.

Dominique, looking bedraggled and somewhat like a street urchin, with her rumpled clothing and her uncombed hair, came to the gates of the garrison, speaking decisively to the guard.

"Take me to Colonel Marceau at once."

"Now who would you be, acting like you are some fine lady that the colonel would want to see?" the sentry asked, giving her a shove that sent her sprawling to the ground. "Get off with you, island rubbish!"

She stood up with as much dignity as she could gather, straightened her soiled linen shirt and glared at the soldier. "Inform Colonel Marceau that Mademoiselle Dominique Charbonneau insists on seeing him."

With doubt on his face, he now looked at her closely. "You do not look like her."

"Well, I am. Open the gate and admit me at once, or be prepared to face your colonel's rage."

He shrugged, opening the gate, and allowing her to enter.

This time Dominique had no escort, but went straight to Colonel Marceau's office, and to her relief, no one tried to stop her.

The colonel was not present, but Corporal Parinaud

was there, and he was seated in his commanding officer's chair with his boots propped on the desk. When he saw Dominique, he quickly came to his feet, with a wide grin.

"I see you got my message," he said, doffing his hat and dipping into a mock bow. "If you are looking for the colonel, he's in Capesterre on important business for the governor."

"Is General Richepance here?" Dominique asked, thinking she might at last be able to see the governor without interference from Colonel Marceau.

"He is in Paris and has left Colonel Marceau with complete authority to govern the island in his absence. There's been some rioting in the south, or else the colonel would be here to greet you himself."

Dominique glared at the man she disliked almost as much as his cruel superior. "When will Colonel Marceau return?" she asked coldly.

The aide scratched his head and then clamped his bicorne hat back in place. "I do not know for certain. But he said I should tell you, if you happened to come here, that your grandfather has been escorted home."

Dominique watched the man carefully, hardly daring to believe what she had heard. "And my brother?"

"You know," he said with a smirk. "That is the humorous part in all this. You see, your brother was never actually here. It seems he had friends who got him off the island before we could arrest him."

Dominique felt her legs go weak, first from relief that Valcour was safe and her grandfather was at Windward Plantation, and then because of all she had suffered from the machinations of Colonel Marceau.

She could sense there was more that Corporal Parinaud had not told her. He was taking particular delight in forcing her to drag information out of him.

"Then my grandfather is safe, and did not suffer from his imprisonment?"

"He was taken away in a coach this very day."

"Unharmed?" she pressed.

"Mademoiselle, the officers do not tell me everything, since I am beneath their notice. However, I did hear some of my friends mention that when the old man was escorted home, the plantation house was to be burned as punishment for your brother's crimes against France."

Dominique gasped and took a hurried step backward. "What are you saying?"

"If I was you, I'd get to Windward Plantation with all haste." His laughter was tinged with amusement. "The troops cannot be more than a few minutes ahead of you, so perhaps you may be able to save a few of your possessions."

She looked about her frantically, wondering how she would get to her grandfather in time. She must find a horse so she could take the shortcut and arrive ahead of the soldiers.

Fear for her grandfather gave wings to her feet as she ran out of the fort, unmindful of the curious glances that followed her. She must go to Bartrand Dubeau; he would help her.

She burst into Bartrand's office at the Exchange, grateful to find him there.

It took the startled Bartrand a moment to recognize the granddaughter of his old friend.

"Help me, please!" she cried, gripping his shirtfront frantically.

"In God's name, what has happened to you, Dominique?" he asked, slipping a supporting arm about her frail shoulders. "I have been looking for you."

"Bartrand, Colonel Marceau has been holding my grandfather prisoner."

"I know," he said sorrowfully. "When I found out, I tried to get Jean Louis free, but they would not even admit me to the garrison. Then, I went to Windward Plantation looking for you, but no one could tell me where you were. I searched everywhere, but without success."

"Bartrand, I have no time to explain, but I need a horse and I need it now!"

He nodded. "Come, I will saddle two horses. I am coming with you."

She looked at him gratefully. "We must hurry!"

19

As they rode along, Dominique told Bartrand some of what had happened to her since the night of Valcour's birthday party, of course leaving out the most intimate parts. She saw his anger flash, but he made no comment. There was little opportunity for conversation because they were now riding single file through the swamp, the quickest way to Windward Plantation.

At last, coming out of the swamp, they galloped past the dense forest as if time were the enemy. Dominique was frantic to reach her grandfather, and just at sunset they were within sight of the plantation. Her heart lightened—the house still stood, rising majestically above the treetops.

Their harried trek had brought them to the back of the house. "We are ahead of them," Dominique said as they slowed their weary mounts to a walk. By the time they reached the front of the house, a coach had arrived with an escort of six soldiers.

Dominique jumped from her mount and ran to the coach, clawing at the door to open it, only to find it was empty. "Grandpapa! Grandpapa, where are you?!" she cried, unable to locate him.

She watched in horror as several of the soldiers began lighting torches and tossing them into the house. Voracious flames were licking at the structure, igniting it like a tinderbox.

Dominique cried out when she saw her grandfather stumble up the steps and enter the burning house. She could not remember running, stumbling, falling, and clambering to her feet. She only knew that she had to reach him ahead of the fire.

"Come back, imbecile," one of the soldiers yelled at Jean Louis. "Are you crazed?"

Bartrand was just behind her, but when he tried to grab her arm, Dominique pushed him away.

When she entered the house, the soldiers took no interest. They mounted their horses and rode away, having accomplished what they had been ordered to do.

Dominique felt the heat of the fire on her face when she dashed through the burning door. She realized at once where her grandfather would go—to his bedroom, where the portrait of her grandmother hung on the wall.

The bottom floor was so smoke-filled that she could not find her way, but instinct guided her to the stairs. The flames were leaping higher, singeing her clothing and making it difficult to breathe; but that did not stop her.

In the distance, she could hear Bartrand calling out to her, but she made no attempt to answer him. Her only thought was to save her grandfather.

The heat was so oppressive that it scorched her face, but she had reached the stairs and was ascending them while flames passed hungrily over the aged wood. She could hear the sound of glass windows exploding from the inferno, and the once beautiful red curtains at the front window were crumbling to flying bits of black ash.

"Grandpapa!" she cried, hoping she could reach his room ahead of the fire. "I am coming, Grandpapa!"

She tripped and fell, then dragged herself upright, thinking it was impossible to get past the wall of flames that stood between her and her grandfather—but that would not stop her from trying.

Heat such as she had never known parched her throat with each breath she took. She suddenly felt the floor give way beneath her and she was falling downward.

"Grandpapa!!" she screamed, and her last thought was of falling into the raging flames below.

Bartrand, who could see nothing in the smoke that was as thick and hot as the breath of hell, heard Dominique scream and ran in her direction. He saw at once that the stairs had collapsed beneath her. He scooped her up into his arms, praying that God would give him the strength to carry her to safety.

Once he had her outside, he lay her on the grass near the fountain, and he could see that she was still breathing. With dread in his heart, he returned to the house. He had to try to save his friend, and it just might be possible because the east wing had not yet caught fire.

Bartrand hurried inside and made his way up the stairway at the back of the house, rushing down the smoky corridor to Jean Louis's bedchamber.

Surprisingly, this part of the house had not yet been touched by flames, and Bartrand found his friend lying beneath the portrait of his dead wife, his unblinking eyes resting lovingly on her face.

Using all his strength, Bartrand lifted Jean Louis in his arms and discovered that the wasted body weighed little more than a child's.

The inferno was coming closer now, ravaging and destroying everything in its path as it grew in intensity.

Bartrand hurried to the back stairs and made his way

outside. He lay his old friend on the grass beside Dominique, not knowing if either one of them would live.

Helplessly, he glanced up and watched the grand old plantation house burn, the red flames lighting the dark sky. In the distance, Bartrand could hear the thundering of horses' hooves—the neighbors must have seen the fire and were coming to help.

Reluctantly, he placed his hand on the pulse point at Jean Louis's throat and discovered that he was dead. With a heavy heart, he lowered his old friend's eyelids. There was no time to grieve—not yet. He had to hide Dominique, and he had to do it quickly because he did not trust Colonel Marceau—not after all he had done to this family.

Lifting Dominique in his arms, Bartrand mounted his horse and rode away into the night. Others would see to Jean Louis.

Bartrand took Dominique to his hunting lodge, and placed her in the care of his gamekeeper's wife, Ineaz. The woman was wise in the ways of herbs and healing, and he trusted her more than most doctors.

"Take care of her," he instructed the old woman.

Ineaz merely nodded absently. Already her hands were dipping a clean strip of linen into a pail of water. Then she turned sagacious eyes on the young girl. "I will do what I can."

It was dark by the time Bartrand returned to Windward Plantation. By now the house was little more than charred and glowing embers. The neighbors were walking around as if in a daze. They had many questions that Bartrand did not feel inclined to answer.

He stood over the body of Jean Louis, feeling sorrow in his heart. He had been a good man, and many would mourn his passing, but none more than Bartrand.

It was much later that he returned to the lodge to find Dominique's hands and most of her face bound with clean white cloths. He was concerned because she was still unconscious.

"How is she, Ineaz?"

"She has burns on her face and hands, and a bad one on her leg. Beyond this I do not know."

For two days, Dominique languished in a shadowy world filled with horrors, real and imagined. Hurtful hands tortured her, making her drink foul-tasting mixtures, and rubbing equally foul-smelling salves and creams on her burns.

Wildflowers bloomed in profusion outside her window and colorful butterflies fluttered fancifully on the warming sea breeze, but Dominique did not know or care in her twilight world. Somewhere in her subconscious, she knew that to take notice of life would bring unbearable pain.

Was it only her imagination, or was Judah beside her, his eyes accusing and unloving?

Someone—a woman—was urging her to fight to live. But to do as she asked required too much effort. It was far more peaceful in her quiet, dark world.

Judah heard the anchor grinding downward, the ship now merely riding the restless waves, rather than being swept along by them. He had no notion where he was because in his darkened hell he could not gauge night from day or discern the passing hours.

Somewhere above him a door opened, emitting light so bright that he felt as if his eyes had been stabbed with tiny needles. He heard someone descend the wooden ladder and braced himself against the wall to await whatever came.

Rough hands gripped Judah's shoulders and flung him forward. It took all his strength to keep his balance.

"Climb the ladder," came a crisp French order.

Judah had no choice but to do as he was told. He had not known how weak he was until he reached the top step and found himself panting for breath. He had been given nothing to eat but watery gruel, which he had refused. Now he wished he had eaten the disgusting concoction.

When he stood on deck, he weaved with each pitch of the ship, so he planted his feet wide and tried to focus on his surroundings. Although it was an overcast day, his eyes burned and watered from the meager light.

"So," a venomous voice said in heavily accented English, "at last we have the elusive Captain Judah Gallant."

There was sneering laughter from the Frenchman. "What no man could accomplish was brought about by the silken arms of a woman. Tsk, tsk, Captain. You fell for the oldest game since Eve induced Adam to partake of the forbidden fruit."

The Frenchman's words stung as no torture could have.

"Who are you?" Judah asked the man, who was no more than a shadowy outline.

"Permit me to introduce myself, Captain." He flourished a bow. "I am Colonel Marceau. After word of your capture reaches Bonaparte, I shall surely be invested as one of his elite guard."

He grabbed a handful of Judah's hair and jerked his head upward. "You do not look like much at the moment, but there is a great prize on your head."

Judah's vision was beginning to clear and he could see the face of his tormentor. He had always surmised that you could tell much about a man by his manner of dress, and this one went in for the flamboyant—the elaborate, oversized epaulets and gold braid were in questionable taste. Judah guessed just how to strike at the man because he was obviously a swaggering braggart.

"I have oft wondered about the ability of a man who must call upon a woman to do what he cannot. Is this the kind of behavior Napoleon admires in those who serve him?"

The open-handed slap came so fast that Judah had not expected it and had no time to brace himself. In his weakened condition, he fell to his knees, where the man kicked him repeatedly.

But Judah felt little of the pain inflicted by the Frenchman. He was thinking of aqua eyes and arms as soft as a dove wing, hair silken to the touch, and lips that muddled a man's reasoning while betraying him.

For what reason had Dominique lulled him into passiveness even at the cost of her own virtue? he wondered. At least he had taken something from her that no other man had had. She would remember him for that, if for nothing else.

Judah was pulled to his feet by two guards, and he soon found himself in a boat heading for the island. He was still in the Caribbean, he knew that much, but he could not identify the location.

"Do you see that great fortress perched atop the hill, there?" one of the French soldiers asked tauntingly.

Judah did not answer, but stared straight ahead as if he had not heard.

"That is where you will draw your last breath," he said, laughing at the thought. "I am sure you have heard what we French do to pirates."

Still, Judah did not answer. He forced himself to think of soft, silken lips that had so easily spoken lies.

Another soldier poked Judah in the ribs with the barrel of his pistol, disappointed when Judah did not react. "I believe Colonel Marceau will not have you executed right away. *Non,* you are a prize he will want to parade around as his trophy."

"What place is this?" Judah asked at last.

"As for as you are concerned, it is hell, Monsieur."

It was a week after the fire that Dominique opened her eyes and focused them for the first time. She blinked in astonishment, wondering where she was. The place was unfamiliar to her, but she felt safe.

A door opened and a gray-haired woman entered, and when she smiled, Dominique could see that her two front teeth were missing.

"Where am I?" Dominique asked.

"You are in the hunting cabin of Monsieur Dubeau, and you have been very ill, but you will recover."

Dominique raised her hands and found them bandaged. She could feel something sticky on her face, and there was questioning in her eyes as she looked at the woman.

"Do not be distressed. What you feel is my own cure for your burns."

Suddenly Dominique stared at her bandaged hands. She began to scream and tried to climb out of bed. "Grandpapa! Where are you?"

The woman rushed to Dominique, and with a strength that took her by surprise, forced her back into bed.

"Monsieur Dubeau is just outside. I will call him for you, if you will lie still. He will answer all your questions."

Dominique nodded weakly.

It was some time before Dominique was able to stop

crying. Bartrand had explained to her that her grandfather was dead and Windward Plantation had been destroyed.

She was still dazed as she put her anguished thoughts into words. "It is my fault that grandfather is dead, Bartrand. I can only think that Colonel Marceau burned Windward to punish me for not doing as he asked." She shook her head as tears spilled from her eyes and ran down her cheeks. "Do you understand why I could not betray Judah Gallant?"

"I understand," he said kindly, "and so would your grandfather. I knew Jean Louis better than anyone, and he would have been proud that you did not follow the dictates of a man like Colonel Marceau."

"But—"

He held up his hand to silence her. "Your grandfather raised you and Valcour not to give in to tyranny. Put your mind at rest, Dominique, and know that he would not have wanted to live to see Windward Plantation burned—it was his life."

"What will I do now?" she asked. "I dare not remain on Guadeloupe."

"It is safe for you to remain here for a time. When you are stronger, I have friends who will help you escape."

She laid her bandaged hand over his. "You have always been so good to me, Bartrand. Would that I could repay you."

"Hush and rest for now." He stood. "I shall visit you again tomorrow. Do as Ineaz tells you; she is a good nurse. And do not leave the lodge because I do not want anyone to know that you are here. Colonel Marceau has spies everywhere, and we do not know who to trust."

She nodded. The last thing she wanted was to fall victim to that monster again.

"Ineaz has told me that the scars on your face will

eventually disappear because they were not severe. But she is not so certain about the scars on your hands or your leg."

"It does not matter." Dominique smiled with some of her old spirit. "I will still manage to turn a man's head."

Bartrand's eyes were sad. "Rest and grow strong."

He left, and Domonique felt so alone in her fathomless sorrow.

20

Ineaz had removed all Dominique's bandages, but for the one on her leg. She held a mirror out to Dominique so she could study her image. "It is a blessing that there is almost no scarring, Mademoiselle Charbonneau, which is a wonder since you were so badly burned."

Dominique pushed aside the mirror, sickened by the red scars on her face. "Please tell me that I shall not always look like this, Ineaz."

The woman looked at her assessingly. "I vow to you that the scars on your face and hands will fade with time and hardly be noticeable. But the burn on your leg is deep, and that is the one that troubles me the most. It has not yet healed, and will still be very painful for a time. I fear that scar will always be a reminder of that horrible day."

"I need no reminder—it was the day grandfather died." A despondent Dominique lay back against her pillow. "I do not really care about myself; my life is over. But I wonder every day about my brother and where he could be. I pray that Valcour is safe."

The old woman frowned. "I believe he is, or you

would have heard. And one day, you will want to live again—I tell you this because it is true."

Dominique looked at the kind-hearted woman who had been her faithful nurse for many weeks. "I have not the words to thank you for your care. What would I have done without you, Ineaz?"

"I am only repaying a kindness that your grandfather once gave me. Monsieur Jean Louis Charbonneau saved me and my five children from starvation. He also encouraged Monsieur Dubeau to give my husband work. That was more than twenty years ago. Since that time, my children have grown up, never knowing another hungry day, and neither have my grandchildren."

Dominique's eyes filled with tears. "My grandfather was an exceptional man."

Ineaz nodded. "Now, I believe Monsieur Dubeau has arrived. Shall I send him in?"

"*Oui*," Dominique said, pulling a soft shawl about her shoulders.

Bartrand handed Dominique a bouquet of blue-red orchids, and for a moment their aroma took her back to the night she had lain beneath the moon with Judah.

"Thank you, dear friend, for all you have done," she said, raising her hand to Bartrand.

"Hush now, there is no need for thanks between us. We are like family, are we not?"

"I have always thought so, as did Grand . . . my grandfather. Thank you all the same."

He dismissed her gratitude with a wave of his hand. "I want to speak to you of other matters. You must leave Guadeloupe as soon as possible. In the absence of General Richepance, that madman, Colonel Marceau, becomes daily more bold in tormenting our people."

Dominique shivered. Colonel Marceau was capable of extreme cruelty. "What has he done now?"

"He prepares a great celebration to his genius, a garish display where he brags that he will march a notorious pirate down the streets of Basse-Terre as an example to all those who would flout his authority."

She stared at Bartrand a moment, fearing to ask, but needing to know. "Who is the pirate?"

"The American called Judah Gallant. I thought you knew. It is said that you were instrumental in his capture."

Dominique frantically grabbed his hand. "Oh, Bartrand, please tell me it is not Judah? Can there be a mistake?"

He looked at her strangely. "There is no mistake. The American is the colonel's prisoner. It is said that he was captured when he came ashore at Tobago. Marceau apparently believes you helped in some way."

"But you know I had nothing to do with it." She shook her head. "You must help me find Captain Gallant's ship, the *Tempest*."

"What are you saying?" Bartrand asked, vigorously shaking his head. "I will not help you in this."

"You don't understand. I must get to Tobago as soon as possible!"

"What nonsense is this?" Bartrand said, standing up and moving away from her in agitation. "I will not hear of such a thing! You are still too weak to even leave your bed."

"Help me in this, Bartrand. And do not ask questions that I cannot answer. All I can say to you is that Captain Gallant is not a pirate, and I will help him escape, with your assistance or without it."

Incaz, who had come into the room, added her opinion. "You should listen to her, Monsieur Dubeau. I believe she will do this alone if you do not help her."

"You are hardly fit to travel," Bartrand reasoned, hoping to thwart her foolhardy scheme.

Dominique slid off the bed and stood, allowing the long shawl to drop about her. "I am well enough for this," she said with determination. "Please leave so I may dress."

At last, Bartrand nodded reluctantly. He had followed Dominique into a burning building, so he knew that when she was intent on doing something, she would do it. "I will see what I can arrange," he said with a resigned sigh. "I shall return in the morning."

Dominique nodded, unable to speak past the tightness in her throat.

Ineaz went to a chest beside the bed and fumbled about until she found what she had been seeking. She held a jar out for Dominique's inspection. "If artfully applied, this will hide the scars on your face."

Suddenly Dominique did care about her appearance. She had found vanity because of her love for Judah, only in as much as she wanted to be beautiful for him. "I will wear the cream until the scars heal, and I thank you for understanding how I feel, Ineaz." Dominique dropped onto the bed, still feeling weak.

"I only hope that the man is worthy of your sacrifice, Mademoiselle."

In the noisy, smoked-filled taproom of the Blue Dog Tavern, Dominique went from table to table, speaking to each man. "I am a friend of Judah Gallant's, are you?"

Although she wore the clothing of a man, she fooled no one. There were hoots and several lewd suggestions, but no one admitted to being Judah's friend. Then she saw a man sitting at the back of the room, and she recognized him as the one who had met with Judah the first day she had seen him.

William York watched the woman approach him and he thought she had the kind of timeless beauty that would last after she was no longer young. He did not know what she was doing in a place like this, but she was certainly not the kind of woman who would offer herself for a price.

He was surprised when she stopped at his table and further puzzled when he saw desperation in her turbulent eyes.

"Monsieur, I know you are a friend of Judah Gallant's and I need your help."

He looked at her distrustfully, having realized who she was. "You are Miss Charbonneau, are you not?"

She fell into the chair beside him in relief. "Then you know me?"

He took a long drink from his tankard of ale before answering. "I know no good of you. You are a French spy!"

She reached across the table and gripped his hand. "Listen to me, please. A hideous man, Colonel Henri Marceau, has taken Judah prisoner, and he now languishes in a cell on Guadeloupe! I cannot even guess what he might be suffering, but the colonel is capable of anything."

William had remained on Tobago even after he learned that Judah had been captured, hoping that he might discover where he had been taken. Thus far, he had learned nothing, and now this woman was trying to convince him that she wanted to help him, when he knew her for the enemy.

"Why should I believe you?" he asked in a deadly calm voice.

"Because you must! I want to help save Judah's life. You must take me to the *Tempest*."

"I have no reason to trust you."

She looked at him in exasperation. "You cannot save Judah without my help, so you will have to trust me."

William studied her carefully, and he could see the desperation in her turquoise eyes. "I have no choice, have I?"

"Then come," she said, standing. "We must hurry. Is the *Tempest* nearby?"

"It is."

She tugged at his hand. "Let us leave now!"

For the first time, William York stood aboard the *Tempest*, but there was not the rush of joy he had always imagined. Her captain was missing, perhaps even dead. He watched Dominique Charbonneau speak to the crew that had gathered about.

"There is no reason you should trust me, but I hope you will. Allow me to answer all your questions before you ask them." She looked at each face in turn. "Yes, it is true that I was sent here to help the French capture your captain, but I swear to you, I had nothing to do with his eventual arrest."

"How do we know you weren't sent to lure us all into the hands of the French?" one of the men asked.

Tom Beeton shoved the man out of the way. "'Cause she says so—that's why. Me, I'm a'going with her."

"Why should we help the cap'n and put ourselves in danger?" another man questioned.

"I'll tell you why you should help him, and I am giving away state secrets when I do," William York said. "Judah Gallant was never a pirate, as most of you thought. He was on an assignment for the United States government, and you were all helping him."

There was mumbling of disbelief, until William spoke again.

"I'll tell you something else. Captain Gallant has asked for, and obtained, a pardon for every one of you, no matter your crime. When you go home to America, because of his insistence, you can walk the streets as free men, indeed as heroes of your country."

There was a long silence while every man considered William York's words.

Tom turned to Ethan. "What do you say to this, Doctor?"

"I say we go to Guadeloupe and free our captain," Ethan replied. "I say we put our trust in Miss Charbonneau and let her lead the way."

There was a loud shout of approval as each man voiced his support.

"I did not come here without a purpose in mind," Dominique told them. "First, I will warn you that Colonel Marceau, who has jurisdiction over Guadeloupe at the moment, is vicious and dangerous. I cannot promise that we will win, and should we fall into his hands, he will be merciless."

"Tell us your plan," William urged. "We are all aware of the danger."

"I will want you to come with me, Tom," Dominique replied, looking at the others carefully. "The fewer there are of us, the less suspicious we will be. Doctor, I would also like it if you accompanied us. Judah may be injured and need your skill."

"How can we break into the fort and rescue Judah with so few men?" Ethan questioned.

"We shall not force our way in, but go there by invitation," she said with assurance. "I shall use Colonel Marceau's own bloated sense of vainglory against him." Then she added quietly and with less bravado, "I hope."

That night, when Cornelius took the *Tempest* out to sea, he navigated a course for the isle of Guadeloupe.

And at Dominique's direction, he sailed to an uninhabited side of the island and dropped anchor in the turbulent waves.

"You must not stay here, but lie off the shores out of sight," she told Cornelius. "Look to this beach each night, and when I am ready for you, I will build a signal fire."

A short time later, Dominique joined Ethan and Tom in a small boat, and they headed for the island.

When they reached the shore, one of Bartrand's men joined them. They were soon aboard a rickety cart that would take them to the hunting lodge, where they would plan their final strategy.

Dominique silently blessed Bartrand, for he had provided her with everything she had asked of him.

Corporal Parinaud handed the colonel a sealed letter, which he raised to his nose, inhaling the lingering scent of perfume. He glanced at the name scrawled across the envelope and smiled.

"I wondered how long it would be until Mademoiselle Charbonneau contacted me."

He broke the seal and read:

Colonel Marceau:
I hope you are as happy as I am about the capture of the notorious pirate, Captain Gallant. I wonder if my friends and I might be allowed to view the prisoner. You see, they do not believe that scoundrel is actually under your custody.

He glanced at his aide. "Most probably Mademoiselle Charbonneau wants to claim her reward. Well, it was my plan and not hers that led to his arrest."

The colonel continued to read, and then he smiled.
"No, she does not want the reward, she only wants me to
parade the pirate before her friends so she can gloat.
Listen to what she has to say."

> I have told my friends that you deserve the
> reward since it was your brilliant strategy that
> finally ended the black-hearted pirate's marauding
> and preying on the innocent. I beseech you to
> allow us to see the man so we can make certain
> that we have nothing more to fear from him.

Marceau laughed as he glanced up at his aide. "My little bird now sings a sweeter song. Let this be a lesson for
you, Parinaud. Women respect forcefulness in a man.
Oh, they may cry and moan at first, but in the end they
are all the same, be they refined, like Mademoiselle
Charbonneau, or a milkmaid."

"The plan was brilliant, Colonel," Parinaud said with
false sincerity, "and Mademoiselle did play an important
part in the capture. After all it was she who sent him to us."

Marceau waived this aside. "I will shower her with
compliments before her friends, and that will appease
her." He stuffed the letter in his uniform jacket. "I have
decided to have a banquet for Mademoiselle Charbonneau
and her companions this very evening You will deliver
the invitation to her at once."

"Colonel, the servant who brought Mademoiselle's
letter said his mistress is residing with the Dubeau family, since her home burned down during her absence."

The colonel stroked his chin. "It appears she has no
notion that it was by my orders that Windward
Plantation was destroyed. Strange, I would have thought
someone would have told her." He shrugged. "Ah, it is
of little matter. What can she do, after all?"

Corporal Parinaud was too shrewd to admit that he had informed Mademoiselle Charbonneau that her plantation was to be burned.

"Yes, a banquet to show my accomplishment to these haughty islanders, who think they are superior to me," Colonel Marceau said with satisfaction. "General Richepance is anxious to remain in France, and what better man could be named as his replacement than myself?" He rocked from his heels to his toes. "I shall make a much better governor than Richepance—you will see. You will all see."

Dominique was dressed in a lovely blue silk empire gown with puffed sleeves. She had taken care to cover her face with the cream Ineaz had given her, so the scars would not show, and she wore lace gloves to hide her hands.

She had to smile at Tom, who wore yellow satin trousers and an equally bright green cutaway coat with long narrow tails. He kept tugging at the frilly shirt and grumbling about looking unmanly, and what his friends would say if they could see him so prettily dressed.

Dominique laughingly set the green beaver hat atop his head. "I can only wonder where Bartrand came by the clothing. You will certainly draw attention tonight."

Ethan, who was elegant in formal black trousers and cutaway, tilted his chin arrogantly, speaking to Dominique in perfectly enunciated French. "I only hope my friends do not learn that I am to be in the same room as that ruffian pirate, Judah Gallant."

Dominique smiled her approval. "Your French will do very well, Ethan."

"What about me?" Tom asked, staring with distaste at the lace handkerchief Dominique had handed him.

She and Ethan exchanged woeful glances. Not only did Tom not speak French, his English was also questionable.

Dominique had a sudden inspiration. "I know! You shall be mysterious, Tom." Her eyes sparkled with mirth. "I shall introduce you as an Austrian. You must act pompous and lofty, as if you are above dining with a mere colonel . . . and above talking to him."

Tom looked displeased as he stuffed the offensive lace handkerchief in his pocket. "I would sooner cut the man's throat."

Dominique laughed. "That you must not do."

Monsieur Dubeau, who had just entered the room, looked them over with a dubious eye. "This is bound to fail, Dominique," he said, shaking his head. "How can I convince you that your plan is too dangerous?"

"You fret too much, Bartrand." She brushed her lips against his cheek. "Have no fear, we will succeed, and we shall meet you at the appointed rendezvous."

"What will you do if Colonel Marceau becomes suspicious?"

"He will not," she said with assurance. "I know his weaknesses. He is a vain man, and I shall provide the flattery to lull him into complacency."

"I still think I should come with you," Bartrand argued.

"I will need you on the outside should anything go wrong," Dominique told him.

She offered Ethan her hand, and Tom came to her side.

"Gentlemen," she said, attempting to disguise her feeling of trepidation. "Shall we go?"

21

As Colonel Marceau watched the door, the only thing that gave away his nervousness was the clenching and unclenching of his hands behind his back. He had waited for tonight for a very long time. To have a member of the elite willingly accept an invitation to dine with him was something even General Richepance had not been able to accomplish.

He frowned, wishing he had not been so demanding of Mademoiselle Charbonneau when they had first met. But apparently she did not blame him, or she would not be attending his dinner.

"Ah, Mademoiselle Charbonneau," the colonel said when he saw her arrive. "Such a pleasure to see you again." He looked with interest at her two companions.

"Your Grace," Dominique said, curtseying to Tom, "may I present Colonel Henri Marceau to you?"

Tom looked down his nose and fanned the air with his lace handkerchief. It was easy for him to look bored because he did not understand what they were saying in French. He acknowledged the colonel by the merest nod of his head before moving away.

"Who was that?" Marceau asked, obviously impressed

with such a well-dressed gentleman. "You called him
Your Grace!"

Dominique pressed closer to Colonel Marceau and
whispered behind her fan, and suppressed a shudder of
horror as his cold hand brushed against her arm. "I am
not supposed to say," she told him, moving just out of
his reach. "Think of him only as Rudolph Hapsburg."

Marceau's eyes widened. "Hapsburg, but surely that
is the name of the royal family of Austria!"

"Shhh," Dominique whispered, "he would rather not
be associated with the family that spawned France's
beheaded queen. You do understand?"

"Yes, of course," Marceau sputtered, "but anyone
who looks at him can tell he is a man of great consequence. Would that I knew the name of his tailor."

Dominique raised her fan to hide a smile. Then she
closed it with a flourish. "I would not ask him such a
question, Colonel. You know how the royals are."

"Oh, yes— yes indeed."

Dominique drew in a relieved breath—they had
passed the hardest obstacle, Tom.

Now Ethan joined in the conversation. "So good of
you to ask us here, Colonel Marceau. I have cherished
the thought of seeing this vicious pirate paraded before
us." Ethan pretended to look worried. "Will we be safe,
do you think?"

"Have no fear, Monsieur," Colonel Marceau said with
swaggering confidence. "Captain Gallant is in no condition to harm anyone. I have seen to that. Besides, he will
be in chains and I will have a guard on either side of
him."

"But still—"

"You will find he has little fight left in him. Even
should he be able to stand on his own, he would be no
threat to anyone." The colonel indicated the door to the

dining room. "Come, shall we dine? The entertainment comes later."

Dominique sat beside Colonel Marceau, listening to his embellished accounts of the apprehension of the dreaded pirate, Judah Gallant. If he were to be believed, he had captured the captain in person and single-handedly. She tasted none of the food, and several times had to look away so Marceau would not see the hatred in her eyes.

"Mademoiselle Charbonneau," he said, leaning close to her so the others would not hear, "allow us to extend our condolences. We had heard that your grandfather has passed to the beyond."

She took a steadying breath, knowing she was sitting beside her grandfather's murderer. She managed to keep her voice low because she did not want Ethan or Tom to hear. "Yes, it was a pity, Colonel. I believe you had only released him from your prison the day Windward burned."

"As to that, I am glad to have this opportunity to tell you that while your grandfather resided with us, he had the best of care." He did not tell her this was done because he feared that the old man would die while in his custody, thus bringing trouble down on his head.

"So," she said, trying to keep her tone even. "All the time I imagined my grandfather locked in a cell, he was kept in comfort?"

"That is so, he was. I even had his doctor look in on him from time to time. I can assure you that your grandfather had no reason to complain of his treatment."

Dominique blinked her eyes, forcing a smile. "And what of my brother?"

Marceau shrugged. "I believe that you already know we never actually had your brother in custody." He spread his hands on the table and studied them. "While I am confessing, I might admit that I also invented the notion of the torture box. I never actually had that either. It is just an effective ruse that I use from time to time."

It was all Dominique could do to smile at him. "You are too clever. Was it you who sent me the anonymous note telling me Valcour had been arrested?"

"Indeed. I saw no other way to get you here. And to be precise, he was almost in our custody, but he was spirited away from the island. When you came here looking for him, I realized that you had no part in his escape."

"You are a genius. But what made you decide to use me to get what you wanted?"

"As I told you, you are a very beautiful woman. And I was certain that you could help us trap Captain Gallant, which you did." He looked at her closely. "You understand why I had to do what I did?"

"You told me on our first meeting that great men must often resort to the unseemly to obtain their aspirations."

He nodded. "Exactly so!" He took a drink of wine and wiped his mouth on his sleeve. "I am becoming very important, Mademoiselle Charbonneau." He patted his jacket pocket, then removed a letter. "I have here a letter from the minister of war himself." Distracted by loud laughter at the other end of the table, Marceau absently tried to tuck the letter into his pocket, not noticing that it fell to the floor.

Dominique pretended to drop her napkin, and when she bent to pick it up, she also scooped up the letter. Artfully, she tucked it into her reticule, then turned to Ethan, and lowered her voice so that Marceau could not hear.

"Be alert, Ethan. I will soon ask him to bring Judah here."

Ethan nodded. "He is a braggart and a popinjay, " he said with a contempt he could not conceal. "I cannot bear the sound of his voice."

"What's that you said?" Colonel Marceau asked, resentful of being left out of any conversation.

Dominique gritted her teeth, but managed to smile. "My friend was just remarking on your manner of speech."

Marceau preened. "I have oft been told that I should be an orator, but you see, I chose instead the military life."

"Such a loss to the literary world, I am sure," Dominique said flatteringly.

"Quite so," Colonel Marceau agreed. "Quite so."

Judah had been beaten so many times that he no longer felt the whip. His swollen face was covered with bruises and dried blood, and there were open wounds on his back. Every time he moved, pain shot though his ribs. No matter how often they beat him, he would never tell them where to find the *Tempest*.

He was hungry, not having eaten in days, but mostly he was thirsty because they had offered him no water.

When the cell door opened, he did not even bother to look up, but when he was doused with a bucket of cold water, he came to his feet, reaching out toward his tormentor as far as he could, being chained to the wall.

"French bastard!" he said through clenched teeth.

"Well, now that just shows that Americans have no appreciation," the Frenchman said to his companion, who had just soaked Judah with a second bucket of water. "We are here to get you groomed and curried so you can be displayed before Colonel Marceau's important guests. I'm told one of them is a beautiful woman, and you wouldn't want her seeing you looking less than presentable."

"*Oui*," his companion said, snickering. "It is the woman who put you here, pirate."

Judah raised his head and cried out, closer to breaking than at any time in his captivity. "No, not her! Surely not her."

It was all Dominique could do to show no emotion when Judah was led into the room in chains. She felt a comforting hand seek hers beneath the table and saw understanding in Ethan's eyes.

She blinked back tears when she watched Judah stumble, and when the guard used the chain about his wrists to jerk him to his feet, she had to turn away. At last, she raised her eyes to Judah's face and found him staring at her with such hatred that it chilled her heart.

She must not falter now or all would be lost. Drawing in a shuddering breath, she rose to her feet, ready to play her part. Although it would be a most difficult accomplishment, she must appear uncaring and cruel.

Judah's vision was blurred and he was not sure how long he could stand without falling. He looked at no one but the woman who had betrayed him. He had not known it would cause him such agony to see her again. There was a part of him that wanted to break her, to make her beg for mercy for what she had done to him, and there was another side—that part of his mind that he tried to suppress—that wanted to hear her say that she had not betrayed him for money.

Dominique walked slowly toward Judah while all eyes followed her. Laughingly, she turned back to Colonel Marceau. "Send the guards away, I am uncomfortable with them listening to my every word."

Colonel Marceau was in a jovial mood and ready to indulge Dominique's smallest whim. He nodded, and the guards withdrew. "You are very courageous, Mademoiselle Charbonneau. Many women would swoon and faint at the sight of this man, in fear of their lives. He is the most notorious pirate ever to draw breath."

She sauntered around Judah and came to stand in front of him. "I do not fear him." She laid a gentle hand on Judah's arm, and he jerked away. "He," she said, shattered by the hatred she saw in Judah's eyes, "does not look so fierce to me."

She wanted to cry, to take his head and hold it against her breasts, to heal his wounds and his heart and body. She wanted to assure him that his suffering would soon end and that she would take him away from this horrid place.

But of course she could not.

"Do not stand so close," Colonel Marceau warned. "He might still have enough life in him to reach out to you."

"He seems subdued," she said, taking her fan and tapping Judah on the shoulder. "Would it not be more humiliating for him to stand before us without benefit of restraint, knowing he is still within your power?"

Marceau eagerly agreed. He produced a key and unlocked the chains that fell to the floor with a clatter.

"Mademoiselle Charbonneau," Marceau bragged. "This man has been whipped like a dog and tortured for his crimes, but he is still stubborn and will not give us the information we want. Perhaps we should enlist your help again."

Marceau shook with laughter and grabbed a handful of Judah's hair and turned his head so he was forced to look at Dominique. "Look upon the face of the woman who was essential in your capture."

"Go to hell," Judah said, fighting against the waves of sickness that washed over him, threatening to drag him down into a tide of unconsciousness. He must not show that weakness before Dominique, no matter how much she taunted him.

"You know this woman as Mademoiselle Charbonneau," Colonel Marceau continued. "But I christened her Delilah going out to bring Samson to his knees—and she has done that as well as her ancient counterpart."

Judah's eyes were burning with a fury that gave him a momentarily surge of strength. "So easily she toppled me."

Dominique could feel a sob rising in her throat. She could not endure much more, and Judah was weakening before her eyes. They would have to act now!

"Shall I show you how I did it, Colonel?" she asked, moving closer to Judah.

"*Oui*," Colonel Marceau said, enjoying himself immensely. "I would like that."

With a flourish, she produced a small dagger that she had concealed within the folds of her fan.

The colonel only laughed when he saw the weapon. "Surely you did not use that toy on the great Judah Gallant."

Suddenly Judah was not watching her. He had glanced at the table, and through a haze of pain, he was baffled by what he saw. Ethan dining with the enemy; Tom in that ridiculous apparel! He must be more delirious than he had thought.

Judah turned back to Dominique and watched as she ran a delicate finger down the edge of the dagger. "Tell me, Colonel," she said, moving to the Frenchman and placing the point of her dagger at his throat, "what would you do if I applied pressure to this . . . toy, as you called it? I can assure you that it is sharp enough to slit a man's throat."

He was still laughing, but there was a touch of nervousness about his laugh now. "So this is what you did to him?"

"No, Colonel, this is what I am doing to you. I can slice your windpipe before you can call for help. Do you understand me?"

He swallowed convulsively. "You must be careful, Mademoiselle, that is dangerous."

Her eyes pierced his. "I am glad you realize that."

Tom climbed over the table and rushed forward, and Ethan quickly followed.

Tom produced a larger, more deadly looking knife and placed it at a now trembling Colonel Marceau's throat. "The lady's got it right, Frenchman. Make a sound or move a step, and I'll slit your gullet."

Colonel Marceau dropped to his knees, his eyes wild with terror. He reached out to grab at Dominique, but Tom pulled him back by the seat of his trousers and yanked him to a standing position.

"Help me, Mademoiselle Charbonneau," the colonel pleaded. "Your friend is a madman!"

"Not a madman, Monsieur," she told him, "but a bloodthirsty pirate who would like nothing better than to plunge his knife into you. If you do as you are told, I may be able to restrain him. If not—" She shrugged. "Who can tell what he is capable of."

Ethan slid a supporting arm about Judah, as he spoke to the Frenchman. "You are going to help us get out of here, Colonel. So listen well and obey. You will stay alive a lot longer that way."

For a moment, Colonel Marceau saw hope and a chance to escape. "You cannot get past the sentry at the gate."

Ethan shrugged. "If we do not leave here alive, you do not leave here either. Do I make myself understood?"

Dominique opened the door and glanced into the hallway. "There is a guard just outside."

Ethan grabbed Colonel Marceau and brought his face forward, almost even with his. "Order that man to have our coach brought to the front. Tell him that you are going with us."

"But—"

"Tell him now, or I'll let Tom loose on you."

That threat was all Colonel Marceau needed to make up his mind. He looked fearfully into the eyes of the man he had mistaken for royalty. What a fool, what an imbecile he had been. "I will do as you say," he agreed. "But do not let that crazed man at me."

Dominique took the cloak Ethan had worn and slipped it about Judah's shoulders. She then took Tom's ridiculous green hat and placed it on Judah's head, pulling it low over his forehead to disguise his features.

"Are you able to walk unaided?" she asked, looking into Judah's bewildered eyes.

He could only nod. But when he tried to take a step, he staggered and fell to his knees.

"Cap'n," Tom said, hurrying to his side, "kinda act like you was in your cups—you know—like you had too much libation. Then you can lean on me, and they won't think nothing about it."

"We'll ask the same of you, Frenchman," Ethan said. "I'll be walking so close to you that when I take a breath you'll feel it. If you're wise, you will convince your men that you drank too much because my pistol will be sticking in your ribs."

Colonel Marceau nervously licked his lips and nodded.

Dominique was surprised at how easily the plan

worked. Soon the carriage was on its way through the gate of the fort, and in moments they had left Basse-Terre behind.

Glancing back, she was relieved to see that no one followed them. Tom had positioned himself near the driver, his pistol primed and ready in case of trouble. The coach bounced over rutted roads, and they were soon joined by two outriders, who were heavily armed.

Ethan examined Judah by the lantern light that swayed with the motion of the coach. "Thank God he is unconscious, or the ride would be too much for him to endure."

Dominique kept a pistol leveled at Colonel Marceau's heart because she did not trust him not to attempt to jump out of the coach. How cowardly he was without his guards around him, she thought with contempt.

"You are very clever, Mademoiselle Charbonneau," the Frenchman said. "But how do you think you will escape this island?"

She smiled. "If I were you, I would wonder how you are going to make your way back to the fort."

"What are you going to do to me?"

"I have a friend who will take you to the great swamp, where he will leave you."

"You will not kill me?" the colonel asked hopefully, relief showing on his face.

"Not outright, but I doubt that you will find your way out of the swamp. If you are not eaten by some wild animal, or slain by natives, drowned by quicksand, or some such malady, you may make it back to the fort alive, but not before we have long fled your reach." She smiled when she saw how pale he had become, and could not resist taunting him further. "If you do manage to return, I wonder what your superiors will do to you for allowing such a valued prisoner to escape? Perhaps you should consider leaving Guadeloupe as well."

There was no further time to talk because at that moment the coach came to a halt and a hooded man, leading a riderless horse, awaited them.

"You know what to do." Dominique told the newcomer. The hooded man merely nodded. "Make certain no one sees you as you take Colonel Marceau to the place we discussed."

Again there was a nod.

"Why do we let him live?" Tom wanted to know, as he climbed down from the coach and yanked the Frenchman from his seat.

"I want him to live," Dominique said, without pity for the man who was responsible for her grandfather's death and Judah's torture. "I want him to live, so that every night he can look over his shoulder in fear of retribution."

Colonel Marceau fell to his knees and his body shook with great sobs as he reached out his hand. "Have pity, Mademoiselle Charbonneau."

"I do not think so." She leaned close to him and whispered, "One day you will look behind you, and my brother will be there. Think about that, and be afraid, Monsieur."

A cringing Colonel Marceau was yanked forward and thrust upon the waiting horse, his hands tied behind him.

Dominique nodded to the hooded man, knowing it was Bartrand Dubeau. "Thank you, dear friend. Take care of yourself."

He rode off into the night, leading a cowardly Colonel Marceau, who was still begging for mercy.

Dominique got back in the coach and fell on her knees beside Judah. "How is he, Ethan?"

"Malnourished, bruised, beaten. I do not detect any broken bones. Beyond that I cannot tell."

She gently touched Judah's face. "Will he live?"

Ethan smiled sadly, wishing he could see that kind of love in Dominique's eyes when she looked at him.

"Have no concern—he will live. It takes more than this to kill a man as stubborn as Judah."

She pressed her lips to a bruise on his forehead. "Yes, much more."

22

It was after midnight when the coach moved down an overgrown lane and pulled to a stop. Tom and Ethan helped Judah out and supported his weight while Dominique dismissed the coachman and the outriders. They had not been waiting long before a dark figure that took the shape of a man on horseback arrived, seemingly out of nowhere. He led four horses and silently handed the reins to Dominique, then departed just as quickly as he had come.

"What now?" Ethan inquired, looking around for direction. "Judah cannot ride in his condition. One of us will have to carry him in front of us. I suggest it be you, Tom, since you are the stronger."

Dominique looked up at the sky and saw the ominous clouds gathering overhead. "It was my plan to get Judah to the *Tempest* tonight. But there is a storm coming, and we must find shelter until it passes."

Between the three of them they managed to get Judah upon Tom's horse, and the big man supported his captain with ease.

Dominique placed her hand on Judah's chest to assure herself that he was still alive. "We had best hurry," she said with urgency. "Storms come up quickly on this island."

After she was mounted, she guided Ethan and Tom through a seemingly endless forest.

It was so dark now that Ethan wondered how Dominique could find her way. After an hour of steady riding, she called for them to halt.

"Mark me well, gentleman—from this point on, the two of you must follow me exactly," she warned, her eyes reflecting a worried expression. "We have come to the swamp, and I do not want you to leave the path for any reason. It is very treacherous and dangerous for those who are not familiar with it."

A strange silence enveloped them, but for an occasional whinny of a horse, or a jingle of a bridle. After they had been riding for the better part of an hour, Dominique became aware that the sky had grown darker still and the storm was almost upon them. Jagged lightning flashed across the sky, and the soft breeze was now becoming a strong wind.

On they rode, past ghostly trees that had been misshapen by the prevailing winds, and stagnant water that smelled of sulfur.

Tom had been watching the sky and was becoming concerned. Being an experienced sailor, he knew in his bones when a storm would strike. "It's going to be a big blow. I can always tell."

Dominique halted her mount. "I am more certain than ever that we cannot rendezvous with the *Tempest* tonight. Even if we could signal the ship, the men could not get close to the island without being crushed on the rocks."

"What do we do?" Ethan called out, forced to raise his voice to be heard above the howling of the wind.

"I know a place," Dominique said. "Follow me."

She led them out of the swamp and up a steep hill of volcanic rock. They had not gone far when the first heavy raindrops began to fall.

The horses slowed to a walk on the slippery surface of the granite slope, Tom tightened his grip on the captain.

At last Dominique reined in her mount. "It's not far from here," she said, nodding toward the hill that rose high above them.

"Here?" Ethan asked, puzzled.

"There is a cave just ahead," Dominique said, straining her eyes in the darkness. "It's too steep to ride from here, so if the two of you can carry Judah, I will lead the horses."

Dominique dismounted and grabbed the reins of the horses. "Let us hurry," she urged.

As gently as they could, Tom and Ethan lifted Judah from the horse, one supporting his shoulders, the other his legs. With difficulty, they managed to follow Dominique up the steep incline.

By now, it was raining harder and the wind was so strong it felt like it might tear them from the slope. The last few steps were straight up, and the two men struggled with Judah's weight. At last, they made their way to an overhanging ledge, and Ethan slumped against a boulder to catch his breath.

"How much further?" he groaned.

Dominique pulled a spidery bush aside to reveal a dark cavern, which she entered, leading the horses inside. "This is where we shall remain until the storm passes. Since I know my way around and you don't, stay by the entrance until I light a torch."

Soft light soon flickered on the rock wall of the cave, and she beckoned them inside.

Ethan looked at the high cavern with passageways leading off in two different directions. "At least it's dry," he observed. "Let's lay Judah by the far wall," he told Tom.

When this was accomplished, Tom removed his cutaway and placed it beneath his captain's head. "I never thought this fancy bit of foolery would be useful," he observed.

"Tom," Dominique told him, bending down to Judah, "you must take the horses down that passage. It leads to another cavern with a natural spring."

Tom gathered the trailing reins, and paused for a moment of satisfied reflection. "I doubt that Frenchman found shelter tonight." His amused laughter followed him into the second cavern.

Dominique hovered over Judah. He was so pale, and so still. "How is he, Ethan?"

"When he awakes, he will probably be in great pain. If only we could reach the ship, where I have the supplies to treat him properly."

"We dare not venture out in this storm, Ethan. To do so would be foolhardy. Is there not something you can do to help him here?"

He was thoughtful for a moment. "Have you a petticoat?"

She nodded and rushed to a dark corner. A few moments later, she returned with a white lawn petticoat and extended it to him with a slight tinge to her cheeks.

Ethan pretended not to notice. With practiced precision, he began to tear the fine material into strips. "Can you bring that torch closer so I can see what I'm doing?"

She quickly did as he asked, staking the torch in the deep sand on the floor of the cave. Soft flames danced across Judah's face, and she dropped to her knees. "Shouldn't he have regained consciousness by now?" she asked with concern.

"Not necessarily. I suspect he is more in a deep sleep

from exhaustion as much as anything else." Ethan frowned when he touched Judah's forehead and found he was burning with fever. "Can you help me?"

Dominique nodded, taking one of Judah's hands in hers. Even though he was unconscious, she could feel the strength of his hand. She watched as Ethan ripped Judah's shirt, and gently turned him to his side. She gasped at the deep, angry lacerations she saw on his back.

Ethan's face was grim. "All I can do is bind his wounds for now. The rest will have to wait until we get him out of here." As he worked, he shook his head, angry with himself for his own negligence. "I should have foreseen this. I should have brought more supplies."

Dominique gently touched Judah's face. "Oh, Judah," she said brokenly. "Judah, my dearest."

Ethan looked at her for a long moment. "What will you do now? Will you come with us?"

Sadly she shook her head. "I cannot do that. I belong here. Someone I love is in danger—" She shook her head, refusing to tell even Ethan any more about her private life.

He saw the great sadness in her eyes as she looked down at Judah.

"Is there some way I can help you?" Ethan asked.

She shook her head. Her home had been burned, she did not know where to find her brother, and she was sure that she would be arrested if the soldiers at the fort found her. "No one can help me," she said at last.

Ethan nodded down to Judah. "When he is safely aboard the ship, he will want to know what happened to you."

"Then you will tell him . . . tell him I . . . love someone else."

He had watched her with Judah and knew that she was not telling the truth. "I know you love Judah."

Her brilliant turquoise eyes sought his and he watched tears form there.

"He must never know. To be near me would only bring about his destruction. It is my fault that he was captured."

"I cannot believe that, and he won't either. Not after what you did tonight."

She reached out and placed her hand lightly on Ethan's sleeve. "But you must make Judah believe that I betrayed him. Otherwise, he would come searching for me, and that would put him in grave danger again. Colonel Marceau is not his only enemy."

Ethan was silent for a long time. He knew that Judah loved Dominique, but he also believed that love could bring about his downfall. "If he believes you betrayed him, I will do nothing to correct that assumption, for I do not even know the truth."

She avoided his eyes. "The truth is that I came aboard the *Tempest* for just that reason."

Now Ethan was studying her closely, reaching for her and pulling her into the light. "What in the hell happened to your face? Come closer so I can see better."

Her hand went to her face and she turned away from him. The rain must have washed away the cream that hid the scarring.

"'Tis nothing that should concern you, Ethan."

"And I say it is." He grabbed her face and turned it to him, examining it closely, running his finger over an angry red scar that ran across her cheek. "In my professional opinion, I would say these are burn scars. Dear God, what happened to you, Dominique?"

"Nothing I am willing to talk about."

He stared at her with disbelief. She had been terribly

hurt, and should even now be in bed recovering. "I care about what happens to you. Allow me to help. I am your friend, you should know that."

"You can help me more by watching over Judah." She shook her head. "He must not continue with what he is doing, it is too dangerous."

Ethan stood and offered her his hand, pulling her to her feet. "You know Judah, he is just as stubborn as you. What a pair the two of you would make."

She crossed the cave to stand silently at the entrance, not caring that she was getting wet. The wind howled like the scream of a woman.

Tom appeared beside her. "There will be a lot of destruction on the island," he said with a shake of his head.

"Thankfully though," Dominique said, "it was not a hurricane. But these violent tropical storms can sometimes do almost as much damage as a hurricane. We can only hope it blows itself out by morning."

Her brow furrowed with worry and she spoke softly. "I hope the *Tempest* is riding out the storm."

"Ah, you needn't worry about her," Tom stated with pride. "She's a fine ship."

Dominique suddenly smiled. "I wonder how Colonel Marceau is faring in the swamp. If he is wise, he will take shelter in the open and risk the rain and wind rather than hide beneath a tree that will likely topple onto him."

Tom grinned as he thought about how terrified the cowardly Marceau must be. "You should have let me slit his throat."

Dominique placed an elegant hand on his arm and squeezed it, which brought a brightness to his eyes.

"Dear Tom, you are one of the finest men it has been my pleasure to know."

He felt pride swell inside him that she should have such a fine opinion of him. He had not been a good man, or even an honorable one, before he met her. She had brought out that which was best within him. He wanted to tell her this, but she turned away and walked to the captain.

Dominique sat beside Judah, watching the rise and fall of his chest, and she thought that there might be more color in his face. Soon, he would be safely aboard his ship, and out of her life forever.

Ethan awoke when someone shook him. He glanced in puzzlement into the eyes of Dominique's friend, Bartrand Dubeau. He raised up, noticing that Tom and Judah still slept. However, Dominique was not there.

Bartrand read his mind. "Have no concern, Dr. Graham, she has come to no harm."

Ethan rose slowly, still trying to shake off the much needed sleep. "Where is she?"

"She has merely gone to visit an old woman who will give her medicine for Captain Gallant's wounds." Bartrand glanced toward Judah. "As a doctor, can you say that he is strong enough to travel?"

"No. He is still very weak—too weak, really. I wish we had more time for him to rest and mend," Ethan confessed.

"There are other problems. Soon there will be soldiers tearing this island apart looking for the four of you," Bartrand said, his eyes narrowed reflectively. "I believe it would be better for the captain if he remained here until he is able to travel on his own."

"Perhaps," Ethan agreed hesitantly.

"Then he shall have a week. I am here to lead you and

the other one, Tom, to the place where you are to signal your ship to come for you."

"I do not want to leave Judah."

"You have no choice in the matter, Doctor," Bartrand stated firmly. "Trust me to do what is best for all concerned. And know this about me: I shall always do what Dominique wants. She wants you and Tom safely aboard the *Tempest*, so that's where you're going."

"And the captain?"

"She will take care of Captain Gallant until he is strong enough to join you. You know this about her."

"Yes, I do. And I can see the sense in what you say," Ethan admitted. "If I don't rendezvous with the *Tempest*, I expect the whole crew to swarm over the island looking for us, and likely end up in the garrison cells themselves."

"One week hence, I shall send you word of where you can meet your captain." He stood up. "I believe you and your friend should leave before Dominique returns."

"May I know why you are helping us, Monsieur Dubeau?"

"Because you are important to Dominique," he said simply, "and she is important to me."

"Will they be safe here?" Ethan wanted to know, still reluctant to leave.

"None but a few know of this cave, and they will not tell. I can assure you that the French at the garrison are not aware of its existence."

Ethan moved across the cave and bent down to Judah, who had just opened his eyes.

"How do you feel?" he asked, tightening the binding about Judah's shoulders.

"Like hell." He licked his dry lips and looked about the cavern with drowsy interest. "Where am I?"

"Safe," Ethan told him. "Are you hungry?"

"So . . . weary." Judah's eyes drifted shut and he was again wrapped in the arms of blissful sleep.

Ethan stood, his eyes on Bartrand. "I am not certain I should leave the captain. I could send Tom back to the ship with a message."

"That will not do. It will be easier for Dominique to guide one person through the swamps than to guide two. And because the island was hit hard by the storm, everyone will be concentrating on the damage to their property. Therefore, we shall meet few who will question who you are.

"Wake your friend, Doctor," Bartrand said. "Then the three of us will leave."

23

It was strangely quiet as Dominique sat beside Judah, watching him sleep. He had hardly stirred when Bartrand and Ineaz's husband had lifted him to place him on a soft straw mattress. Ineaz had helped Dominique clean Judah's wounds and apply healing cream, then they rebound his ribs.

He had awakened just enough for Dominique to spoon nourishing broth into his mouth, but he did not open his eyes, and he did not speak, and she said nothing to him.

It was now late afternoon. The others had gone and Dominique rose and walked across the cave to stand at the entrance. A gentle trade wind cooled her face while she gazed upon the beauty of her island. She could see all the way to the sea from this lofty vantage point.

Between her and the sea was the mangrove swamp, teeming with wildlife, an amphibian world that meant death for those who were unaware of its dangers. Her grandfather had often taken her and Valcour exploring there when they were young. He taught them about the perils and the beauties of those swamp. Now she knew them as well as some might know their own land.

She glanced just beyond the swamp, where a mist hung over the tropical forest that was heavy with lush vegetation. The brilliant colors were dominated by the exquisitely flamboyant flame trees. Beyond that were waterfalls and hidden coves that were home to the fresh-water crayfish that had been one of her grandfather's favorite foods. Her eyes swept past the forest to the beautiful white sandy beaches sheltered by high banks of coral, kissed by turquoise-colored sea. There again was danger to those who did not know about the storm tides. Many a ship had been dashed on the rocks there.

This had once been her home, her sanctuary, but no longer. Her grandfather was dead, Valcour was still missing, her home burned, and the crops were rotting in the fields.

In that moment, she heard Judah groan and relief made her giddy. Turning, she approached him slowly.

Judah seemed groggy at first, and then his vision cleared and he saw her. He seemed confused. "Where am I? In hell?" he asked bitterly.

"You are safe," she answered him without hesitation. "You were brought to this cave, and be assured that no one can find you here."

Sudden realization came over him, and he sat up, his dark gaze on her. He was struggling to stand, but was too weak. "Why are you here?" he demanded, falling back on the straw mattress.

She rushed forward and held her hand out to him, but he shoved her away and struggled to his feet on his own. "You have not answered me. Why are you here?"

"To help you."

He stood on unsteady legs and reached out to brace himself against the rock wall. "You want to help me," he said with irony. "I believe I have had enough of your help."

"Judah, allow me to—"

He stepped away from her, his body corded with tension, his eyes bright with a feral light. "How did I get here?" His voice was cold and demanding, his manner distant.

"We brought you here."

"We? Define we?"

"Do you remember nothing about—"

Anger clenched like a tight fist within him. "Ah, yes, you want me to remember," he interrupted. "I believe you had played Delilah to my Samson. I do recall Colonel Marceau bragging about how you brought about my destruction."

She wanted to cry, to beg him to understand what she was trying to tell him. "Is that all you remember?"

"Bits and pieces, nothing I can hold on to." He glared at her. "I remember enough." There was ice in the hard tone of his voice. "You betrayed me."

She felt as if her heart had been wrenched from her body. "Please, Judah—"

He would not listen, but moved toward the entrance and stood there, silently trying to get his bearings. His gaze naturally went to the sea, watching the perpetual motion of the waves slamming against cliffs and sending a fine spray of water high into the air. From this vantage point the water and sea seemed to merge with the sky.

"What is this island called?" he asked without turning to her.

"You are on Guadeloupe."

"I have never been here before."

Suddenly, Judah felt dizzy and leaned his head against the stone wall; she ran to him and slipped her arm about his waist.

"Lean on me and I will help you to the mattress."

It did not help his temper any that he was too weak to

protest. He leaned heavily on her and almost fell onto the mattress.

"Go away. I must sleep."

And he did.

It was night when Judah awoke, and the light of lanterns danced on the walls of the cave. His mind was clear and he felt stronger. He turned his head and saw Dominique lying nearby on a straw mattress, her lovely eyes closed in sleep.

Judah watched her for a time, trying to fathom what had happened—why was he here, and why with her?

He slowly stood, taking pains not to wake her. He closed his eyes against the pain and then straightened to his full height.

Quietly, he made his way across the cave and out the entrance, standing on a wide ledge. He had no way of knowing whether it was a sheer drop-off or there was a path. He was a prisoner here as surely as if he had been placed in a cell, for he had no way to leave this cursed place.

"Judah."

He turned to find Dominique standing just behind him. He restrained the impulse to grab her shoulders and wrench her forward.

"When does the ignominious Colonel Marceau appear?" he asked, watching her eyes. Was that pain he saw in those shimmering depths?

With a careless flip of her elegant hand, Dominique whisked a strand of hair from her face. "As soon as you are able, I will guide you to a place where you will rejoin your crew."

"I do not trust you." An insolent smile curled his lips. "I wonder if you are capable of telling the truth?"

Fierce pride would not allow her to seek his understanding. "I, Captain," she injected, "can recite the truth
as long as I am of a mind to. Or if it is your wish, I can
quite successfully weave a tapestry of lies."

"So I've noticed. What I don't know is why." He
watched her closely, trying to read the truth in her aqua
eyes. "Did you betray me for money?"

"I did not betray you."

He wanted to believe her, but he would never trust a
woman again, especially not this one. "Do not think that
I will be so easily duped by you again."

She straightened her shoulders and merely looked at
him.

"Are you finding it difficult to face your accusers,
Dominique?" In spite of his anger, his lips caressed her
name.

"You will believe what you want to believe, so I shall
save my breath," she told him.

In a sudden move, he gripped her head between his
hands, holding her still. "Then I will kiss the lies from
your lips."

She tried to turn her head away because it was his
anger talking, not love. "No, Judah," she pleaded. "Do
not do this."

Against his will, he gravitated closer to her, laying his
rough face against her smooth one. "You are like poison
to me. I have prided myself on being a man of strength,
but you were my one weakness." He was disgusted with
himself because of his admission. "I cannot tear you
from my heart, but I will exorcise your ghost."

His hands were rough as they went to her hair, and he
loosened the pins so it cascaded down about her face.

"Judah no, not this way. I—"

He shook his head as if to clear it. "Perhaps another
time. I find I am not as strong as I thought." He stum-

bled to his mattress and threw himself down, glad for the sudden pain that took his mind off Dominique.

She was instantly beside him. "You are hungry and must eat to regain your strength."

He raised up onto his elbow. His voice was low and oh, so richly male. "What have you to tempt my appetite?"

The words formed hoarsely on his lips, for she could tell by the fury in his eyes that he was not speaking of food.

"Chicken, cheese, fruit."

His lips curved into an almost smile, half wistful, half teasing. "That will have to do until something more tempting comes along."

She went to a basket near the back of the cave and carried it to him. Sitting down beside him, she laid out the food. "You will find everything quite delicious," she said, avoiding his gaze. "Ineaz prepared it for you, and she is a good cook."

For the first time he noticed that Dominique was wearing leather gloves. "Are you going riding?" he questioned.

She quickly moved her hands behind her back. "You should eat, Judah. You have taken very little sustenance since we brought you here."

"So good of you to care," he said, his words laced with sarcasm. Then his eyes dropped to the food she had spread before him, and he chose a succulent chicken leg, taking the meat between his strong teeth. "And who is this Ineaz that I have to thank for the feast?"

Dominique raised one delicate shoulder in a shrug. "Just one of the many people who have helped you."

"I can well forgo this kind of help." His tone was measured, his eyes without warmth. "I seem to have a vague memory of Ethan, then there was Tom in some preposterous yellow and green jester's attire. Was that real, or did I merely dream it?"

She couldn't keep from smiling. "It was not a dream. Tom was glorious. He even convinced Captain Marceau that he was of royal blood."

"The devil you say."

"I can assure you it is true. One day you will have to hear Tom's version of what happened."

By now Judah had hungrily devoured the chicken and reached for a chunk of cheese. "What happens next? Do we live here like primates, eating, drinking, . . . " he nodded to his bed, "mating?"

She raised her eyes to his and hoped he could not see the misery she was feeling. "You will not be here nearly so long as that. When you are stronger, I shall lead you to your ship."

He raised a doubtful eyebrow. "You will pardon me if I am skeptical. My past association with you has done little to inspire trust."

Dominique tossed her head, and her mane of dark hair swirled about her face like a curtain of midnight. "Well, Judah, I am all you have. Whether or not you trust me is of little importance, is it?"

He had never seen her looking more beautiful, although she was dressed in the ridiculous trousers and shirt that she had worn aboard his ship. "How is it that the hand that brought about my downfall is also the hand now held out to rescue me? You can see where I would be confused, Dominique. But tell me, all the same, what you have in mind for me."

She stared at him, hoping he would not know how her heart was breaking. "As soon as you are strong enough, we will leave here. Our trek will take us through the mangrove swamp to a small fishing village, where Tom and Ethan will be waiting for you. It is a difficult journey with steep mountains, deep gorges, and many waterways. Do you think you will be up to it?"

He was feeling stronger after having eaten, but he had not recovered enough to make the trek that she described. Even so, he would not allow her to see his weakness. "When do we leave?"

"We thought you would need a week. Do you find that satisfactory?"

He lay back on the mattress and closed his eyes. "What choice have I?" He turned his back, indicating that he no longer wanted to talk to her.

With a heavy sigh, Dominique gathered up the remaining food and placed it back in the basket. Then she left the cave and made her way down the slope to the makeshift pen where their two horses were kept. She mounted one and rode down the hill.

She did not return to the hideaway until after dark. When she entered the cave, Judah grabbed her, his hands biting into her shoulders.

"Where in the hell have you been?"

Dominique shrugged out of his grasp. She was weary, and had wounds of her own that still pained her. Her leg hurt her the most. All she wanted to do was crawl on her mattress and sleep.

When she brushed past Judah, he grabbed her arm. "Where did you go?" he asked once again. "Were you cavorting with my enemies?"

Vexed by his obvious suspicion, she glowered at him. "I had to make further arrangements to get you off this island, Captain. Just remember this, we are not on board your ship here and you are not in command. *I am!*"

Judah's body became rigid, his lips compressed in a disapproving line. He yanked her forward, then taking her hands in his, he noticed the fear in her eyes as she jerked them free. He was certain that she was hiding something from him.

"Remove your gloves," he said bitingly.

She twisted away from him and backed against the wall of the cave. "No. I will not."

In two strides, he was standing before her, blocking her between his body and the cave wall. "Give me your hand!" he demanded.

She shook her head, lacing her fingers tightly behind her.

"Dominique, don't make me force you."

"Why should it matter to you? It has nothing to do with you."

"You are concealing something from me," he said with certainty. "It appears to me that a glove would be a perfect place for a lady to keep something she wanted to hide."

"It is nothing like that," she said in a rush. "I merely. . . hurt my hands—"

Judah's mood appeared more temperate, and he touched her cheek, then allowed his hand to drift down her arm, to placate her. He heard her gasp as he took both hands in his, removing the gloves, first one and then the other. He examined each glove and found nothing. Then he glanced up at her and saw that she had pressed her hands behind her back.

She cried out as he grasped her hands, pulling them forward and then turning them over so he could see what she was hiding.

He stared disbelievingly at the jagged scars on each palm.

"My God, what has happened here, Dominique?"

24

There was anguish in Dominique's eyes. "As I told you, it has nothing to do with you."

He wanted to raise each hand to his lips and kiss them. She must have suffered a great deal, but how? Why?

She freed her hand from his grip. "You are probably hungry. I will get you something."

He was still puzzling over her injuries. Why did she not tell him how she had been hurt?

"I am not helpless," he said at last. "I took care of my own hunger."

"Very well," she said, going down on her knees at the basket. "I am hungry."

He watched her closely, trying to decide what was real and what was illusion. Was she holding him here so she could turn him over to the enemy, or was she helping him escape as she had said? He didn't know what to believe anymore.

"Where did you go today?" he asked.

She was taking a drink of water and paused to look at him. "To see a friend."

"And?"

"He warned me that the soldiers are combing the island looking for you and me. We will have to leave sooner than we thought. Will you be strong enough to start out tomorrow?"

He still didn't trust her, but he had no choice. "If you can make it, so can I."

She sat down cross-legged and peeled a banana, biting into it. "Then you had better rest because the journey ahead is an arduous one that will require strength and endurance."

He dropped down beside her, taking the banana from her and tossing it back in the basket. His eyes swept her face as if he could read truth there. She looked so like an angel, so beautiful, so desirable.

With an anguished cry, he bent forward and his hard mouth plundered hers, cutting off any protest she might have made.

At first Dominique tried to resist the desire she had for Judah, but her body went to his like a small bird being caught in the fury of a hurricane.

He broke off the kiss and took her hand, pulling her to her feet.

Knowing what he had in mind, she shook her head.

"You are no stranger to my bed, why do you hesitate?"

"It is best that we do not "

He placed a lean finger to her lips, his eyes drawing her like a magnet. "Come to me. It has been so long since I touched you." His hand trembled as his fingers sifted through her hair. His eyes fastened on her lips. "I have dreamed and ached for you. It didn't seem to matter that you probably betrayed me."

She shook her head, but he merely smiled. "Have you missed me as I have you, Dominique?"

Suddenly she nodded in acquiescence.

They floated down to the straw mattress and she closed her eyes in surrender.

Dominique's body welcomed his with a longing that was like pain. Their lips touched and hot flames seemed to spark between them. Their hands met, laced, clasped, as if they were grasping for something they had once had but lost.

When she drew back, wanting to confess her love, his magnificent face, which had once reflected love for her, now seemed the face of a stranger. The blue eyes that had once softened with love were now cold.

His body stiffened, and so did his grasp on her hands. "How easily you overcame your resistance to me," he murmured, his words wounding her at the same time that his hands wreaked their magic as he stroked and caressed her into submission.

Her mouth followed his, and his kiss robbed her of any shred of resistance she might still harbor.

He could tell by the brightness of her eyes and the gasp that escaped her lips when he stroked her most private core that she wanted him. When he mounted her and slid between her thighs, she opened her legs, eager to receive him. With gentleness, he slid inside of her to find for himself and give to her unspeakable bliss.

Dominique pressed her face against his, having been made breathless by his heated passion.

Judah's voice came to her like the crack of a whip, stealing any illusions she might have that he still loved her.

"Don't make any more of this than it was, Dominique," he whispered in a deep voice, as if he guessed what she was feeling. "This was merely flesh satisfying the lust of flesh."

She rolled away from him and came to her feet, reaching for her discarded clothing. She swallowed several times before she found her voice. "There is a pond nearby, where I intend to wash every part of me that you touched."

He watched her walk away in her naked glory, wishing he could call back his cruel words. He knew he had hurt her and he knew why: he had once given her his love, and she had used it against him.

As Dominique swam in the warm waters beneath the tropical night, tears pooled in the corners of her eyes. Never again would she give herself willingly to Judah Gallant.

She did not go back to the cave but curled up on the downy soft grass and closed her eyes. The sounds of her beloved island finally soothed her aching heart. With precious sleep came reprieve from her tortured thoughts.

Judah was finding it difficult to sleep. He considered going in search of Dominique, but reason told him he would never find her. After tossing on the mattress for over an hour, he got up, left the cave and sat upon a protruding boulder that gave him a good view of the valley below.

It was dark and the stars glistened like thousands of fireflies. Leaning his head back and bracing it against the rock face, he closed his eyes. He could still feel Dominique's presence because she was so much a part of him. He relived the wonder of taking her body to his, and his desire for her flamed alive within him once more.

Would he ever get over wanting her? Needing her? he wondered torturously.

It was still dark when Dominique entered the cave to find Judah lying back on his mattress, his dark head resting on his folded arms. He looked at her and then turned away as if her presence was of no interest to him, but she saw the tautness of his jawline, and the tension in his body.

"Have you eaten?" she asked, dropping a canvas pack on the floor of the cave.

"I'm not hungry," he said stiffly, reminding her of a little boy who had not gotten his way.

"I suggest that you fortify yourself, Judah, because what faces you will be more taxing to your strength than anything you can imagine."

He resented her having this power over him, and he could not have said why. "I will decide when I am hungry," he said, as if to demonstrate that he at least had control over his own food intake.

"Very well. Just remember you were warned." She dropped down beside him. "Remove your shirt please."

He sat up and looked at her though veiled lashes. "So early in the morning? Are your needs so insatiable?"

She flung her head back, reminding him of a stone goddess. "Captain Gallant, you will rot in hell before you ever touch me again. I merely want to apply repellent to your skin, but if you want to catch yellow jack or some such disease, it is on your head."

He looked at the thick, tarlike substance she held out to him. "You don't have any on you."

"But I will. And so should you. The part of the island we will be traversing today is infested with mosquitoes. We will also be traveling through the swamp, which is worse."

He nodded, seeing the sense of her argument. He unfastened his shirt and turned his back to her without another word.

Dominique deftly applied the foul concoction to his back and shoulders, taking care not to aggravate his wounds, and trying not to think about the corded muscles that tensed beneath her fingers. At last she handed him the jar. "I will leave you to deal with the rest. Be sure you put a generous amount on your arms and face. I'll wait for you outside. I suggest you hurry; it will be sunup in two hours."

He didn't know if he wanted to shout at her or take her in his arms and hold her against his heart.

He did neither, because she left the cave.

When he joined her, her face was blackened with the repellent that made her aqua eyes stand out even more.

When she saw him staring at her, she managed a smile. "Not what one would wear to a fashionable ball, hmm, Captain?"

His lips dipped just the merest bit, almost into a smile. "I believe you would look good in whatever you wore," he replied without thinking.

"Why, Captain, a compliment." She tossed her head and spoke in a mocking tone. "I shall just treasure your warm sentiments until my dying day."

His eyes pierced hers, and he was white-lipped with anger as he resisted the urge to crush those taunting lips beneath his.

"If you will follow me down the slope, I'll take you to the horses," she told him. "We shall ride until we reach the swamp, and then we must go on foot."

Judah glanced to the east, where the sun was spreading its first streaks of red across the sky. "Surely there is a faster way to get to the sea than through the swamps," he stated, watching her closely.

"Our plans have changed, and we will be traveling to the south of the island."

"Why is that?"

"Because the French are looking for you, so we are forced to take the longest and most difficult way, where they cannot follow."

He glanced down at her and their eyes locked.

"You could always turn me over to them again," he suggested.

She glared at him in anger, wishing she could damn him to hell. With amazing control, she pushed such thoughts aside. "What a tempting notion."

Before he could reply, she turned away and moved down the slope at a steady pace, and he hurried after her.

When they reached the horses, there was a man waiting for them. He was an older man, and his eyes were less than friendly as he looked at Judah.

"You will not remember my friend," Dominique said, "but he knows you. He will ride with us until we reach the swamp, then he will take the horses away with him."

It had not escaped Judah's notice that she had failed to introduce the man to him, so he took matters into his own hands. "I do not know your name, sir."

"Names are not important," Dominique intervened, saving Bartrand the trouble of answering. "But time is. We must be away from the high road before the sun is fully risen. I suggest we ride fast."

Judah knew how a fish felt out of water. Give him a ship and a battle and he would fight it and win. But he did not know this island and he did not know friend from foe. He gnashed his teeth, gripped the reins, and mounted his horse, riding to catch up with Dominique and her silent friend.

They galloped down the road with only the slight lightening of the eastern sky to guide them. Judah used this time to think about his situation. He had already decided that Dominique and her friend were not taking him to the French, or else they would not go to all this trouble.

He was equally certain that Dominique had helped the French capture him the first time. That was something he could never forgive, no matter how she tried to make up for it now by getting him off the island.

The sun was well up when they turned off the main road onto a trail, without slackening their pace. They dismounted once to rest the horses, and Judah reached into the canvas bag and took a chunk of cheese, which he washed down with cool water from a waterskin.

Nothing would have induced him to admit to Dominique that he was ravenously hungry—he would not give her that satisfaction.

He felt her hand lightly touch his shoulder.

"Here, Judah," she said, handing him dried meat and fresh fruit. "You will need more than the cheese."

He couldn't bring himself to meet her eyes, but he noticed that there was not even a glint of mockery in her voice, only concern.

He took the offering and devoured it greedily.

Soon they were mounted again and riding down the incline through a heavily wooded area.

Judah saw vast banana trees, mango trees, and the distinctive scarlet blooms of the flame trees. They left the flat lands and were riding through gentle rolling hills, where a profusion of wildflowers sweetened the very air he breathed. He glanced up at the dazzling azure sky and thought this was surely how paradise must have been.

They had now reached a valley that was dotted with fields of sugarcane, tobacco, and some other crops that he could not identify. The practical side of him, because of his family's export business, could see the fortune that was to be made in transporting those crops to an insatiable Europe. He could better understand why the French and the English coveted these islands.

They walked the horses for a while to rest them, and Judah followed Dominique, watching her hips sway gracefully and her dark hair ripple in the slight breeze. Every muscle in his body was tense and there was no denying he wanted to make love to her. It nettled him that he had to rely on her to get him off this cursed island.

He stumbled and caught himself, thankful that she had not noticed. He had to concentrate on keeping pace with Dominique; she was like a healthy young mare, strong and persistent. And damn it, he was not her equal in this land that was so foreign to him.

25

It was late afternoon when the weary travelers reached the edge of the swamp.

Dominique dismounted and went to Judah. "Are your wounds paining you? If you do not feel well, there is a hidden glade nearby where we can rest for the night."

Although he was in pain and he could not recall ever being so weary, he shook his head. "I can go on as long as you can."

Silently, she turned from him and he watched her approach the older man. Judah wondered what Dominique's relationship was with the Frenchman. It had become apparent throughout the day that the man was no mere guide—he was a born gentleman.

Dominique watched Bartrand dismount and begin unfastening the ropes that held the supplies she and Judah would need on their trek. When he placed them on the ground, he turned to her.

"Are you certain you are well enough for this, Dominique? I still say you should have given yourself more time to recover."

She smiled, taking her index finger and rubbing it

across the tarlike substance on his face. "My worst concern is what this concoction will do to my skin."

"This is no jest, Dominique." There was a slight rebuke in Bartrand's voice and more than a little irritation. "I could lead him through the swamp."

"You are dear, Bartrand, but we both know that you would be hopelessly lost within an hour. You do not know the swamp as well as I do."

He conceded with a stiff nod. "I will go to the rendezvous and warn Captain Gallant's men that the meeting place has changed. Have a care and be alert at all times. I will expect you to meet us in three days."

She picked up one of the packs and strapped it across her back, then handed the reins of her horse to Bartrand. "I will be there."

Bartrand rode up to Judah and watched him dismount. He could see by the grimace on the young captain's face that he was still in great pain. He had to admire him, though, because he had not once complained.

As he handed Judah a pistol, he stared long and hard into his eyes. "Take care of her. She has suffered enough on your account."

Without waiting for Judah's reply, Bartrand yanked the reins from his fingers and rode away, leading the two horses.

Only after the man was lost from sight among the foliage of the thick fern forest did Judah turn his attention to Dominique. He saw her push a pistol through the belt around her waist, then she caught his eye.

"We can rest awhile before we enter the swamp, if you would like."

He looped his fingers around the pack on the ground and drew it up to his shoulder, feeling the pain in the weight of it, but not letting it show. "I am ready to go on if you are."

"Captain Gallant," she said, her expression unreadable behind the thick repellent she had smeared on her face, "you are a commander of men, and strike terror in the hearts of your enemy. But be warned, you are in my world now. If you want to stay alive, you will do just as I say."

She seemed so small, so vulnerable as she stood there, her courage like a beacon across a darkened sky. It entered his mind that his life had been dull and uneventful until he met her. "I will do as you say," he answered. "You lead and I follow—for now."

It was damp and hot in the mangrove swamp with its uneven and inhospitable terrain. Judah walked along on spongy ground, leaving pooling footprints behind him. The swamplands, while treacherous, were also a thing of beauty. The fragrance of brilliant colored flowers in every hue of the rainbow sometimes dominated the decaying, rotting smell of the stagnant swamp water.

Dominique turned to him for a moment. "At this point, step in my footsteps and nowhere else."

He had to lessen his stride to match her small steps, and he was again reminded how vulnerable she was. She stopped once and shifted her pack from her left to her right shoulder.

"Let me take that," he said, reaching for it.

"No," she answered. "We will each carry our own. It is a rule my grandfather taught me."

Judah had learned that it would do no good to argue with Dominique. He wondered vaguely if her grandfather had taught her stubbornness and defiance as well.

Once she stopped and held up her hand, waving him quietly around a clump of needle-sharp grass.

He placed his hand on his pistol and she smiled, shaking her head. "No need for that. It is merely a bird nest filled with hatchlings. I did not want to disturb them or their mother will desert them."

He mumbled under his breath and she turned to look at him. "What did you say?"

"Translated, I said how can the same woman who can help fire a cannon in a sea battle have the gentleness to care about some damned baby birds?"

She looked at him, puzzled. "What has one to do with the other? One was war, the other is respecting other species that we share the earth with."

"I know, I know. Your grandfather taught you that."

"Yes, he did. No matter how we might like to believe that we are the most important species on earth, we do have to share it with others." So saying, she moved away and he had to hurry to catch her.

After what seemed a lifetime of trudging in the waterland, they emerged into a magnificent meadow surrounded on all sides by steep volcanic cliffs.

"There is a waterfall that pools into a river just ahead," Dominique told him. "It is suitable for bathing, if you are of a mind to."

What he wanted to do was fall on the cool grass, close his eyes and sleep. He dropped his pack and sat down to catch his breath.

"It is not usual for you to walk, is it?" she asked with sympathy.

"Why should I?" he growled. "I have a ship."

"And no doubt a horse and carriages, when not at sea."

"Of course. I live in a civilized part of the world, where everyone has one form of transportation or another." He waved his hand to indicate the rugged terrain. "It's not like this."

She decided not to argue with him. No doubt he was weary and hurting from his injuries. She would try to be tolerant. "Today was difficult, but tomorrow will be even more trying. We will have to climb that cliff." She nodded in the distance, and he looked at the sheer rock face.

"That's impossible!"

"I can assure you it is not. I know a trail, but it will be steep, with deep drop-offs."

Judah stood and stared down at her. "If you will point the way to the waterfall, I would like to bathe."

She was unloading her pack. "Follow the sound of the water and you cannot miss it."

He clamped his jaw together tightly. He had not even heard the sound of water until she called his attention to it. Grudgingly, he admired her. She was strong of will and body. He'd had a damned hard time keeping up with her today, although he would never admit it to her.

As Judah walked away, Dominique watched him out of the corner of her eye. He had been in a lot of pain today, she knew that. But she had to push him hard and get him off this island where he would be safe.

After Judah had bathed in a shimmering pool fed by a waterfall, he felt better. His muscles ached and his ribs were troubling him, but it felt wonderful to wash the sticky repellent off his body.

Being a seafaring man, Judah was accustomed to the sun lingering on the horizon, but here, sunset came with a suddenness that took him unawares, leaving him with only a quarter moon to light his way back to camp.

When he arrived, he found a campfire glowing and food arranged upon a clean white cloth. A thick blanket had been laid out for his bed. Dominique straightened from where she was spreading her own blanket on the opposite side of the fire.

"You are just a wellspring of competency, aren't you?"

He meant it as a compliment, but she had grown accustomed to his criticism and shrugged.

"We all do what we must." She moved to stand over him. "You had better let me put ointment on your wounds and rebind your ribs."

He nodded, having nothing else to say. Her hands were gentle as she applied the medicine. But she tugged hard and tightly wrapped his ribs. When she had finished, she stood away from him.

"I know today has been difficult, but I would not have pushed you so hard if it weren't important."

"I know."

"You should eat now. I am going to bathe."

Judah managed a smile. "I would rather go with you."

She merely shook her head, and he watched her until she disappeared behind the thick foliage that screened his view.

Dominique purposely waited until she thought Judah would be asleep before she returned to camp, and he was.

She lay down on her blanket and stared up at the stars. In two more days, Judah would be reunited with his men and she would probably never see him again. That thought made her very sad, but they were never meant to be together. Too much had been against them from the beginning.

The burn on her leg had been hurting her all day, but now it throbbed and ached. She was afraid the pain would keep her awake, but, exhausted, she soon fell asleep. She was up the next morning before Judah awoke, so she would have time to apply the hideous repellent to her face. Not that it was necessary now that they were away from the swamps, but she still didn't want him to see her scars.

"Good morning," Judah said, coming to his feet and staring at Dominique's blackened face. "Nothing will induce me to smear that stuff on myself again."

"It is your decision," she said, pushing the stopper into the bottle. "I laid out your breakfast." She looked apologetic. "I'm sorry that you have to eat dried meat and cheese again."

He sat down beside her and took the water she offered him. "I have seen times when I would have welcomed such a meal as a feast."

"When you were at sea?"

He nodded. "Once off the coast of Panama a storm came up and blew us off course. It was the worst storm I had seen, then or since. It didn't let up for six days, and when it was over, we were a long way from land and weak and exhausted from fighting to keep the ship afloat. Our food was all but gone and our fresh water was depleted."

"What did you do?"

"Just when we had given up hope, we spotted sails in the distance."

"American?"

He took a bite of dried meat and chewed and swallowed it before answering. "English."

Her eyes showed her eagerness. "Did they give you food and fresh water?"

"Let's just say we took what we needed, and let it go at that." He crumbled a bit of cheese in his hand and studied it for a moment. "I might add that they had pressed twenty Americans into sea duty, and we took them away with us."

Dominique gathered up the remnants of food and stuffed them into the canvas bag. "I have seen the ruthless side of you and I have seen your gentleness. Which, I wonder, is the real Judah Gallant?"

"Which would you expect?" he asked, tossing the bits

of cheese to a brightly colored bird that was trilling in a nearby bush. "I am a black-hearted pirate."

Dominique would not tell him that she knew he was nothing of the sort, and that she knew he was working for his country's government. "We had better leave. Already the day is hot."

Judah made certain the campfire was out and soon they began the steep trek up the volcanic cliffs. Once they climbed across a place where the cliff had broken away and there was a sheer drop-off to the crashing waves below.

They traveled until noon, and then Dominique suggested they find shelter beneath an overhanging ledge. She offered Judah the waterskin, but he pushed it back to her, indicating that she should drink first.

She raised the water to her lips and drank deeply. He smiled when she wiped her mouth on the back of her hand, forgetting she had the repellent on her face.

"Dominique," he said, taking the waterskin, "you do not need that repellent. I have not been bothered by insects, and I don't have it on me."

"I . . . It will keep my face from becoming sunburned."

"I see. I forget that women go to great lengths to keep their skin pale. I had noticed on board ship that you had a sprinkle of freckles across your nose." His eyes met hers and his voice became deep. "I found the freckles most intriguing."

She leaned her head back and closed her eyes, basking in his nearness. How would she bear it when she had to watch him leave? She needed to know more about his life, so she could imagine what he might be thinking and doing when he was gone.

"Tell me about your wife."

"Mary was pink-cheeked and blonde, with lovely brown eyes. Her mother and mine grew up together.

They had always planned and hoped that we would one day marry."

"Did you marry to please them or yourself?"

Judah was surprised to find that he could now talk about Mary without guilt. But he did not want to. He wanted to know about Dominique. "I would rather speak of you," he said, artfully turning the conversation in her direction. "Are there many beaux that pay homage to your beauty?"

He watched her take a deep breath and look past him at the shimmering sea. "As I told you before, too many to count."

"What will you do when I am gone?"

She was glad he could not see the pain she felt at his words. "I have not thought that far."

"Will you go home?" He tried to imagine what her life had been like before he'd met her. She was still a mystery to him, and he wanted to know more about her. "You do have a home, do you not?"

She decided to answer him evasively. "Guadeloupe has always been my home."

"Were you happy here?"

She smiled, remembering her grandfather's gentle teachings and his firm guidance. "I had a wonderful childhood."

"And you left this island to go to Tobago to work in the Blue Dog Tavern?" There was doubt in his tone, and accusation in his eyes.

Dominique stood. "I believe we should leave now. I know a place we can stay that will be far more comfortable than where we spent last night."

She noticed he was slow in rising and realized he was still in pain. Even so, they had to hurry. "We must walk fast so we can be there by early afternoon," Dominique told Judah. "Then you can rest."

26

The sun made shimmering spears of light through the graceful flame trees that arched down the long avenue. As weary as he was, Judah paused, struck by the beauty of this tranquil setting. Off to his left was a pond spanned by a wooden bridge, and black swans drifted lazily on the mirror-bright water.

"What place is this?" he asked, turning to Dominique, who stood beside him, her eyes moving almost caressingly over the scene.

"It's called Windward Plantation and was once a home to someone I knew. It is deserted now, and no one will mind if we pass the night here."

"No one lives here?" he asked in amazement, wondering why anyone would desert such a beautiful plantation.

She pointed to the end of the lane, where the trees fell away to a rolling lawn that was overgrown and neglected. "There is all that is left of the manor house."

He gave a low gasp when he saw the two charred chimneys rising ghostlike out of the blackened ruins—all that remained of what must have once been a magnificent residence.

"It is a pity. Were you close to the family that lived here?"

He had been watching her eyes, and he saw incredible sadness reflected there.

"Yes. I knew them very well."

Suddenly jealousy tugged at his heart and suspicion crept through his thoughts. "Someone you loved?" he demanded.

"Yes."

"Why did they not rebuild? Surely it is shameful to abandon such a magnificent plantation."

She dropped her pack and stood there, trying not to cry. The last time she had seen her home it had been on fire. It hurt to stand there while memories of the happy times she had spent with her family wove their way through her mind.

At last she could find her voice to answer him. "The master of the plantation died as a result of the fire. His grandson cannot be located."

"You love the grandson?" Judah asked with painful understanding.

"I love a man called Valcour." She shouldered her pack and walked down the lane. "We shall stay tonight in the overseer's cabin."

Judah walked beside her, sensing her troubled thoughts. He resented any man who could make her feel so deeply. He said nothing as she stopped before the ruins of the house, her eyes tracing the skeleton of the once magnificent stairway.

Then she nodded toward an overgrown path that led away from the ruins. "We should not stand in the open; someone may see us."

Judah's lip curled in contempt as they walked past a row of deserted cabins. "It would seem the slaves took the opportunity to run away."

Dominique glanced at the scowl on his face. "Surely you do not believe in slavery?"

"No, I don't. Do you?"

"Of course I do not believe in such an atrocity, and neither did . . . the master of Windward. He engaged only paid laborers to work his fields. When he died, the laborers obviously moved on to another plantation."

"I am not a farmer," Judah said, glancing toward the sugarcane fields that were being reclaimed by the encroaching vegetation. "But I can see this land is going to ruin."

Dominique gave a deep sigh. "There is no help for that." Her eyes took on a faraway look, and glowed with affection. "Perhaps one day Valcour will return and—" She shook her head. "Let us find out the condition of the overseer's cabin."

Valcour, Judah said to himself. The name of the man Dominique loved. Yet they had not been lovers, that he knew. He did not want to ask, but he could not help himself. "Where is this Valcour?"

They had reached a cabin larger and finer than the others; this one even had a front porch.

"I do not know," she answered, looking up at him. "No one does."

What price it had cost him to possess her body and not her heart. He had been a fool to offer her marriage— a mistake he would not make again.

Dominique climbed the porch steps and, grasping the doorknob in her hand, threw open the door. There was a satisfied gleam in her eyes as she looked back at Judah.

"It seems my friends have been here before us and made everything ready."

He came up behind her. The one-room cabin was larger than he'd expected. It was clean and scrubbed, smelling like beeswax. There were two cots spread with clean linen, and food in abundance on the table.

"We can be thankful that you have friends who are willing to help you."

"Yes." She dropped her pack on the floor and ran her hands through her tousled hair. "You would not be here now if it were not for my friends."

Judah grasped her shoulders and turned her to him. "I would be aboard my ship, if not for you."

She pushed his hand away and moved to the table, picking up a slice of fruit. "Soon you will be back on board the *Tempest* and your experiences here will be no more than a vague memory, perhaps something to one day tell your grandchildren about."

"And what do I tell them about you?" he asked in a poignant voice. "Shall I tell them how we made love?"

Dominique raised her face, her eyes locking with his. "You can tell them that you once met a sea siren, and for a short space of time you listened to her sad song."

Without a backward glance, she scooped up her pack and left the cabin, walking slowly past the blackened plantation house. Happy memories went though her mind like splashes of color, like the Christmas her grandfather had given her the horse she had coveted for so long. That horse had long since died, but the memory was still sweet.

She took the path that led to the river and stood on the banks, recalling the many times she and Valcour had fished there. Valcour, her beloved brother and childhood companion—where was he? Was he safe?

She glanced down at her reflection in the mirror-bright river and gasped at what she saw. How hideous she looked with her face smeared with the repellent. Going to her knees, she doused her face in the water, rubbing until the ghastly concoction was washed away.

Then she stared at her face in amazement. Ineaz had been right, the scars on her face were beginning to heal and fade. Of course they were still visible, but not nearly so noticeable as she had imagined.

On an impulse, she slipped into the river, diving deep and coming up some distance beyond shore. She loved the way the cool water soothed her skin. She floated on her back and gazed up at the darkening sky, knowing she should return to the cabin, but she didn't want to, not just yet.

She smiled, remembering her grandfather. He was so much a part of Windward Plantation that she could still feel his presence. He had cleared the land and built the house, then raised a family here. This land was in her blood, and she was sure it was in Valcour's as well. But she could not stay because the French had probably already been here searching for her, and they would surely return.

She swam to the bank and pulled on her clothing. It was almost dark and there was still something she must do. When she was dressed, she took her pack and walked down a well-worn path that led away from the river to the back of the stables. She paused at the flower garden that was choked with weeds and picked a bouquet of white orchids, her grandfather's favorite.

When she reached the place where so many of her family had been buried, she knelt beside the grave that had been so recently dug. Laying the flowers on the gently sloping mound, she lowered her head and clasped her hands, allowing the tears to flow freely. Seeing her grandfather's grave made his death seem so real. Somewhere in the back of her mind she had not admitted that he was really dead. Now she would have to accept the truth.

"Oh, Grandpapa," she lapsed back into French as she

always did when speaking to him. "I miss you so desperately. I am sorely in need of your guidance."

She stayed beside her grandfather's grave for a long time, and then she finely stood, saying her last good-bye.

She hurried in the direction of the cabin. There was no telling what Judah might do if he thought she'd left him.

Judah had paced the floor, gone out to sit on the porch steps and finally, in frustration, had thrown himself onto one of the cots, fully clothed.

Where was that woman?

Dominique was concerned when she found the cabin dark. "Judah!" she cried frantically, fearing that something had happened to him. Oh, why had she ever left him alone? "Judah, where are you?"

She felt hands grip her in the dark. "It's all right, I am here," he told her soothingly, his earlier impatience all but gone.

"I thought . . . that . . . Well, when the cabin was dark, I thought they had captured you again."

"I was going to ask where you have been, but I can feel you are wet, and I would say you bathed."

"Yes." She turned from him and fumbled in the dark until she reached the table. She then lit a candle and stepped away from it so he would not be able to see her face.

"We should rest."

He was staring at the way her dark, wet hair clung to the sides of her lovely face. Then against his will, his eyes dropped to her wet shirt, where he could clearly see her breasts through the thin material. He felt a stirring deep inside and took a step toward her.

Dominique was busy deciding what to pack for the trip tomorrow and was totally unaware that she was torturing Judah.

"We will be parting tomorrow, will we not?" he asked, taking another step toward her.

"You will rejoin your ship, and then you must leave these waters as quickly as possible." She turned to find him standing just behind her, his eyes, oh so mesmerizing. She quickly raised her hand to her face, fearing he had seen her scars, but apparently he had not because he made no mention of them.

"I know you said you would never let me touch you again, Dominique." His voice sounded hesitant, unsure. "Could I . . . hold you just this last time?"

With a strangled cry, she went into his arms and closed her eyes as they wrapped tightly about her. She pressed her cheek to his rough shirt and wished she could freeze this moment in time.

"Tomorrow I shall never look upon your face again," he whispered against her ear. "And there is something I want to say to you. You have drawn a veil across your life that I cannot see past. You have given me nothing to hold on to."

She didn't answer; she could not have spoken at that moment for the lump that had formed in her throat.

"To say that meeting you has been a pleasure is not exactly accurate," Judah continued.

"I know I have been trouble to you."

She could feel him shake with silent laughter. "An accurate statement."

"What did you want to tell me?" she asked, hardly daring to breathe, and hoping he would say that he still loved her.

"It's merely this: I know you tried to convince me that you had been with other men, Dominique, but I know I was the first."

She was still in his arms and she clung to him, partly because she wanted to be there, and partly because she could not have looked into his eyes at that moment. "How did you know?"

Oh God, he wanted to be with her at that moment, but he stood rigid and tried not to think about how desirable she was. "A man knows these things, Dominique."

"How can that be?"

He hooked his index finger and raised her chin, his probing eyes somehow gentle. "It is impossible for a man not to know, Dominique."

She pulled back and looked at him in bewilderment. "You let me go on pretending and making a fool of myself? Why did you do that?"

"You should ask yourself why you tried so hard to convince me that you were a soiled dove. I have never been sure why you came to my ship in the first place."

"That no longer matters. It is in the past; let it remain there."

Dominique did not know how it happened. One moment she was looking into his eyes, wishing he would kiss her, and then with a throaty sigh, his lips crushed hers.

His hands ran roughly up and down her back, then he pulled her shirt from her trousers, gently touching her breasts. She did not pull away when his hand jerked at the belt to her trousers and his hand slipped inside, touching and caressing her into submission.

"Just once more," he said, lifting her in his arms and carrying her to his cot, where he came down beside her. He did not leave her as he flung off his clothing, but continued to kiss her mouth, neck, breasts until she quivered for more of him.

"I did not mean for this to happen," she said in a trembling voice.

"I have had to fight my desires to keep from ravishing you," he admitted.

He slid his hand down her leg to the inside of her thigh and softly spread her legs. "Say no and I will stop."

She shook her head and offered him her lips.

His breath caught in his throat, and he entered her with just the tip of his hardness and looked into her eyes, which were blazing with passion.

"You can still stop me."

She arched her hips upward and forced him inside her.

He trembled and quaked, grabbing her to him. "I cannot stop now, little siren."

Together they rode the waves of passion, each knowing this was the last night they would have together. And when he finally did withdraw from her, they were both exhausted and emotionally drained.

"Stay with me," he said, kissing her swollen lips.

"Do not ask it of me." She sat up and pushed her tumbled hair from her face. "I cannot."

"You are the most unpredictable and maddening woman it has been my misfortune to meet. The mystery of you grows and nettles me more profoundly with each passing day. Does anyone know the real you?"

"Only Valcour."

The ache he felt at her words was like a raw wound. "Oh yes, the man you love," he said with mockery and an edge of anger to his voice. "What would he feel if he knew you had given yourself to me?"

There were parts of her life she must keep secret, even though that seemed to annoy him.

"Would you like me to put medicine on your injuries?" she asked, changing the subject.

"No, I would not."

"Very well. Tomorrow night you will be aboard the *Tempest* and Ethan can continue your treatment." She dropped down on the other cot and closed her eyes, wishing her leg did not ache so badly. She feared it was getting worse.

"Good night, Judah," she said sleepily.

He walked outside, deciding it was best to put some distance between them. There was very little light from the moon, but he found his way to the burned manor house, where his eyes swept over the grotesque shadows it cast against the night sky. There was a story here and it involved Dominique, but he would probably never learn the details.

After a while, a light rain started to fall and he walked back to the cabin.

Tomorrow he was going to sail for home, and he was different from the man he'd been when he started on this adventure.

His life had been changed forever by an aqua-eyed little siren who had given him back his soul. How could he leave her when she was so much a part of him?

Did she not feel it too?

27

The first streaks of sunlight seemed to strain to invade the land through the heavy mist. Dominique silently crept down the porch steps and hid in the shadow of a climbing vine that wound itself around the drainpipe.

She had heard a noise and wondered why it had not awakened Judah. Perhaps it was because she slept lightly, knowing the danger that stalked them until she could get him safely on board his ship.

She saw the outline of a man and slammed herself against the house, wishing she had had the foresight to bring her pistol. It was too late to go back and get it, and besides, the intruder might hear her if she moved.

"Dominique."

She heard the man call her name softly.

"Dominique, where are you—answer me."

Drawing in an impatient breath, she stepped from her hiding place. "Philippe, what are you doing here? It isn't safe for you to be seen with me."

He watched her approach, and she could see the horror on his face. It took her a moment to realize that it was the sight of her in trousers that had shocked him.

"What in God's name are you doing dressed like that? Have you no notion what the neighbors would say if they—"

She held up her hand and silenced him. "I am fighting for my life, Philippe, and all you can think about is the way I'm dressed. Let us just say I have a flawed character and leave it there."

He still looked at her with displeasure. "If you do not care what others think, I do."

The fire of anger surged through Dominique's veins and she was fast losing patience. Bartrand had been right: Philippe was a bore. "Did you come here this morning, Philippe, to instruct me in the proper way to dress?"

He looked momentarily ashamed. "No, you know that's not why I am here. I have been concerned about you."

"How did you know where to find me?"

Unknown to them, Judah had come out of the cabin and was moving toward them with his pistol primed and ready. He had been awakened by voices, not knowing if they were friend or foe.

Philippe walked to Dominique and took her hand in his, raising it to his lips. "I knew if I came to Windward often enough you would be here sooner or later. I have been out of my mind with worry about you. I heard about your home burning and how you rushed inside to save your grandfather and were burned."

Judah now knew how Dominique had gotten the scars on her hands. She had been burned, and it was somehow connected with the tragedy at this plantation. This must have been her home. Why had she not told him? he wondered.

By now a soft rain was falling, and Dominique felt a rush of tenderness for Philippe. He was, after all, an old friend, and he was there out of concern for her. "You can see for yourself that I have not suffered any lasting harm."

"I am sorry about your grandfather," he said softly, pulling her to him.

Dominique laid her head against his shoulder, needing his comfort. "I miss him so much," she cried as Philippe's arms tightened about her.

Judah felt as if he were eavesdropping and would have left, but for some reason he seemed rooted to the spot. At last some of the mystery from Dominique's past was lifting. He surmised that the man who held her in his arms would be Valcour, the man she said she loved. That thought was like a stab at his heart.

"It was foolhardy to come back here. Colonel Marceau has had men watching the roads. He expects you to return to Windward."

"I know that. That's why I came by the swamp."

"Are you crazed, Dominique? You know how dangerous the swamp is."

"As you can see, I made it without any disasters." She placed her hand on his arm. "You should leave now. I have other things to do."

He grasped her arm and pulled her to him. "No, you don't. You are coming home with me so I can take care of you—although I cannot imagine what mother will think of your outrageous behavior."

Angry at his pompous displeasure, she slipped out of his grasp. "I want you to leave—now."

He set his jaw in a severe line, his eyes sparking with fury. "I am not leaving without you."

Judah stepped into the open, his arms folded across his chest, his eyes riveted on the man. He spoke in flawless French. "The lady says she wants you to leave. If I were you, I'd listen to her."

"Who the hell are you?" Philippe asked.

Judah sneered at the man, still believing him to be Valcour, whom Dominique had spoken of so lovingly. It was difficult for him to see anything to admire in this man. "Just think of me as someone who is intervening on the lady's behalf."

Philippe felt unbridled rage as he looked at the stranger, his eyes going to the cabin and then back at Dominique with understanding. "The two of you spent the night together." It was not a question, but an angry statement.

Telltale color stained Dominique's cheeks. Still, she raised her head and met Philippe's eyes unflinchingly. "What I do does not concern you."

Philippe took a step closer to her, and there was genuine love in his glance. "But you have been hurt. Bartrand told me you are still unwell. You should be in bed, where someone can see to your health."

Judah jerked his head around and looked at Dominique closely. If she was ill, she had hidden it from him.

"Come home with me," Philippe pleaded.

"No, I will not endanger you and your family. You know I have powerful enemies, and if you help me, they will become your enemies as well."

"No one will find you. I will keep you safe."

She shook her head, wanting him to leave. "Go now, if not for your sake, then for mine. You are a danger to me by just being here. Anyone could have followed you here."

"What will you do?" Philippe asked in defeat.

"It is best that you do not know. That way, if you are questioned, you can be truthful when you deny any knowledge of my whereabouts."

He took her hand and raised it to his lips. "I will wait

for the day when you return." There was questioning in his expression. "You will return?"

She felt a rush of affection for Philippe. After all, he only wanted to help her. "Yes, of course." She gently kissed him on the lips.

Philippe touched her face, raising it to the thin light. "Dear God, what has happened to your face?"

She ducked her head, feeling ashamed of her appearance. "I was burned, remember?"

Philippe shook his head. "Do you think that matters to me?"

"Please go. Now is not the time to speak of this," Dominique begged Philippe.

He nodded grimly, and turned to his horse that was tied nearby.

His eyes were soft as they swept her face. "Are you safe with this man?"

"*Oui.*"

Philippe mounted his horse and stared at her for a long moment. "I'll go, but it isn't finished between us."

She watched him ride away and resisted the urge to call him back. With him went her last tie with her old life. Philippe belonged to the past that she could never recapture—and she felt he knew it as well.

She was startled when Judah spun her around and looked closely at her face. Beaded drops of rain ran down her cheek and he could clearly see scars there. In agony, he shook his head. "Why did you not tell me that you had been hurt?"

"It matters but little."

Softly, like a lover, he traced one white scar across her forehead. "What happened?"

"I cannot talk about it. Please do not ask me any more questions."

"Valcour knows what happened."

She looked at him in puzzlement. "Valcour?"

"The man who just left."

Laughter bubbled up inside her. "Judah, that was not Valcour. That was Philippe Laurent."

"He's in love with you."

"He will get over it." She walked toward the cabin. "The hour grows late. We should leave at once."

He caught up with her. "Not until you tell me what happened to your face."

She merely shrugged. "I played with fire and got burned."

At that moment, there was the sound of riders approaching, and Judah pushed Dominique between the cabin and a row of flowering shrubs. They both waited tensely until they saw Bartrand leading two horses. He quickly dismounted and hurried toward the cabin.

Dominique ran to him. "I did not expect you until this afternoon."

"You must leave now," he said, pushing her toward a horse. "I am only minutes ahead of Colonel Marceau's troops!"

She dashed into the cabin and picked up her pack, throwing it across her shoulder. Then she quickly went outside to find Judah already mounted.

"Leave by the fields," Bartrand told them. "I shall make sure that you left nothing suspicious behind in the cabin, then I will try to draw the soldiers in a different direction."

His words struck terror in Dominique's heart, not for herself but for Judah. She tried to hide her panic and the need to flee. "What of Colonel Marceau?"

"He has incurred the governor's displeasure, as you might guess. General Richepance has given him another chance, however, and that is to capture you and the captain."

When they were ready to ride away, Bartrand grabbed Dominique's reins and spoke to her hurriedly. "After you see the captain safely on board his ship, go to my lodge. I have made plans to get you off the island. If the French find you, it will mean your death."

She nodded. "I understand. Please be careful Bartrand; you know the kind of man Colonel Marceau is."

"I can take care of myself, and you do the same."

Judah turned to the older man. "Why should Dominique be in danger? Is it because she has helped me?"

There was resentment in Bartrand's eyes as he gazed upon the man he blamed for Dominique's troubles. "Yes, because of you. Now go! The sooner she is free of you, the sooner I can protect her."

Judah was still not satisfied. "How do I know you can keep her safe?"

"You don't, and neither do I. Much in life is left to chance."

"Then let us be gone," Judah told Dominique. Already a plan was forming in his mind. He would leave nothing to chance as far as her safety was concerned.

They rode across rows of sugarcane rotting in the fields, past rusting sugar mills, and across a shallow, but wide river. On they galloped, and Dominique would often glance behind them to see if they were being followed.

It was raining harder, but they did not slacken their pace. Dominique silently thanked Bartrand for providing them with what she knew was his best horseflesh.

After a while, they left the fields behind and entered a forest thick with foliage, but there was a clear-cut path they followed.

When they reached a clearing, Dominique motioned that they should stop. "The horses need a rest," she said, dismounting.

When she loosened the girth on her mount and led

him to a clear pool to drink, she glanced at Judah. "We should let them graze for a short time."

He was strangely silent and merely nodded as he led his horse to the water.

"Judah, I am sorry that we had to leave so quickly and I picked up the wrong bag. I'm afraid we do not have any food, and in your weakened condition, you still need nourishment."

He whirled on her. "Damn it, Dominique—stop it!"

She looked bewildered. "What—"

"Stop coddling me." He came to her in two strides and gripped her hands. "Do you think I am addled-brained that I do not know you are hurt yourself, that you need nourishment as well, that you need someone to care for you?"

"No, I—"

Judah took her face between his hands, his eyes moving over the scars that Philippe Laurent had brought to his attention. "Tell me what happened."

Dominique nervously licked her lips, afraid that he found her hideous. She tried to pull away, but he held her firm.

Judah bent his head, and his mouth softly traced each scar. "Little siren, what have they done to you?"

It took all her strength to turn from him. "Please do not ask me any questions, for I will not tell you." She went to her horse and led him away from the water to a patch of grass.

Judah followed her, unwilling to let the subject lie. "Why must everything always be so secret with you? You have me gnashing my teeth in frustration."

"After today, you can put me from your mind," she reminded him.

"I don't think so." He lowered his hands. "Tell me about the danger Bartrand spoke of."

"I will not discuss this with you, Judah."

"No matter. I shall make certain you are safe before I leave this cursed island."

She laughed softly. "I do not believe that will be possible. The sooner you are gone, the safer I will be."

After a while, they mounted their horses and continued through the tropical forest. The sun was going down when they finally reached the sea. The sand was black on this side of the island, and huge cliffs made it almost impassable, but for the trail Dominique had brought them across.

She dismounted and began stacking driftwood on the beach. She was so engrossed in her own actions that she did not notice that Judah had unsaddled the horses and removed their bridles, tossing them upon the sand.

By now, it was dark, and she proceeded to light the dried wood.

"All we have to do is wait," she told Judah. "It would be best if we stayed away from the fire. I do not think we have been followed, but it is wise to take every precaution."

He was staring out at the sea, and she wondered if he was feeling the same soul-wrenching sadness that she felt because of their parting.

"I have to admit that you are the most capable woman I have ever met. Whether it's swimming to a ship in the middle of the night, manning a cannon, or riding through a swamp. If there is another like you, I have yet to meet her. Is there no end to your daring, Dominique?"

"I am not very brave, Judah," she said, letting out a soft sigh. "There have been many times of late when I have been frightened beyond reason."

"Even the bravest heart knows when to fear. But fear did not stop you, did it?"

"Shh," she said, straining her eyes in the darkness. "Did you hear something?"

Judah listened for a moment, and then he nodded. "I hear the sound of oars. Someone is coming."

Soon they both heard a boat cutting through the waves, and Tom's voice called out as the boat touched the shore.

"You here, Cap'n?"

28

Dominique turned to Judah, and there was relief as well as sadness in her voice. "You are safe now—you must go."

Deep wrenching loneliness coiled inside him at the thought of parting with Dominique. And how could he leave her behind, knowing that she was in danger?

With a suddenness that startled her, he scooped her up in his arms and held her against him. "You are coming with me."

She looked at him in bewilderment. "What are you saying? I cannot go with you."

"I will not abandon you to the mercy of your enemies. How could you think I would?"

"But if I leave, then Valcour will not know where to find me when he returns," Dominique protested.

Judah's face was masked by darkness, but she could feel his displeasure. "Your Valcour has not done much to protect you until now. You are coming with me, and I will hear nothing more about it."

Tom had come ashore, along with six other crew members, and he ambled up to them, looking from one to the other. "Dominique. Cap'n," he said with a vast smile. "We feared we'd never see you again."

Judah waded toward the boat, while Dominique wriggled in his arms, trying to get down.

"Let me go!" she demanded.

He glanced down at her with a dark look. "Damn it, Dominique, be still! I'm stronger than you are, so don't fight me."

"But—"

As he stepped into the longboat, he tightened his hold on her, knowing that she might bolt if she got the chance. "Put out the fire and take us to the ship, Tom," he ordered.

If Tom thought the captain was acting strangely since he carried a reluctant Dominique, he did not show it. Those two were oft times at odds. "Aye, Cap'n."

Only when they were a safe distance from shore did Judah loosen his hold on Dominique. She wanted to tell him that his actions were outrageous, but she could not do that with his crew listening. However, by the stiffness of her body, she managed to convey her displeasure to him, all the same.

Dominique could feel Judah's implacable attitude, and it only made her angrier. How dare he take it upon himself to force her from her home? She could not wait to vent her anger on him.

Judah laughed softly as the small craft cut its way through the cresting waves. "I know what you are feeling." He pressed her against him. "I am sure you will tell me all about it when we are alone."

She said nothing, but merely rested her chin on her hand. Oh yes, she had plenty to say to Judah Gallant.

Tom bent down beside her. "You all right, Miss Dominique?" he asked with concern. "I been worried about you."

"I am fine." She saw no reason to drag poor Tom into her quarrel with Judah. While he admired his captain, she had little doubt that he would quickly take her part, and might even try to help her get back to Guadeloupe.

The crusty seaman plied his oars, knowing that something not right here, but he could not think what it was.

At last, out of the darkness, like a ghost ship, loomed the *Tempest*. There were no lights on deck save one small lantern that had guided the oarsmen to her.

Judah lifted Dominique in his arms and climbed the rope ladder. He set her on deck and called out orders.

"Raise sails and catch the wind, Cornelius. I want to be away from here before day breaks."

"Aye, Captain," came the sound of a familiar voice.

In spite of her anger, Dominique felt like she had come home.

There was the sound of scampering feet as every man knew his job and rushed to do it.

"Tom," Judah said, as he moved hurriedly toward the quarterdeck, "escort Miss Charbonneau to her cabin and then find the doctor straight away and send him to me."

"Aye, Cap'n."

It was dark, so Tom took Dominique's hand and led her down the companionway to the cabin she had occupied before she shared Judah's—and that suited her just fine.

"I'm glad you made it back safely," he said.

She realized that Tom must have expected her to return to the *Tempest*. "Thank you, Tom."

"Sorry I can't light your lantern 'til the cap'n says so."

"I will be fine, Tom."

He hesitated at the door. "I'm right glad you're here."

"Good night, Tom."

She heard him close the door behind him and lay back on the bunk, feeling heartsick. What would

Valcour do when he returned and found Windward burned, their grandfather dead, and her gone? Then there was Bartrand—he would not know what had happened to her, and would worry unnecessarily.

She felt the ship catch the wind and it seemed to glide upon each crested wave. The *Tempest* was under way, and a part of her was glad to be on board.

Ethan entered Judah's quarters. A lone candle gave off the only light. He set his medical bag down on the desk and grinned at his friend. "Thank God you are safely on board. After we left, I wished I had insisted on remaining with you."

"You need not have worried. Dominique was most capable."

"I am sorry I didn't get to say good-bye to her. She is an exceptional woman."

"You'll get your chance, she's on board the *Tempest*."

"What!?" Ethan said with amazement. "How did you manage that? I had the feeling she wanted to remain on Guadeloupe."

"I took that decision out of her hands."

"I see." There was unspoken accusation in Ethan's voice. "Remove your shirt; I want to examine your wounds."

Judah went to his desk and sat down, feeling bone weary. "Do not worry about me. I want you to examine Dominique. I believe she has burn injuries, but I have no idea how severe they are."

"I know about her burns. I saw them for myself."

"Did she tell you what happened?"

"No. But I have never admired a woman as much as I admire her. She has troubles, Judah. I don't know what they are, but they were bad enough to make her stow away on this ship."

Judah could not help the jealousy that took possession of him. "Perhaps you should be her champion."

Ethan looked at his friend's dark scowl. He had known Judah long enough to guess what he was thinking and feeling. "Don't think I would not take her in a moment if she cared for me. She does not. We both know it's you she loves."

Judah hung his head for a moment, and then when he glanced up at Ethan, there was misery in his eyes. "You are mistaken, Doctor. Dominique loves a man named Valcour. She admitted as much to me. Hell, there was even a man named . . . Philippe. It seems he loves her, too. The men seem to flock to her like insects to a bright light."

"Ah well, not you, though."

Judah glared at him, but said nothing.

"Why have you brought her on board the *Tempest*, Judah?"

"Because she was in danger on Guadeloupe." He stood up and began pacing back and forth. "Damn it, she refuses to tell me anything."

Ethan's voice took on a serious tone. "What are your plans for her?"

"I have no plans. For the moment, it is enough to know that she's safe."

"Where does the *Tempest* sail?"

"Home, to Boston."

Ethan lifted his medical bag and walked to the door. "I will report back to you after I have examined Dominique. Then I will dress your wounds."

"I will be waiting to hear about her condition."

Ethan moved carefully across the deck, picking his way through the darkened shadows. He still felt that Judah and Dominique were meant to be together, no matter that there was a man somewhere called Valcour.

He had observed Dominique when she saw how badly Judah had been tortured by Colonel Marceau. She had looked at him the way a woman looks at the man she loves.

He rapped lightly on Dominique's door and heard her voice bid him enter. The cabin was in shadows, and she called to him.

"Is that you, Tom?"

"It's me, Ethan."

Suddenly, she threw her arms around him. "I knew you would come. Oh Ethan, I am so worried about Judah. Have you examined him? Is he all right? Is he in pain?"

"Slow down," Ethan said, laughing. He was more certain than ever that Judah and Dominique belonged together. Each worried more about the other's hurts than their own. "When I left Judah, he looked weary and haggard. With a few day's rest, he will be himself."

"Oh." He could feel the tension leave Dominique's body. "You cannot imagine what Judah has been through these past three days. It's a wonder he made it at all."

"Allow me to light the lantern," he said, putting her from him. "Then we can see each other as we talk. I think we are far enough from shore to risk it."

Soon the cabin was aglow with warm light. Dominique smiled at Ethan. "You seem no worse for your ordeal."

"I had it easier than you and Judah, remember?" He was watching her as he spoke. When he lifted the lantern to hold it close to her face, she turned her head away.

"How are your burns?"

"I have no complaints." Then she clutched his shirt-front. "Will there . . . Is my face permanently scarred?"

"I would say not. Perhaps only slight scarring. And

even that may fade in time." He lifted her hands and observed that they seemed to be healing nicely. "Were you burned anywhere else, Dominique?"

She lowered her eyes. "My leg. It does hurt sometimes," she admitted. "Could you give me medicine to put on it?"

"May I see it, Dominique? I am a doctor, you know?"

She nodded, bending to raise her pant leg. She gritted her teeth and cried out in pain as the fabric brushed against the wound.

Ethan dropped to his knees and removed the bandage that must have been clean when first applied, but was now a filthy rag. Then he gasped as he turned the leg to the light. "Dominique, this is a very serious burn. It should have been cleansed and dressed daily."

"I had no time. Judah was in danger."

His eyes were kind as they rested on her face that showed such inner beauty, courage, and strength. "Dominique, what were you thinking?"

Her eyes were fever-bright. "I . . . could not have gone another day."

"You did not tell Judah about this burn, did you?"

"No. He had enough to worry about as it was."

"I am going to have some hot water brought in for you. After you have washed the leg as best you can, I will return to cleanse your wound and apply healing ointment. You are going to stay in bed and do nothing for at least a week."

She did not bother to argue with him. She was so weary, she thought she could sleep and never waken.

He touched her head. "You have a fever."

She only nodded.

He walked to the door, and on impulse turned back to her. "Dominique, who is Valcour?"

She yawned and closed her eyes, too weary to think clearly. "He is my brother."

It was just after the changing of the midnight watch that Ethan found Judah at the helm of the ship. Even in the waning moonlight, he could see the pleasure plainly written on his face—Judah had been created to captain a ship.

"Ethan, come join me. This is what I missed most while I was on the island."

"I had thought you would be weary after your long ordeal."

"Rest can come later. First, I will set the *Tempest* on her homeward journey."

"I have just left Dominique," Ethan said worriedly.

"How is she?" Judah asked, concerned by his tone.

A cloud had passed across the dim moonlight, casting Judah's face in shadows, so Ethan could not see his friend's reaction to his announcement. "Not good, I fear. She is very ill."

"You there on watch, come to me!" Judah called out. When the man hurriedly appeared, Judah shoved him to the wheel. "Keep her on course." Then he turned to Ethan. "I will see her for myself."

Ethan had to run to forestall Judah as he descended the quarterdeck. "She is sleeping, Judah. It is best not to wake her."

Judah gripped him by the shoulder. "Then tell me what ails her."

"Let us go to your quarters and I will tell you all."

Judah nodded.

When they entered Judah's cabin, he turned to his friend impatiently. "Well?"

"You know about the burns on Dominique's face and hands."

"Yes, yes."

"But you do not know that she has a severe burn on her leg. I can only guess at the pain she endured while leading you to safety. I am a man, and I do not think I could have endured it."

Judah closed his eyes. "She never spoke of it."

"I have known many women," Ethan said softly, "but Dominique is the most loyal, brave, and forthright of them all."

Judah lowered himself onto his bed as realization hit him. "All the time that she was worried about my health, she was suffering. God in heaven, I showed her no mercy, no kindness." He leaned his head in his hands, and devastation swept over him when he remembered how hard Dominique had pushed them both to get him safely off the island. "How ill is she, Ethan?"

"The leg is bad right now, but I believe with daily dressing, I can stop the infection."

Judah raised tormented eyes to his friend. "Do everything you can to help her."

"Of course I shall."

"Valcour," Judah said, "is most fortunate indeed to have the love of such a woman."

"Indeed. He is a most fortunate brother."

Judah looked confused. "What do you mean?"

"She told me that he is her brother."

Many emotions played across the handsome plane of Judah's face. "Her *brother!*"

"That is what she told me."

Then Judah's jaw tightened and he stared into space. "I wonder what game she is playing now," he said, more to himself than to Ethan. "I must not allow her to—"

"Damn you for the fool you are, Judah!" Ethan walked to the door and wrenched it open. "I have no time to spend on fools."

Judah bowed his head. There were too many thorns in his heart to ever trust a woman completely. He lay back on the bed and closed his eyes. But there was softening there as Dominique wedged her way into his thoughts.

29

The Tempest made her homeward journey, sailing out of the sun-kissed waters of the Caribbean toward the brisk Atlantic. A cold north wind swept across her bow and waves crashed before her in a frenzy. Bright shiny days gave way to dark overcast skies.

Dominique had never known such cold. She shivered in her cabin while fever ravished her body. Ethan spent most of his time with her, and her only other visitor had been Tom, who worriedly hovered near her cabin.

Judah purposely stayed away from her because he was fighting a battle within himself, and it was a battle he was losing. Twice a day, Ethan reported Dominique's condition to him, and it seemed the whole ship's crew waited and hoped for her recovery.

After a week, the fever broke and Dominique began to take nourishment. Within the next two days, her strength returned and she began to walk about the cabin.

One morning, she opened the door to find Ethan carefully carrying what appeared to be a woman's gown, a broad grin on his face.

"I have a surprise for you," he told her.

"What is it, Ethan?" she inquired curiously.

"Clothing. Fashionable, and warm enough for you to endure the cold."

He placed his bounty on the bed and watched her face brighten.

"Oh Ethan, it is so lovely. I do not even want to know whence it came." She ran her hand across the blue brushed-velvet gown, which felt lush and soft against her fingers.

"You are right: you don't want to know how I came by this plunder." He chuckled, glad to see her face flushed with happiness after all the pain she had endured. "I have a few other things for you that the crew donated." He picked up a silver-handled mirror and handed it to her. "There's a hair brush, a warm cloak . . . But I will leave you to inspect everything at your leisure."

Dominique rushed at him and threw her arms about his neck. "Thank you, dear Ethan. Thank you so much!"

"I have an invitation for you," he said.

She looked at him, hardly daring to breathe. She had not seen Judah since the night he brought her on board the ship, and she hoped the invitation was from him.

"The captain requests the honor of your presence at dinner tonight. If your engagement card is not full, of course," Ethan teased.

He watched a frown form on her brow and she hesitated. "Will you be there?"

"I was not invited."

"Then I shall not go either."

"As your physician, I advise you to accept the captain's invitation. It will lift your spirits."

She wanted to go—oh, how she wanted to. Dare she? "You may tell the captain that I shall be there."

Ethan raised her hand to his lips and smiled in understanding. She did not know that he saw into her heart and recognized the love she felt for Judah. It was a beautiful and rare gift, and he hoped Judah would treat it as such, or even recognize it as love.

"He will think you beautiful, Dominique," Ethan said, responding to her unanswered question. "I shall call for you at eight to escort you. That gives you three hours to make yourself ready."

After Ethan left, Dominique held the velvet gown out for inspection, wishing she had a full-length mirror so she could see herself. Judah had only seen her looking ragtag and disheveled, and she wanted him to think she was pretty.

With distaste, she picked up the ragged trousers, tossing them in a heap and vowing that she would never wear them again. Her eye caught something that had fallen from one of the trouser pockets, and she bent to retrieve it.

It was the letter that Colonel Marceau had dropped the night they rescued Judah. She had forgotten all about it.

She studied it for a moment, trying to decide whether to toss it out the porthole or read it. It was addressed to General Richepance, not the colonel, as he had claimed. She felt no guilt as she began to read:

My dear General,
I am taking a great risk in passing on information to you that has come to me in the strictest confidence. I overheard a conversation between Bonaparte and his generals. Of course, as you can imagine, they did not know I was within hearing, or they would not have spoken so freely, knowing I am opposed to the notion. Our beloved leader has decided to sell the entire Territory of Louisiana to the Americans. He will soon ask for the American minister, Livingston, to come to France to begin

bargaining. As of yet, the Americans know nothing
of this. Bonaparte is quite pleased with himself and
declared that by increasing the territory of the
United States, her power will be immense and she
will one day become England's seafaring adversary
and humble British pride. I do not have to remind
you that this is to be kept in the strictest confidence.

Dominique read the signature: Charles Talleyrand.
She had never heard the name and did not know who he
might be. She quickly reread the letter a second time,
realizing the importance of it—at least to an American.

At exactly eight, Ethan rapped on the door. When
Dominique whisked it open and stood with the lantern
light behind her, her hair in a halo of light, he was sure
he was looking at an angel.

"You are beautiful," he said softly.

She turned around in a circle so he could see her in
her finery. Her hair had been curled in ringlets and
pulled away from her face with ivory combs. Made in the
empire style, the blue velvet gown could have been created for her, so well did it fit. Her cheeks were flushed
with excitement, and he thought her the most beautiful
woman he had ever seen.

Ethan reached around her and took the matching
cloak off a hook. "It's cold." He draped it about her
shoulders. "You will need this."

As she walked across the deck, she had to stop every
few paces to greet one of the crew. If she but knew it,
they were all her willing slaves. She stopped before the
sailmaster and curtsied. "I have not forgotten the gown
you made me, Hennings. I loved it every bit as much as
this one."

He grinned, looking pleased. "I reckon you are about the prettiest lass I've seen."

She thanked him with a nod. Then she felt a small tug at her cape and turned to Tom.

"You are a sight, Miss Dominique. We've all been worried about you." He looked her over carefully. "Are you well?"

"I am." She looked at each rough, unshaved face of the men that surrounded her, thinking how she had come to care for them. "I want you all to know that I am well."

They smiled and nodded.

Ethan led her toward the quarterdeck, and she paused with her foot on the first step. "I should not have come."

His hand tightened on hers. "Scared?"

"Terrified."

"I am going to tell you a secret, and if you repeat it to the captain, I'll deny saying it. He's more afraid of you than you are of him."

"Me? Why?"

He urged her forward. "I'll leave you to find that out for yourself."

When they reached the captain's quarters, Ethan held the door open for her and pressed his hand against her back, urging her inside.

Dominique almost lost her courage when the door closed behind her at the same time that Judah entered the dining room. He wore the uniform of an American naval captain: form-fitting trousers, a crisp white, high-neck shirt, and blue jacket trimmed with gold buttons. His midnight-colored hair lay smooth across his tanned forehead, and she ached to touch the velvet strands.

Neither had spoken as they stood there looking at each other. Remembering his manners, Judah came to her and removed her cloak, his hand lingering against the back of her neck.

Then he just stood there, looking at her in the soft candlelight. Her blue gown fit snugly across the breasts and dropped in soft folds from the empire waist. Her dark hair was a sharp contrast to her white skin, and her blue eyes were enhanced by her long, silken lashes.

"Dominique," he said her name like a caress. "You take my breath away."

She glanced down at her scuffed boots, which peeked from beneath her gown. "I still have no shoes," she said, wondering why she could not think of something clever to reply.

"No matter what you wear, you turn heads."

"Thank you, Judah." She looked him over carefully. "Ethan says that you have recovered."

"I have indeed. Thanks to my able guide and nurse." He held the chair for her. "Shall we dine?"

For some reason, Dominique felt shy. Perhaps it was because she was more herself than she had been at any time since meeting Judah. It had been easier to communicate with him when she had worn the baggy sailor garb.

"I see you wear the trappings of an American naval officer, Captain. Is this the real you?"

"Who can say?"

"Does this mean you will not be sailing the seas in search of French plunder?"

He rested his hand on the white tablecloth and she stared at his long, tapered fingers. "I'd like to think so. The price on my head was getting too high for my comfort."

"Did you find what you were after?"

"Did you?"

She ducked her head. "Not as of yet." She laid her

hand on his. "Why did you take me away from my island?"

"You were in danger," he said simply.

"But I must return. Someone will be going to Guadeloupe looking for me. I must be there for him."

"Your brother."

"Yes. But how did you know?"

"Apparently, you spoke of him in your delirium."

Her face paled. "What else did I say?"

Judah tilted his head back against the chair and appeared to be studying the overhead beams. "If you told Ethan any of your deep, dark secrets, he has not related them to me."

"You must put me on the first ship sailing for Guadeloupe, Judah. I must be there for my brother when he returns."

"You would not be helping him if you fell into Colonel Marceau's hands."

"You know that I have friends who will hide me."

"So you do."

Dominique thought of the letter she had tucked into her boot. "I will strike a bargain with you, Judah."

His lips twisted in irony. "Now, why should I worry when you get that look in your eyes? Can it be that I recognize it as the expression of a predatory cat about to pounce upon its prey?"

"Hear what I have to say. And if it is to your liking, I will exchange what I have, for my freedom."

He rested his elbows on the table and sank his chin into his clasped hands. "You are not my prisoner."

"Then will you agree to put me ashore at the first available port, with enough money for my passage back to Guadeloupe?"

"Allow me to counter your offer with one of my own." He watched her face closely. "I once asked you to marry me, and I now repeat that offer." He saw her beautiful aqua eyes widen with disbelief and then something else he could not read.

She hid her trembling hands beneath the table. "What would I have to gain from such a connection?"

He gave her a bland look. "I am a man with considerable wealth, and contrary to the impression you may have gotten because of my pirating ways, I have a respectable name to give you."

"Do you think me so mercenary that I would marry a man for wealth and a name? If I had been so inclined, I could have married a dozen times over by now."

"Yes," Judah said, his eyes on her face, "yet none but I can say that they bedded you."

She lowered her head, her face flooded with color.

"You have me puzzled, Dominique. You say you will not marry for money or position, and yet you gave me what you would take to a marriage, your virginity. Some day, perhaps you will tell me why."

She took a moment to gather her thoughts. He was very clever, and she must not let him conquer her pride. "I do not know why you would want to marry me, Judah. You certainly know no good of me."

He smiled. "Do I not?" Then his eyes locked with hers. "Let us just say I am in need of a wife, and I have already tested your   charms and found them more than adequate to keep me rushing home to you each night."

Dominique stood, her eyes flaming with anger, her breasts heaving with indignation. "How dare you say these things to me! I can see why you might think I am a woman of loose morals, since that is what I wanted you to believe. But I have no desire to compete with your memory of your dead wife."

"Pray God you do not think that is what I want," Judah said in exasperation.

Dominique knew she had to leave before she began to cry. "I am more than you think I am." She rushed out of the door and walked shivering into the night air, stopping only to catch her breath. A black mist of dread engulfed her. Judah could not know how desperately she wanted to be his wife.

She was startled when she felt something soft and warm go around her shoulders and drape to her feet.

"You forgot your cloak," Judah said, tying the bow beneath her chin. "Come back with me. I will hear this bargain you propose."

30

Refusal swelled tightly in Dominique's throat, but she mutely allowed Judah to escort her back to his quarters, with his steadying hand at her elbow. Once inside, she turned to him.

"I will not marry you!"

Judah indicated that she should sit on the green leather bench against the wall, and when she complied, he sat beside her—but not too close.

"Well, Dominique," he said at last, "you must not make a hasty decision because you have not heard all you have to gain by marrying me."

"I daresay it will not be to my advantage. I am aware that you loved your wife, Mary. I will compete with no lost love of the man I marry."

"There are no ghosts that stand between us, Dominique. There never was." He reached out to her, and then his hand dropped away, and she could not know of the significance of his next words. "If Mary's ghost haunted me at one time, those feelings are now buried with her."

She wanted him to speak of love, like the love she felt for him. "The absence of feelings is no reason for me to take you as my husband, Judah."

"I am coming to that part." He stared down at his hands for a moment, and if Dominique had not known him better, she would have thought him nervous. "I am not without influence. If you were my wife, I would call on that influence and bring it to bear in locating your brother."

He had taken her completely by surprise. She had not expected this. "How much influence?"

He was quiet for a moment. "Considerable."

"I do not know how I could ever have mistaken you for a pirate. Who are you, really?"

He took her hand and turned her toward him. "My name is Judah Tarrance Gallant. I live in Boston, Massachusetts. I am a shipbuilder by trade, and I am half-owner of Gallant Shipping, along with my only relative, my brother, Jason—I already mentioned him to you. What else would you like to know about me?"

"I have seen you in many different disguises—a French captain, a pirate, and now an American captain. Who is the real Judah Gallant, and why did you masquerade as a pirate, when I know you are not?"

She saw his eyes flicker just the merest bit. "Forgive me, but I cannot discuss that with you. You will have to take my word that I am indeed considered respectable."

There was indecision in Dominique's eyes. "You can really help me find my brother?"

Judah smiled, raising her hand and brushing his lips against her delicate fingers. "Could I do worse than you have, thinking you could save him by running around pretending to be a . . . strumpet?"

Suddenly laughter bubbled out of her, taking him by surprise. One of the things that endeared her to him most was her ability to laugh at inane situations. "Deception has risen between us with the solidness of a brick wall. Will we ever know one another?"

"I believe we shall," he answered. "If we give ourselves the chance." He had a few unanswered questions
of his own. "Can I assume that you have no deep feelings
for the man you call Philippe?"

"Philippe?" Dominique asked in surprise. "We have
known each other since childhood, but he and I are not
suited. We never have been, although he will not believe
it."

"Is there anyone else?"

"No."

"Then pray tell me something more about yourself. I
only know bits and pieces."

She was silent for a moment, then relented. "My
name is Dominique Charbonneau, and I was born on the
island of Guadeloupe. My brother, Valcour, and I were
raised by our grandfather, Jean Louis Charbonneau. As I
told you before, my father was French, my mother
English. They have both been dead these many years."
Her eyes misted over and she hurriedly continued. "I
believe you have already guessed that Windward
Plantation was our home and my grandfather died in the
fire that destroyed the house."

"Tell me how he died," Judah said, sensing she
needed to talk about it.

"I tried to save him." Now tears swam in her eyes.
"But you see, I arrived too late. I ran in after him and the
stairs collapsed beneath me. Had it not been for
Bartrand Dubeau, I would also have perished in the
fire."

Judah gathered her to him, feeling his own body tremble at how close he had come to losing her. "You need
someone to take care of you. You certainly have not
been doing very well on your own."

She blinked away her tears and was content to lie there
with her head on his shoulder. She felt safe with his strong

arms around her. She wanted to say yes to his proposal. But why did he want to marry her? She had to know.

Dominique drew back and looked up at him. "You want me because I satisfy you physically?"

He tried not to smile. "In part—a great part."

"Is that enough reason for two people to be joined in marriage?"

"I have heard of worse reasons." He thought of his own marriage to Mary. "Because of close family ties and because it is expected of one, for instance."

He took both her hands in his and drew her to her feet. "What do you say, Dominique? Will you do me the great honor of becoming my wife?"

She could not speak; her throat seemed to have closed off.

His eyes were probing, seeking, as if drawing an answer from her, and she could only nod her head in acquiescence.

He looked startled. "Are you saying you will?"

Her voice was hardly audible. "Yes."

He drew her to him, and she lay her face against his shoulder.

"You will not regret it, Dominique. You need taking care of, and I intend to see that you are."

She stepped back. "You . . . do not feel you are honor-bound to . . . to—"

His lips dipped into a smile. "Make a virtuous woman out of you?" He shook with laughter and pulled her back in his arms. "No, my wonderful, imperious Dominique. I do not marry you out of anything nearly so noble as duty. It is mostly selfishness on my part."

This was the man she had dreamed of as a girl; the man she wanted to be with for the rest of her life; the man she loved wholeheartedly. He had once loved her—at least she thought he had. Could she win his love again?

"When will we be married?" she asked, reluctant to move out of his arms.

"Soon," he whispered, his lips brushing her neck. "Very soon, I think."

She braced her hands against his chest and looked up at him. "You have not asked what my bargain would have been."

He stepped away from her. "Forgive me. I believe you had something you wanted to offer me for your freedom and passage money home?"

"Yes. But now I give it to you as a wedding present."

He watched with interest as she bent to lift her gown and dipped her hand in the top of her boot, removing a letter.

"I believe you will be interested in this," she said, handing him the letter.

"What is it?"

"Do you know a Frenchman by the name of Charles Talleyrand?"

"Of course I do. He is Napoleon's foreign minister. At least he was when last I heard."

"The letter is from him to General Richepance. It was somehow in the possession of Colonel Marceau. Knowing his greed for intrigue, I can imagine that he obtained this by ill-gotten means."

Judah looked at the letter with mounting interest. "How did you come by it?"

"The night we rescued you from Colonel Marceau, the letter fell from his pocket and I managed to retrieve it without him knowing."

Judah's eyes slid over the page, then he glanced at Dominique as if he could not believe what he was reading.

She watched him, and the emotions that played across the handsome plane of his face.

At last, he raised his eyes to her face and just stared at her.

"Is it important?" she asked.

"Important? *Important!* I cannot tell you what this means." He turned the letter over to look at the seal to make certain it was genuine. "I must see that this gets to the president at once."

"The . . . the president of America?"

"Yes. Thomas Jefferson."

She smiled at him. "You do have important friends, Judah Gallant."

"So you won't think I boast overmuch, you should know that I am not personally acquainted with the president. My contact with him is through William York. Mr. York is Jefferson's friend."

"Will they help me find my brother?" she asked hopefully.

Judah took her in his arms and swung her around while he laughed with an abandon she had never before seen in him. "Will they help you? For this letter, they might just offer you half the kingdom!"

Suddenly, he stopped and looked at her for a long moment. "Lady mine, you are a maker of dreams." His hand brushed down her cheek to rest at her throat. "Are you real, or will you disappear from my life as quickly as you came into it?"

"I will not leave you unless you want me to," she said solemnly.

He bent his head, his lips very near hers. "That will never happen, Dominique. I fear you have agreed to a pact that will bind you forever."

When his lips curved over hers, she clung to him, her heart beating, her knees weak, and happiness swelling within her.

Judah broke off the kiss much too soon for her, and

backed away from her, dropping his arms. "I must not do that again."

"But, I—"

He placed his finger to her lips. "Oh no, my little temptress. Now that you are to be my wife, I will show only the deepest respect."

She glanced through the door at his sleeping quarters.

He read her thoughts, as he had done so often. "Yes, I want you in my bed. But mostly, I want you to know the man I am and not the man you thought me to be."

She smiled. "You are not the pirate who carried me to his bed?"

"Oh lady, you do so sorely tempt me." His bold stare and flashing smile tugged at her heart. "Go now, Dominique, unless you want me to finish what you started."

She could see by his slow smile that he knew what she was feeling. She looked into stormy blue eyes and could read his thoughts as well—they made her blush.

Then he seemed hesitant, as if his mind was on another matter. "There is but one thing I will ask you, Dominique, and then we shall put the past to rest."

"You want to know if I betrayed you to Colonel Marceau?"

"Did you?"

"No. But that was my intention when I first came aboard your ship. I would have done it then, Judah. I would not have liked it, but I would have done it had I not come to . . . to respect you."

"Respect? Is that all?"

"Respect is a great deal." With the swish of her gown, she moved to the door. "Good night, Captain Gallant. You certainly know how to entertain a guest.

It has been a most enlightening evening." She touched her fingers to the her lips and blew him a kiss. "Most enlightening."

31

Dominique awoke to a strange sensation—
something was different. She had come to know the
movements of the *Tempest* so well, and although there
was motion, it was not a forward motion.

Sleepily, she slid out of bed and went to the porthole.
She could see land, a large mass of land, and they were
anchored there. It must be America!

She quickly dressed and brushed her hair, tying her
massive curls back with a scrap of lace.

She answered the knock at her door to find Tom
standing there, smiling.

"Is that America, Tom?"

"That be her right enough. We're off the Virginia
coast at Norfolk."

Since the night she had accepted his proposal,
Dominique had not seen Judah except at a formal dinner, which had been held in their honor by the ship's
cook.

Judah had said they would be married the moment
they touched American soil, and if this was America, it
must be her wedding day!

"Where is the captain?" she asked.

"Well, the cap'n and Doc Graham went ashore near sunup. That was three hours ago."

She was stung with disappointment. Apparently, Judah did not mean to take her ashore with him today. "Oh."

Tom's eyes twinkled. "I'm to escort the bride ashore. I was the cap'n's choice for that honor."

She laughed lightly as she pressed her small hand into his big one. Tom had become so dear to her, and in the absence of her brother, she would have chosen no other escort. "Then this is my wedding day, after all, Tom."

Her eyes dropped to her blue velvet gown, and she wished Judah could see her in a white gown and veil. She raised one foot and studied her scuffed brown boots. Those would be the first thing she would throw away when she had a proper pair of shoes.

"You're getting a good man, Miss Dominique," Tom told her. "The cap'n . . . well he's all right with me." His ruddy face turned red, and he looked at her adoringly. "Course he's getting the prize."

"Why, Tom, what a nice compliment."

"The cap'n talked to us—the crew—last night."

"What did he say?"

Tom led her up the companionway and across the deck. "He told us that he wouldn't be going to sea no more. Leastwise, not like . . . well you know."

She smiled. "Pirating?"

"Well . . . yes. He said there'd be no more of that. And we sort of all promised him that we'd reform our ways, since he got us a pardon and all. I'm not going to disappoint the cap'n."

She was trying not to smile. "I cannot tell you how glad I am to know that."

"He—the cap'n—told all of us that we could still

work for him. Be those who wanted to go to sea, or those who want to work at his shipbuilding yard. Me," he said with pride, "I'm going to work in the shipyard, overseeing kinda like. He said I was a good man."

"And so you are," she said smiling. "Will you be happy tied to the land, Tom?"

He looked serious. "I got me some money put away, and I'll have a respectable position now. It's time I found me a good woman and settled down."

Dominique linked her arm through his. "Some woman will be fortunate to have you, Tom."

He looked pleased, and his chest seemed to swell. Tom could have told Dominique that if he was a reformed man, it was more because of wanting to please her than any other reason. He knew that Dominique had no notion that she had changed many of the men who had sailed the *Tempest*—mostly she had changed the captain.

When the longboat reached shore, Ethan was there waiting for her. He lifted Dominique and set her on dry land. He then led her to a waiting carriage.

"Tom," Ethan told him, "the captain wants you to come with us now. Tell the others in the boat that I'll send the carriage back for them, so they might be in attendance as well." Then he turned his attention to Dominique. "I am the representative for your impatient bridegroom, and I am to escort you to the house of a friend, where you are to be married this very day."

"Not a church?"

"Judah asked me to inquire whether you would find it objectionable to be married by a ship's captain. Later, if it is your wish, you can repeat the ceremony in a church."

Dominique found it fitting that they would be married by the captain of a ship. "I thought a sea captain could only perform weddings at sea," she said in confusion.

Ethan laughed and winked at her. "You know Judah. He leaves nothing to chance. He asked for, and obtained, special authorization. Captain Fletcher will marry the two of you since he is an old friend of the family."

"If that is Judah's wish, I have no objections."

"Then let us be away," he said, handing her into the carriage and beckoning Tom inside. "We are going to a wedding."

The horses clipped along the street, while Dominique's apprehension grew. She did not see the stately homes they passed or the ship channel, where many graceful ships lay at anchor. Her mind was in a quandary. What if Judah was marrying her out of pity? She tugged at Ethan's sleeve. "I have only a small mirror to assist me. How do I look?"

"Breathtaking."

"Ethan, you would tell me the truth, wouldn't you? Am I horribly scarred?"

His eyes went slowly over her face, and he felt a deep ache that she should be so unsure of herself. Then he smiled to himself. That was what made her so different from other beautiful woman. Her beauty had never been a tool for her to use on a man. He doubted that she would ever know how beautiful she really was.

Ethan was taking so long to reply that Dominique was sure he was trying to spare her feelings.

"No," he said at last, "the scars on your face have disappeared completely, and the ones on your hands are hardly noticeable. You are the least scarred woman I know. Have no fear, you will be a beautiful bride."

"Ragtag, you mean."

"As to your wardrobe, I am certain Captain Fletcher's wife will help you. She is eagerly waiting to receive you and usher you off to her rooms to do whatever women do to ready themselves for such an occasion."

The carriage had stopped before a grand house, and Ethan jumped down to assist Dominique. Her foot had hardly touched the ground when a plump, pleasant-faced woman came rushing up to her.

"My dear," her hostess said, taking Dominique's hand. "I am Tessa Fletcher. My but you are lovely. Come with me, around to the side, so the men cannot see you. This is such fun. Just think, a wedding in my house."

"Tessa," Ethan said, "this is—"

"I know, I know. Dominique something-or-other. Come, my dear, we must hurry."

Ethan gave Dominique a sympathetic shrug as the chattering little lady led her away, talking all the while and scarcely drawing a breath.

Dominique was promptly taken to the woman's dressing room, where two servants waited. She stood before a full mirror while Tessa looked her over. "The blue gown is nice, but if only it were white."

"Yes," Dominique said wistfully. "I had always thought I would be married in white."

"I have it!" Tessa cried, going down on her knees and fumbling through a trunk. "Ah ha. Here it is." She held a cream-colored brocade surcoat out for Dominique's inspection. "This was my daughter's before she was married. She was about your size. It isn't white, but perhaps it will do nicely."

She handed it to a servant. "Iron this."

In no time at all, the servant handed the wrinkle-free garment back to her mistress.

Tessa draped the surcoat over Dominique's gown, and a magic transformation took place. It fell in gentle folds across the blue velvet, and it almost seemed as if it had been made for the gown.

"Now, let me see," Tessa said thoughtfully. "You need a veil. I only have dark shawls, and they won't do." She rummaged in her trunk again and came up with a lovely cream-colored lace handkerchief, which she placed on Dominique's dark head, allowing the point to come down the center of her hair in front.

Tessa Fletcher clapped her hands delightedly. "I have done it—you are stunning!"

"Thank you," Dominique said, staring at herself in the mirror. She did look like a bride.

Tessa dismissed the servants with a nod, and when they had gone, she turned to Dominique.

"I haven't much time to speak to you, my dear, but I will talk to you as a mother. Judah Gallant is a fine man from a fine family. After his first wife, Mary, died, we all thought he would never wed again. We are glad that he found you. As to children, I do not know. He was so devastated when Mary lost the child and then died. But surely you know this?"

Dominique swallowed a painful lump. "You do not think he will want children?"

"I only know what he said to my husband, John—but this was right after the funeral, so he may have changed his mind."

Dominique hoped Tessa Fletcher would tell her no more. She wanted to clamp her hands over her ears and shut out the words she had already heard.

"But there, there, dear, I have upset you, and on your wedding day. Pay no attention to my ramblings." The little woman looked doubtful. "I am sure Judah will want children eventually."

Dominique could only stare at her own vision in the mirror. She asked the question that was haunting her—

she had to know. "Did Judah love his first wife so much?"

"It is not my nature to gossip," Tessa said, lowering her voice and leaning closer to Dominique, although there were only the two of them in the room. "After Mary died, he drank heavily, and avoided everyone they had known. It was like he wanted to be in that grave with Mary."

Dominique straightened her shoulders. This was her wedding day, and she would think no more of Judah's dead wife. But as she was led out of the room, and into the formal sitting room, where the ceremony was to take place, she felt that Mary's ghost walked with her.

Captain Fletcher was as tall as his wife was petite. He even towered above Judah. Both men were dressed in formal naval attire. Judah looked decidedly dashing with a gold sash and a saber at his waist.

Dominique approached Judah and looked into his blue eyes, searching for the man Tessa had spoken of— the man who drank too much and wanted to be buried with his wife and baby.

As he smiled at her and took her hand in his, the guests closed in around them.

Dominique hardly heard the words that were spoken, and once had to be prompted by Captain Fletcher to reply.

She was stunned when Judah placed a ring on her finger, and she closed her eyes, hoping it had not been Mary's ring.

Then Captain Fletcher smiled. "You are man and wife."

Judah's eyes were tender as she looked into them. If there was not love between them, there was certainly something strong and compelling. She smiled slightly as his lips brushed hers.

"It's too late to change your mind now, Dominique," he told her. "You belong to me."

There were good wishes all around, kisses on the cheek for Dominique, and hearty congratulations for Judah. At last, Tessa elbowed her way the front of the room.

"Now," she said, taking command. "I have it in mind to arrange a hasty reception, invite a few friends, nothing very fancy."

Judah glanced down at Dominique, whom he held close to him as if she were a part of his body. "You have been wonderful, Tessa, but I am taking my wife back to the *Tempest*, that is if she has no objections." He looked at Dominique inquiringly. "Perhaps you would prefer a reception here."

"No," she said hurriedly. "I mean—"

"There you have it, Tessa," he said, understanding Dominique's reluctance better than she thought. Tessa meant well, but she did talk a lot, and sometimes without thinking.

"Well, it is not my notion of what's proper," Tessa said, her eyes round with disapproval. "All those men around. It's practically—"

"Tessa," her husband scolded, "that is hardly the way a sea captain's wife should talk." He wrung Judah's hand and raised Dominique's to his lips. "Just go and begin your new life together." He winked at Dominique. "And your husband was right when he told me you were a beauty."

Upstairs, Dominique removed the overskirt and handed it to Tessa, but when she would have removed the handkerchief, the older woman stopped her. "Keep that as a remembrance of this day." She kissed Dominique's cheek. "Be happy, my dear."

Judah steered Dominique out of the house and into

the waiting carriage. When they were on their way, he drew Dominique to him, not saying anything, just holding her.

She was the first to break the silence. "Judah, are you happy?"

He flicked a dark curl from her cheek and smiled. "If you had asked me before I met you what happiness was, I could not have told you. Am I happy? Yes, sweet Dominique, I believe I have never known such happiness."

She sighed inwardly, choosing to believe him and not the chattering Mrs. Fletcher.

"Dominique, I am sorry you could not have had a proper wedding."

"I was not disappointed," she assured him, "only . . . "

"Yes—only?"

"I wish Valcour could have been there." She looked into his face. "You will find him, won't you Judah?"

"I have already sent a messenger to Washington to bring William York to me. I want to give him the letter and have him begin the search for your brother."

"Thank you." She saw the *Tempest* riding the waves, and it was like a friend beckoning her home. "What do we do now?"

He arched a brow at her. "Mrs. Gallant, what a scandalous question."

She laughed. "No, I mean what do we do with the rest of our lives?"

"I can only think of tonight." His voice deepened and sent shivers of delight throughout her body. "I will have you in my bed, and by rights, that is where you belong."

His hand moved to her arm, and she wanted to lean her head against his shoulder, but the carriage was too public a place and she dared not.

Suddenly, as if from nowhere, a mist descended on

them, making it impossible to see more than a few paces ahead. Fear, unbridled and strong, encased Dominique's mind. It seemed the clopping of the horses on the cobblestones was echoing over and over, "Mary's husband, Mary's husband."

32

When Judah and Dominique returned to the ship, they found William York impatiently pacing the deck.

The older man greeted Dominique graciously, but with polite restraint. When he heard of the marriage, his face brightened considerably, and he smiled as he wished them happiness.

"I got your message," William said at last. "Your man said it was extremely important that I come at once."

Judah turned to his new bride with regret in his eyes. "Will you excuse us, Dominique? I have much to discuss with William."

She nodded, and Judah caught her arm. "Wait for me in your cabin. I won't be long."

After she had gone, William stared at Judah. "I had no notion Miss Charbonneau was on board the *Tempest*. I would have thought after all that's happened, you would have left her on Guadeloupe. And the marriage—that is a surprise."

"There is much you do not know, William. I married Dominique only this morning."

"Was that wise?"

"It is most probably the singularly most important thing I have ever done in my life."

"Then I congratulate you." William still looked doubtful. "Apparently you know more of her doings on Guadeloupe than I do."

"She is everything any man would want in a wife."

William nodded, considering how different Judah was from when they had first met. It could be that the little French miss was just what he needed. "I wish you well, Judah, but surely you did not send for me to discuss your marriage."

"Accompany me," Judah said, "I have something to show you."

When they were seated in Judah's quarters with the door closed, Judah handed William the letter Dominique had given him.

William read it once, then in shock scanned it again.

"Can this be authentic?" he asked in disbelief.

"I assure you it is."

William seemed in a daze. "How did you come by it?"

"My wife," Judah said simply.

An ecstatic smile smoothed the rough planes of William's face. "God, Judah, this is what I've prayed for. Louisiana joined to our great country!"

"What will you do with the letter?" Judah wanted to know.

William rose to a standing position. "I will leave at once, today. The president must see this." He reached out and wrung Judah's hand. "We chose the right man when we selected you for this mission. I never thought much would come of it, but we have six French ships added to our navy and now this." He slapped the letter against his hand. "This is the prize of them all."

"Do not give me credit for the letter, William. If anyone is to be thanked, it is Dominique."

"Yes. Yes, of course—she is a wonder."

"There is something I would ask of you in return for the letter, William."

"Name it—money—to be commissioned as an admiral—what is your desire?"

"Only one thing—two actually. First, I want to resign my commission at once."

This came as no surprise to William. "I understand, and that will be arranged. I'll take it upon myself to give you leave to return to Boston. But you said there were two things you wanted."

"The second will not be so easily accomplished. I need you to locate someone for me."

"Certainly, my boy. Who is it?"

"Dominique's brother. He is believed to be working with the English—probably somehow connected with the English navy. And probably as a French royalist."

William looked troubled, for it was a difficult task indeed. "Judah, if I did that, I would have to call in an old favor from the British admiralty."

"Then do it! The information my wife furnished you in that letter is worth more than any owed favor from the British."

William nodded his head vigorously. "If it is possible, you shall have it. Write down all the information you have on the young man, and I will begin the search when I return to Washington."

Dominique sat upon the bed, her hands demurely folded in her lap, her eyes on the door, waiting for Judah to appear. She knew he and Mr. York would be discussing the letter from Charles Talleyrand and what it would mean to the United States of America. But it was taking a long time.

It had been an emotional day, and after a while, she lay back on the bed and closed her eyes, falling into an all-consuming sleep.

The cabin was dark as the door opened and Judah entered. The light coming from the doorway fell on Dominique's sleeping form.

Silently, he moved toward her, dipping to his knees and softly pressing a wayward curl behind her ear. She groaned, but did not awaken.

She looked angelic, with the soft light on her face, her small hands clutched before her, almost as if in prayer. Warmth circled Judah's heart as his lips touched her mouth ever so lightly.

She stirred, opened her eyes, and stared at him for a moment. Suddenly, a smile lit her face and she threw her arms about his neck. "I am sorry I fell asleep."

He scooped her up in his arms and held her to him. "I have kept my part of our bargain, Madame," he said, pretending seriousness. "Now you must keep yours."

"What did you do?"

"I brought all the powers that be to search for your brother. If he can be found, my government will do it."

Her arms tightened about his shoulders. "Thank you, Judah."

He nuzzled her neck. "I have a better way you can thank me." He carried her to his quarters, where a lantern burning low was the only light.

She thought he would put her down, but instead, he held her, his lips gliding across her cheek to nestle against the pulsebeat at her throat.

She was vaguely aware that the wind had caught the sails of the *Tempest* and they were moving into open waters, but it did not seem to matter.

Judah turned her, allowing her body to slide down his, and she felt the swell of his need. Trembling, she moved closer to him, pressing her body tighter to his, wanting to feel the unending pleasure he had given her before and would give her again.

"Oh, lady wife," he murmured in her ear, "you do so stir my blood."

His mouth claimed hers, pillaging with a savage passion that made her weak with longing. She knew that he had unhooked her gown, but it made no impression on her mind because his lips were draining her of every thought but him.

Her head was spinning, and she felt herself float down to his bed, with his arm there to cushion her descent. His hot, hard body fit into her curves as if it had been created for just that purpose.

His hands stroked her breasts, then his tongue followed that trail. When she squirmed in his arms, his lips returned to her mouth, his tongue circling, enticing, then plunging deep to draw a moan from her.

Their lovemaking was different this time. He was unhurried, playing her body as a master musician would stroke the strings of a violin to make sweet music.

Just when she thought she could no longer stand the aching want, his hand glided smoothly across her belly, gently nudging her legs apart.

"Judah," she breathed.

"Yes, my love," he whispered against her ear, his voice doing as much as his hands to stir her longing.

"I have never felt this way before."

His hands massaged her, then his finger slid into her silken softness and she groaned, arching her back. "I know, sweetheart."

His lips swept down her throat and across her stomach, and she gasped and pressed her hands against his muscled back.

When he raised his head to look into her eyes, she

wanted to cry at the expression she saw reflected there—the softness, the intensity.

When he moved between her legs, she raised up, her fingers tangling in his dark hair, her lips opening temptingly for his mouth.

His body pressed against hers, and she gasped and trembled as he arched into her, the heat of him swelling inside her, driving deeper, then slower, and deeper again.

"Judah!" she cried, clinging to him. "Oh, Judah."

Just when she thought she could not stand it any longer, her body trembled and erupted in blissfulness.

Afterwards, they lay there, their legs entwined, their heartbeats slowly returning to normal.

Judah's arms tightened about her and he held her as if she were his most precious possession.

Her hand slid over his shoulder and down his back as she remembered the night of her brother's birthday celebration, when she had foolishly dreamed of a man who would sweep into her life and whom she would know at once as her one true love. What she felt for Judah was deep, all-consuming love that would last all her life.

She raised up on one elbow and looked into his face. His eyes were closed, and she wondered what he was thinking. She decided to ask him. "What can be on your mind, my husband?"

He opened his eyes, and she thought they looked misty, or was it a trick of the light?

"I was just remembering," he said.

Now she wished she had not asked. He must have been thinking of his wedding night with Mary. "Oh."

"I was remembering the first time I made love to you, Dominique. I was rough with you that night, and I will always regret that."

Bubbling laughter came from her lips. "Oh, Judah, I

would have you put that from your mind. I set out to,
and did, entrap you. You only believed what I wanted
you to."

"I think of all you have been through, the grief, the
danger, much of which I am certain you have not even
told me. It makes me want to wrap you in my arms and
keep you safe forever."

She sighed deeply and lowered her head to his chest.
"Oh, Judah. The world is so immense, our paths only
crossed by mere chance. I could easily have missed
knowing you."

He raised her face to his. "Such deep thoughts."

She could feel his silent laughter. "What?"

"I was just thinking about the first time I saw you on
board the *Tempest*, and how I wanted to toss you into
the sea."

"And I would have fed you to the sharks."

Laughingly, he lifted her in his arms and carried her
to a tub of water, where he proceeded to step in and sit
down so the water encased them. The remainder of the
night was spent in glorious discovery.

33

Dominique had come on deck because she wanted to catch her first glimpse of Boston, her new home. It was a dull, gray morning and a light drizzle fell. As they entered Boston Harbor, a raw wind struck, making it bitterly cold.

Judah appeared beside her and gave her the special smile that he reserved for her alone. He pulled her hood more securely about her head. "I would have had you arrive in the spring, when the flowers bloom and the weather is not so foul. I fear you will not like Boston, since you are accustomed to the warm tropics. Do you miss Guadeloupe?""

"I will be homesick for a time," she answered as honestly as she could. "But it will pass."

"Then you will not mind the cold?"

She touched his arm. "I have never experienced the cold—not like this. I find it invigorating. I shall love it here. This is my home now—I am a Bostonian—more than that, I am an American."

Pride swelled in Judah at the thought that she was the greatest prize he had won from his pirating.

In that moment, the anchor came grinding down and a thick fog blanketed land and sea. Dominique strained her eyes, but to her disappointment, she could see very little of her surroundings.

Suddenly, she heard Judah laughing, and she looked at him inquiringly.

"It's those damned boots," he said, pointing to her feet. "The first thing I will do is buy you dozens of pairs of shoes so you will never have to wear those again."

She pretended haughtiness. "I have become attached to these boots," she mused. "They took me into sea battles, across swamps, and most importantly, I wore them at my wedding. How can I part with them now?"

Judah touched her pert little nose with his finger. "You are incorrigible, Mrs. Gallant. I wonder if Boston is ready for you."

Ethan appeared beside them. "Well, Judah, we are home."

"Thank God. There were times when I thought we would be blown out of the water or transported to France to be hung." He smiled down at his wife. "I surely never expected to return with a sea siren."

Tom came up beside Dominique, and she linked her arm through his, while his rough face relaxed in a broad smile. "Welcome to your new home, Dominique," he said in a gruff voice. Even now he called her by her familiar name, and no one thought anything of it. He had earned the right.

"Yes, home," she said reverently.

The three men who loved her, all in their different ways, stood about her, ever ready to keep her from any harm that should befall her.

Light from many tapers reflected on the highly polished table as Dominique entered the house on Bowdoin Square.

"Judah," she said turning about in a circle. "It's lovely. It will be hard to imagine you in these surroundings, and not stalking the deck, issuing orders."

"I am pleased that you like it. I was born here, as was my father."

"Did you . . . bring Mary here to live?" she could not help but ask.

"No. She never liked this house. She wanted a bigger one—grander, so I built it for her."

"Will we live here?"

"Do you want to?"

"Oh yes. I will love living in the house where you were born."

At that moment, Mrs. Whitworth entered, looking startled, and then her face flushed with pleasure. "Captain, I did not know you were home." She looked from Judah to the woman beside him, waiting to know who she was. "I would have had the cook prepare all your favorite dishes, had we known you were coming."

"Mrs. Whitworth, I want you to meet your new mistress. Dominique, Mrs. Whitworth has been in this house longer than I have, and you will find her very capable."

The housekeeper's plump face lit from within. "Oh, Mrs. Gallant, I am so pleased to welcome you. If there is anything I can do for you, anything you require, you have only to ask."

Dominique held her hand out and clasped the woman's plump fingers. "You can help me and instruct me. You see, I am new to this country and I do not know all the customs. I will need you to keep me from making mistakes."

Nothing she could have said would have endeared her more to the older woman. The warm glow in the captain's eyes told Mrs. Whitworth all she needed to know.

The captain was happy at last, and that was enough for her.

Mrs. Whitworth smiled her welcome. "Madame, I will do all I can."

Dominique could not have been happier. She met each day with eagerness and looked forward to the nights when she would lie in her husband's arms.

The only thing that kept her from being completely happy was the absence of her brother. She waited each day to hear some word of Valcour, but up to now, there had been nothing.

Judah had generously showered her with gifts, jewels, and clothing, the likes of which she had never seen. He had kept his word about the shoes, and she had every color and style imaginable. However, she could not bear to part with her brown boots, and they had been tucked away in a trunk.

The best gift of all, however, was a white Arabian mare with an impressive bloodline.

The morning was warmer than it had been, but the sky was overcast. Dominique thought it might rain, but she was unconcerned as she rode beside Judah.

Dressed in a burgundy, three-pile velvet riding habit, Dominique set a steady pace on the high-stepping mare. Judah kept even with her on his great striding gelding.

After a time, Dominique slowed the thundering gallop to a smart, sidestepping canter. She patted the neck of the horse in delight. "Judah, she is wonderful!"

It brought him joy to see her so happy. "I'm glad you like her," he said. "She suits you."

Dominique glanced through the bare trees at the strange-looking sky. "I am nervous about the tea I am to attend this afternoon. I do not know these people. I wish you were coming with me."

"Your hostess is Ethan's mother, a most admirable woman. You will find her as kind-hearted as her son. And as for me attending, I do not believe any man would be welcome—it being a lady's gathering."

Suddenly Dominique stared about her, her eyes filled with wonder. She removed her glove and held out her hand. "Is this snow?" she asked, watching the flakes melt as they hit the warmth of her hand.

Judah looked at her with astonishment. "I take it you have never seen snow before?"

"In books."

She slid off her horse and held her arms out as the flakes drifted down, heavier now. "This is magic!" she exclaimed. "And so beautiful."

She raised her head, opened her mouth, and caught a snowflake on her tongue. When she saw that her footsteps made tracks in the newly fallen snow, she spun around in a circle as if embracing the phenomenon.

For a moment, Judah could only stare at her, thinking he had never seen anything as lovely or as innocent as Dominique. If asked to, he could not have spoken for the tightening in his throat. He leaned forward, propped his leg across his horse and just watched her.

She gathered a bit of snow, tossing it up, and allowing it to shower down on her.

At last, she turned to smile at him and paused, embarrassed, when she found him watching her so intently. "It's just that I . . . well it's so beautiful. It's my first snow."

With as much dignity as she could gather, she moved toward her horse. "I suppose we should go now."

Judah jumped down and helped her mount. "I am constantly amazed by your outlook on life. You are teaching me to see everything in a new way."

She looked at him sideways, straightening her back. "You did not enjoy the snow."

"Ah, but I did." He handed her the reins and mounted himself. "Next time, I'll teach you about snowball fights."

Ethan's mother was soft-spoken and gracious as she greeted Dominique at the door. "My dear, I am so glad to meet you. I have heard nothing but praise about you from Ethan. Come in and meet our friends. They have been quite anxious to make your acquaintance."

"Thank you for giving a tea in my honor," Dominique said. "It was most thoughtful of you."

Mrs. Graham's face took on a grave expression, and she looked worried. "I . . . feel I should explain something to you. I did not invite her, but she came anyway."

"So," a chilling voice spoke up from behind Dominique. "This is Judah's little wife."

Dominique smiled hesitantly, not understanding the reason for the woman's obvious hostility. "How do you do, Madame? Yes, I am Mrs. Gallant."

Dominique waited for Mrs. Graham to introduce the other woman, and when she did not, the woman introduced herself.

"I am Nedra Banks," she said guardedly

The name meant nothing to Dominique. "It was nice of you to come," she said, trying to be friendly, but she could feel something dark and disturbing from this woman, whose smile on her lips did not reach her eyes.

"Come, my dear," Mrs. Graham said, and it was obvious that she was trying to get Dominique away from the woman called Nedra.

"You do not even know who I am, do you?" Nedra Banks asked angrily.

Dominique turned to her, confused by her strange attitude. "Yes, you said you are Nedra Banks. Mrs. or Miss, I do not know that."

They entered the formal sitting room, and the voices of the other guests dropped in tone. But Dominique had heard someone say that Nedra should not be there, and she wondered why.

Dominique was introduced to the others, who seemed genuinely friendly, but she could feel eyes boring into her, and every time she looked up, she found Nedra staring at her.

The tea had become an uncomfortable affair, although Dominique could not understand why. When it was time to leave, and her carriage arrived, she was not sorry.

"You aren't leaving us so soon, are you?" Nedra asked, catching Dominique at the door, where she was slipping into her fur-lined cape.

"Yes, my husband will be waiting."

She could not have said anything that would have angered the woman more.

"My sister, Mary, will always be the wife of Judah's heart. I cannot think why he married you."

There were gasps from several ladies, and Ethan's mother rushed to Dominique's defense. "Nedra, you will leave my house this moment unless you apologize to Dominique."

Nedra paid no attention to her hostess because her eyes were on Dominique. "Who is your family?" Nedra asked pointedly, and everyone knew she was trying to embarrass Judah's wife. "My sister, Mary, was a Claborne of Boston."

Dominique wore a placid expression. "I am not certain what you mean."

Harsh laughter emitted from Nedra's throat. "I will

make it clear enough so that even you will understand," she said in a condescending voice. "Were you upper or lower class—judging from your appearance, I'd say lower."

"Let us just say I am not in your class," Dominique answered with dignity. She moved to the door and turned back to Ethan's mother. "Thank you for the lovely tea, Mrs. Graham. Judah and I would like very much to have your family dine with us soon."

"You have not answered my question," Nedra said relentlessly.

Judah was standing in the doorway with another man, and they both heard the venomous grilling. Judah took a step to defend his wife, but the stranger placed a hand on his arm and emerged from the shadows.

The stranger had realized that the woman was attempting to hurt Dominique—and he would never allow that. "Permit me to do this," he told Judah.

Then he advanced into the room. "I believe that I should be the one to tell you about Dominique, since I know her better than anyone."

Everyone's attention was on the newcomer, for his presence was electrifying. He was obviously a man of breeding and culture, as well as handsome beyond belief.

"Dominique," he continued, "comes from a long and proud line of French and English aristocracy, although she would never tell you this herself. Alas, most of her family lost their lives to the French guillotine, so she would never parade their rank before you."

Dominique spun around with tears in her eyes and flung herself into the stranger's arms. "Oh, Valcour, Valcour, I feared you were dead! God has brought you back to me."

Valcour hugged his sister and laughed. "God and the American navy. Imagine my surprise when an American warship came alongside the English ship I had boarded and demanded that I come with them."

He held her to him as he looked back at the woman who had been persecuting his sister. "Madame," he said contemptuously, "just so there will never be any question, if Dominique but chose to flaunt her rank, she could have told you that she is the sister of the Marquis de Charbonneau."

Judah's eyes widened at this bit of news. He wondered why Dominique had never mentioned a title to him.

Nedra's face was drained of color as she stared at the handsome man with the eloquent manners, who was eyeing her with such disdain. "Who are you?"

"I am Dominique's brother." He bowed and tempered his impatience with tolerance. "Allow me to introduce myself. I am the Marquis de Charbonneau," he said, using the title his grandfather had abandoned long ago, but that now rightfully belonged to him.

34

Dominique hardly remembered taking leave of the guests as she was whisked to the waiting carriage by her husband and brother. She clung to her brother's arm as if she were fearful that he would disappear if she did not have hold of him.

Judah stepped back, but Dominique turned to him, holding out her hand. With a smile, he came to her.

"I have so many questions," she said as Judah lifted her into the carriage beside her brother. "Valcour, tell me where you have been and what you have been doing."

"I have been in London," Valcour told her as the carriage moved down the Boston streets. "I was almost arrested by Colonel Marceau, but friends helped me escape."

"British friends?" Dominique asked.

"I cannot tell even you that, Dominique." He smiled at his brother-in-law. "Here's a pretty kettle of fish; I owe so much to Judah for taking care of you, and yet I fear we will soon be on opposite sides in a conflict."

"Not with me, Valcour," Judah said. "I am retired from naval service." His hand tightened on Dominique's. "Your sister has clipped my sails, so to speak."

"I do not have to ask if you are happy," Valcour said, looking into Dominique's face.

Her eyes saddened. "You know about grandfather?"

"*Oui* . . . yes. I returned to Windward to find the house burned and grandfather dead. I was frantic to learn what had happened to you. It did not ease my mind when I went to Bartrand, and he told me some story about you having left the island with a notorious pirate." He glanced over at Judah and grinned. "But we will speak of that later."

"I am sorry you were worried, Valcour," Dominique said softly. "But at last we are reunited."

He glanced at Judah. "You have influential friends, brother-in-law. When the British ship was boarded, I was told that I was being taken by order of the President of the Unites States of America. Imagine my thinking I must be important to draw such a great man's notice."

Dominique laughed with happiness as she leaned over and kissed her husband. "You kept your promise."

His eyes rested on her face. "I will always keep my promises to you."

Valcour saw the love that passed between his sister and her husband. Dominique was well settled, and he no longer had to worry about her.

"Judah has told me much of what happened to you," Valcour said, "and how you came to stow away on board his ship. Here is a bit of information that might please you."

Dominique was curious. "What is it?"

"There was such an outcry from the islanders that General Richepance had no choice but to arrest Colonel Marceau. At his trial, the colonel raved like a madman, when he was stripped of his rank and convicted."

Dominique's eyes narrowed with loathing. "What were the charges?"

"There were many charges, but the only one that should concern you is that he was accused and convicted of the death of Jean Louis Charbonneau."

Dominique let out a long breath. "And his sentence?"

"Death."

"I am not sorry," she said bitterly. "He was responsible for so much suffering."

"Even if he was a monster, I am grateful to him," Judah said, attempting to bring a bit of levity to the serious atmosphere. "Had it not been for him, we would never have met, Dominique."

She leaned her head against Judah's shoulder. "Something good oft can come from something bad." She raised her eyes to her brother. "Do you recall that Grandpapa used to say that?"

Valcour nodded. "Yes, but he was speaking of the swamp, Dominique."

She laced her hand through his, feeling so happy she thought her heart would burst. "So he was."

"How long can you stay with us?" Judah asked. "I know Dominique will want you to remain as long as you can."

"I would like to remain until spring."

Dominique clapped her hands in excitement.

"I would also like to see your shipyard, Judah," Valcour said.

Judah laughed. "So you can tell the British?"

Dominique gasped. She had a horrible thought, her husband and her brother as enemies. How would she bear it? But when she looked at Valcour's face, she saw that he was smiling.

"No matter where I go or what I do when I leave here, I would never betray the country that gives my sister sanctuary, or the man who gave her love."

* * *

Judah had left Dominique alone with her brother so they could talk, and it was much later when she joined him in their bedroom. She had removed her gown and was sitting at her dressing table brushing her hair, wearing only her lawn chemise.

He watched her, seeing that she was troubled, and he waited for her to tell him what she was thinking. At last, she laid the brush aside and came to him.

"You are happy that you were reunited with your brother," he said, watching her face. "And I am glad that the two of you found each other again."

She seemed somehow withdrawn from him. "Today was one of the happiest days of my life, but also the saddest."

"Sad?"

"I did not understand why your . . . why Mary's sister was filled with malice toward me."

Judah tried to think how to answer her, and he decided that she must know the truth. "I wish that you could have been spared that confrontation today, but I believe your brother handled it quite well on your behalf."

She smiled. "Yes, he did. Valcour was always protective of me."

"I have a brother, and it is much the same with us. But I wanted to speak to you of Nedra. What you saw in her today was much the same as Mary's personality, only Mary was more practiced on how to hurt others."

Dominique's mouth rounded in surprise. "But you loved Mary."

"No, I never loved her. I blamed myself for her death because I was at sea when she died, and I blamed myself because I knew our marriage was a mistake even before I married her and still I went through with the ceremony."

"I thought—"

"I know what you thought." He reached out and took her hand, studying it for some time. "I have loved only one woman." He raised his eyes to her. "That woman is you."

She gave a strangled cry and flung herself into his arms. "Oh, Judah, why didn't you tell me this about Mary?"

"Misguided pride, I suppose."

"I have something to tell you, and I do not know how you will feel."

He rested his lips against her forehead as she curled up in his arms.

"What is it?"

"You once told me you did not know how you would feel about having . . . a baby."

He tensed. "Are you telling me that you are with child?"

She sat up, her expression somehow wistful. "Yes, I am. Will you mind very much?"

His breath seemed trapped in his throat. "What would you feel about giving birth to my child?" Her answer was more important to him than he could show.

"Oh, Judah, I do so want this baby. It is a part of you that I can have with me, even when you are not here. I want many children." She raised her eyes to his. "Do you?"

He grabbed her to him, holding her, kissing her face, and wishing his body would stop trembling. He wanted to tell her many things, but he did not trust his voice at the moment.

Tears glistened in Dominique's eyes because she could see by Judah's expression that he was deeply affected by the news of the baby. She pulled away from him and raised her hand to softly touch his face.

"Judah, I feel such pain because you have been so terribly hurt."

He laughed and tugged at the ribbon on her chemise. "There is no hurt left in me. Knowing you has allowed me to live again—to believe again."

"Then you are happy about the baby?"

"Extremely so. Come into my arms and I shall show you the magnitude of my joy."

And she did.

Let HarperMonogram Sweep You Away

SIREN'S SONG by Constance O'Banyon
Over Seven Million Copies of Her Books Are in Print!
Beautiful Dominique Charbonneau is determined to free her brother, even if it means becoming a stowaway aboard Judah Gallant's pirate ship. But Gallant is not the rogue he appears, and Dominique is torn between duty and a love she might never know again.

THE AUTUMN LORD by Susan Sizemore
A Time Travel Romance
Truth is stranger than fiction when '90s woman Diane Teal is transported back to medieval France and must rely on the protection of Baron Simon de Argent. She finds herself unable to communicate except when telling stories. Fortunately she and Simone both speak the language of love.

GHOST OF MY DREAMS by Angie Ray
RITA and Golden Heart Award-winning Author
Miss Mary Goodwin refuses to believe her fiancé's warnings that Helsbury House is haunted — until the deceased Earl appears. Will the passion of two young lovers overcome the ghost, or is he actually a bit of a romantic himself?

A ROYAL VISIT by Rebecca Baldwin
An affair of state becomes an affair of the heart when Prince Theodoric of Batavia travels to England to find a bride. He is looking for a titled lady, but a resourceful and charming merchant's daughter shows him that love can be found where one least expects it.

And in case you missed last month's selections...
KISS ME, KATIE by Robin Lee Hatcher
Bestselling Author
When high-spirited suffragette Katie Jones takes a job at a local Idaho newspaper with her childhood friend, Benjamin Rafferty, she never expects love to be the top story. A warm and touching romance from one of the most beloved Americana writers.

FOR THE FINEST IN
HISTORICAL ROMANCE

MISBEGOTTEN by Tamara Leigh

No one can stop baseborn knight Liam Fawke from gaining his rightful inheritance—not even the beautiful Lady Joslyn. Yet Liam's strong resolve is no match for the temptress whose spirit and passion cannot be denied.

MIRANDA by Susan Wiggs

In regency London, Miranda Stonecypher is stricken with amnesia and doesn't believe that handsome Ian MacVane is her betrothed—especially after another suitor appears. Miranda's search for the truth leads to passion beyond her wildest dreams.

HONOR by Mary Spencer

Sent by King Henry V to save Amica of Lancaster from a cruel marriage, Sir Thomas of Reed discovers his rough ways are no match for Amica's innocent sensuality. A damsel in distress to his knight, Amica unleashes passions in Sir Thomas that leave him longing for her touch.

AFTER THE STORM by Susan Sizemore

When a time travel experiment goes awry, Libby Wolfe finds herself in medieval England and at the mercy of the dashing Bastien of Bale. A master of seduction, the handsome outlaw takes Libby to heights of ecstasy that are hauntingly familiar.